SOME

QUIET

PLACE

kelsey sutton

Woodbury, Minnesota

First Edition
Second Printing, 2013

Book design by Bob Gaul
Cover design by Ellen Lawson
Cover photo by Brooke Shaden Photography

Flux, an imprint of Llewellyn Worldwide Ltd.

Library of Congress Cataloging-in-Publication Data
Sutton, Kelsey.
  Some quiet place/Kelsey Sutton.—First edition.
      pages cm
  Summary: "Seventeen-year-old Elizabeth Caldwell sees, rather than feels, emotions; they're beings who walk among us. The only emotion who engages with her now is Fear, and he's as desperate as Elizabeth is to figure out how she became this way"—Provided by publisher.
  ISBN 978-0-7387-3643-3
[1. Emotions—Fiction. 2. Fear—Fiction. 3. Supernatural—Fiction. 4. Family problems—Fiction. 5. High schools—Fiction. 6. Schools—Fiction. 7. Farm life—Wisconsin—Fiction. 8. Wisconsin—Fiction.] I. Title.
  PZ7.S96828Som 2013
  [Fic]—dc23

                                                      2013005021

Flux
Llewellyn Worldwide Ltd.
2143 Wooddale Drive
Woodbury, MN 55125-2989
www.fluxnow.com

Printed in the United States of America

Acknowledgments

First thanks must go to Beth Miller, my incredible agent, for rescuing me from the slush pile (twice!), for reading every single thing I send and being so enthusiastic about it all, and especially for sending me those pictures of Damon Salvatore on special days and days that I might not have survived otherwise. I don't know what I would do without her.

Thank you to the fabulous team at Flux. Brian Farrey-Latz, for loving this story as much as I do. Courtney Colton and Mallory Hayes, for getting others excited about it. Sandy Sullivan, for catching all those little things I missed. Ellen Lawson, for such an amazing cover. And to everyone else who was involved in this process. I can't wait to work with you all again!

Of course thanks to all my critique partners and cheerleaders: Gabrielle Carolina, Tanya Loiselle, Bailey Hammond, Ella Press, Stefanie Gaither, Skyanne Fisher, Holly West-Hedeen, Ruth Walters, Cindy Cowan, Ashley Levens, and Sarah Dalton. Not to mention all the early readers a few years back on YWS. And if I somehow missed anyone in that list, a blanket thanks to all of you.

Lastly, thanks to my family, for all your love and support. I am truly blessed.

For Wayne and Aneesa

O N E

Fear is coming.

As the day ends and I milk the cows, I wait for another meeting with my old friend. He comes swiftly, speeding over the plains as only one of his kind can do.

Every second that he draws nearer, the cows become more agitated, eyes rolling, hooves stomping the floor. I know his only purpose for making the journey to Wisconsin is to taunt me again. Test my boundaries. See if he can break through the unbreakable barrier. I'm the only human being he can't torment, the only one who can look him in the face and not flinch. To Fear, I've always been a mystery.

"It's late, and I need to go to bed," I call out, making sure to be gentle with Mora's udder. None of our other cows mind the milking, no matter how rough I am, but this one always raises a fuss. I try to make it easier for her, standing to croon nonsensical phrases in her flicking ear. There's no sympathy, no affection, only the understanding that the animal will be more willing if I do this for her.

"Too tired even for a visit from *me*, Elizabeth?"

He leans against the doorway, cool and beautiful. He's timeless, he's seen everything and nothing in this world, and he doesn't grow old or wise. Without glancing at him, I can picture his white-blond hair, envision his black, flowing clothes, feel the intensity of his hot-cold blue gaze.

I don't raise my eyes to meet his, as I know he wants me to. His power, ever-present, ever-changing, sweeps over me. I see a young boy cowering in a dank alley, a woman shivering in a barren room, an old man clutching a gun with his back pressed to a wall. White eyes, trembling lips, utter isolation.

It doesn't affect me.

For a moment, there's only the sound of the milk squirting into the pail. Fear makes a guttural note in his throat, and suddenly there are spiders swarming all over me. Mora shuffles in annoyance when she feels some of them crawling up her hind leg. I study the onslaught crawling down my arms, my front, my feet. They're small and black and their legs look like a writhing tangle of living string.

"You're eager tonight," I observe.

Fear sighs and waves his pale hand through the air. The spiders vanish. "And you haven't changed."

I begin milking again. My hold on Mora is steady and sure. "No."

"Not even a little?" Fear steps closer, and I sense his essence flex and shimmer again as it wraps around me. Nothing. Fear sighs a second time. "What does your terror taste like, Elizabeth?" he asks, breathless now. "What would it feel like to see your eyes cloud over at my touch? To know you tremble at my will?"

I continue my task and don't answer.

Fear is in a talkative mood tonight. He tells me stories, stories I have heard before, stories about the humans he has driven insane with his mere breath. People all around the world at every second of every day know who Fear is, and he relishes it. I listen to every word, feeling my nothingness dig deeper inside of me.

"Why are you the only one who can't let go?" I finally ask Fear when he quiets and simply watches the movement of my hands. Dry now, Mora turns with expectancy in her large brown eyes. I stand again, scooting the stool back, but Fear moves to block me. I tilt my head to meet his gaze, adding, "All the other Emotions gave up a long time ago."

The barn is utterly silent and my voice echoes a little. Fear has to hear the detachment in it, the proof that I'm unreachable. He still doesn't move, but this time when I shift he allows me to brush past him. I untie the rope that holds Mora to the stall and lead her into it for the night.

"Hate," I continue, "Surprise, Disappointment . . . they've all stopped coming."

"They don't have my stamina," Fear says with a smirk. He looks satisfied at my words, as if it mollifies him that he's not the only one who can't influence me. He's smiling that sardonic, sly smile he does so well. He may be the Emotion that causes people to cower or scream or run, but he is much, much more. "Don't you want to know the truth?" he asks, and now he sounds genuinely interested, even though he already knows the answer.

I pick up the full pail. The others I've already put through the hand-cranked milk separator, poured into bottles, and placed in the cooler. Fear waits for me to respond, and I give the answer to him yet again because maybe if he hears it enough times, it'll penetrate. My shoulder rotates with the motions of the milk separator. "No." It's not denial, only truth. The hard, cold, simple truth.

After throwing away the heavy cream and pouring the milk into a bottle, I walk out. Fear saunters beside me with his hands shoved in his pockets. It's still dusk, the sun ducking down in the sky behind wisps of clouds. The fields are dark. The tall corn stalks sway gently, rustling.

"I watch you sometimes, you know," Fear tells me abruptly, taking my attention away from the horizon. We're at the front door of the house. He opens the door for me and stands aside. Entering loudly so I don't startle Mom, I set the bottle down on the counter along with the separator. The milk sloshes within the glass. She looks up from her place in front of the sink.

"Did you close up the barn?" she asks, and as always she's blind to Fear's presence. It's me that causes the shadows in her eyes, her wary tone. She's been looking at me this way ever since I can remember; I frighten her. I heard her tell Dad once that I act unnatural. She wishes I were normal, like every other teenager in Edson. My efforts seem to be futile so far.

I shake my head no. Mom takes both the bottle and

the separator. One for the fridge, one for the sink. I catch the faintest sound of a sigh as she turns away. She opens the fridge door. "Tim will get mad if he notices. Better go do it."

Fear watches the two of us with mild fascination. He's seen it all before, but he never seems to tire of examining me and my life. "She really just wants you to get out of the house," he says. Not cruelly. It's a blatant observation.

I let the screen door slam shut behind me. "I know."

The Emotion follows again, his hair gleaming in the weak light. This time he stares ahead with a thoughtful, almost frustrated expression. A crow swoops overhead. *Caw. Caw.*

"Leave," I tell Fear, entering the barn once more. "Nothing will change." I check to make sure the cooler is shut and lock the side door. I brush past Fear to go out the garage door.

Flames shoot up the walls. The heat throws me back, and I land on my side. There's a brief flare of pain, but then my survival instincts kick in; I jump to my feet and search for an unblocked exit. *Survive.* I run back to the side door, but the floor above me collapses. I barely leap out of the way in time. I spin. All the ways out are guarded by the fire. Hay hisses and bursts. The cows bay in their terror, and my skin sears with heat and pain. I do the calculations several times, but Fear has done them, too, and he has every possible avenue of escape eliminated.

Heat eats up my pant leg, up my side and arm. I drop and roll. The smell of burnt flesh fills the air. I'm burning alive, I realize. The physical pain swiftly grows overwhelming, and tears run down my cheeks. But pain is usually impossible to endure because of the rush of feeling that comes along with it. I should be frantic. I should be screaming with horror.

I feel nothing. I am nothing.

"Stop, Fear," I say with my wet cheeks and smoking skin. Hell continues to crackle around me.

I hear him sigh yet again, doing an excellent imitation of my mother. Then, in the space of a single blink, the fire is gone. Everything is the way I left it, nothing destroyed or charred, although it'll take the cows a while to calm. Power shivers around me. I search for Fear as the burns on my skin close up—it was all an illusion. There he stands, leaning against the wall, arms folded across his chest. It's as if none of it ever happened.

"Who could have done this to you?" Fear muses for the thousandth time. "What could have that kind of power, and for what purpose? You're completely human—I'd know if you were anything else. You haven't been sought out, collected, or studied. Why—"

"I'm going to the house," I cut in. "If you're going to come, fine. But please calm the cows down first. Dad grounded me last time he came out and saw them so riled. He thought I'd done it."

"Why would you care if you were grounded? You never go out."

I don't say it out loud, but it's simple, really. I pretend to care because a normal teenager would. I make any and all attempts to be just that. But I don't want Fear to know this; it'll only encourage his obsession.

"I won't rest until I've tasted your terror, Elizabeth," Fear tells me. He vanishes.

I stare at the wall for a moment, absorbing the absence of danger. No thoughts, no fire, no beings from the other plane to disturb the normality. There is only me, my breathing, and the frantic moans of the cows.

I shut the door.

TWO

I've been told that I cried as a child. I screamed when I didn't get my way. I laughed and pulled my mother's hair. I got into fights with my brother. When I hear these things, it's as if I'm listening to stories about a stranger. The little girl I see in the pictures doesn't really look like me. The physical details are the same, of course. The wild blond hair, the blue eyes, the smooth, sun-darkened skin. But if someone else hadn't said that the little girl was me, I wouldn't have known. It's not that I don't remember being so young... I just don't know how I became what I am now.

There's something missing in the girl I see in the mirror compared to the one in those pictures: a sort of soul. A light inside. Her smile is innocent. When I practice smiling, it looks puny and tight. False. Sometimes I think of it as the Caldwell mark; it's how my entire family smiles, now.

I have knowledge few other humans have. They are unexplained and unwarranted, these ironclad truths. Yet I don't know everything. I may be able to see the creatures that no one else can, I may know about the other plane, and I may understand the natures of humans and animals alike, but I don't have the one thing I should have above all else.

I don't know what it is to feel.

I can't experience the freedom of grief, the abandon of ecstasy, the release of fury. And of course I can't be curious about these experiences.

I don't have the luxury of the people around me. I can't weep, I can't lust, I can't cower in terror, I can't celebrate. Not in a true sense; I've grown talented at the art of pretending. The only sensation I'm capable of—not an Emotion, but something physical—is a sort of... nothingness that's always there.

The next morning, on my way through the kitchen, I pass framed pictures of the little girl on the wall and remember those stories. I adjust the strap of my book bag, contemplating that smile for what feels like the thousandth time. The bright eyes. I turn my back on her and glance at the clock on my way out. Late again.

Closing the screen door gently—Dad is out in the fields with the harvester but Mom is still sleeping—I attempt to put the pictures from my mind.

It's a cold dawn. Fog hovers over the ground. Gravel crunches beneath my shoes. In the distance I see a shadow in the fields, the form of a man. But it's not a man. He stands there, utterly still, and the fog rolls around him. Because that is what he is. Fog. Element. Other. More. I don't just see the Emotions that wander the world—I see everything.

I don't pause to observe; it is something I have seen many, many times before. I throw my bag onto the passenger seat of my truck and hop in.

The engine rumbles as my truck bumps along the dirt road. It's an ancient '96 Chevy; I bought it with most of my babysitting money. The smell of gasoline permeates the air. I roll down the window and listen to the vehicle's peaceful growl, feel the cool morning breeze on my face.

But a few minutes away from the house, my awareness sharpens and the brief stillness falls away. My eyes scan the trees alongside me; I sense something. Something else otherworldly. It's the same sensation as when Emotions are near—my nothingness strengthens, hardens, prepares. But I don't recognize this essence.

The minutes tick by, and I get closer to town. Nothing happens. Nothing appears. When I pull into the school parking lot the clock shows 7:59, and there's still no reason for why my senses are tingling.

I pull the hood of my windbreaker up over my head as I walk toward the school doors. Under my lashes I take stock of my surroundings. There are the Dorseth brothers, roughing each other up near the wall—they're infamous for their drugs and constant suspensions. There are the cliques that I don't take part in. And there, sitting on the wall a little ways down from the Dorseths, is ...

"Maggie," I say, stopping. I instantly take note of the veins beneath her translucent skin, the trembling, the smudges under her eyes. Her ink-black wig shines weakly in the sun. "Maggie, you shouldn't be here."

She puts a book in her bag and stands, grinning. The smile has a contrasting effect; she's wearing so much makeup it makes her eyes look droopy and hopelessly sad. "Well, hello to you too, bitch," she says wryly. "I can tell you missed me."

I know she'll be hurt if I don't reassure her. "Of course I'm glad to see you," I intone, failing to correct the pitch of my voice before the words come out. "It's been a long time," I add, forcing a note of sincerity into the words now. I move forward and hug her. She's like a bag of bones in my arms.

I step back to get a look at Maggie's clothing; her choices seem to be getting more drastic. Today she's wearing fishnet tights and a short skirt, complete with a chain clinking against her thigh. Her feet are covered by thick leather boots that are way too big. Velvet gloves adorn her arms to hide those jutting, pale hands. Her top . . . there isn't much of a top to speak of. But she's so flat-chested that the low neckline is a bit pointless.

"Aren't you going to ask?" Maggie pulls away. I don't respond, offering her a slight shrug. This girl who I call my friend slings her arm around my shoulders, steering me to the front doors. Even sick as she is, her grip is tight. "How I escaped from the asylum?" she presses. Her term for the hospital.

We're drawing stares from others. I meet the gaze of Tyler Bentley, the star quarterback on the team. He barely notices me, but he's looking at Maggie unabashedly. *What is she doing here?* I see him mouth. He doesn't understand. None of them do. They think Maggie is an addict, and she lets them believe it. She even encourages it. She doesn't want anyone to know the truth, because she doesn't want to be pitied.

"Maybe you should go back to the hospital," I say to her now. A friend should be concerned, and Maggie is deep into the cancer, reason enough for worry. Just getting out of bed is probably too much for her.

"So when do I get to see it?" she asks, ignoring me. She's always been like this, jumping from one topic to another. Her lip ring glints.

"See what?"

"Hey, guys, wait up!"

Maggie turns quickly, her expression lighting up. The boy who called out runs toward us, then brushes past, heading for his friends a few feet ahead. I watch Maggie's face fall. I'm not enough for her. She needs more. I know this. And yet where there should be remorse, regret, longing, grief, there is, of course, only me. The black hole, the white canvas, the empty room.

Maggie is already recovering, and she links her arm through mine as we navigate the halls of Edson High. I sidestep what looks like a puddle of soda. "I want to see your newest painting," she asserts. "What are you working on?"

The bell rings overhead. "We'd better go to class," I tell her. She nods, not bothering to force another smile or say goodbye. She's already dwindling.

When the second bell sounds out—last chance to get to class—I stand by my locker and watch Maggie walk away, her tread trembling and uncertain. She'll be going back to the hospital in less than an hour, no doubt. I may be able to understand human nature, and Maggie is stubborn enough to always get her way, but at this moment I can't fathom what her parents were thinking this morning when they let her come back to school.

"Elizabeth Caldwell!" a teacher says sharply as she rushes by. I glance at her and wave, but we both know I'm going to be late again. I gather the materials for class, keeping one eye on Maggie making her way down the hall. In a moment, she'll turn a corner and be gone from sight, probably the last time I'll see her in a while.

I'm still there when she falls.

I hesitate for just an instant. I really should get to first period. *That's not a normal reaction*, instinct nudges. Realizing this, I drop everything and run. The doors and posters on either side of me are blurs. When I reach Maggie's side I go down to my knees, shake her shoulder.

Her skin has a more pronounced sickly tint, and her eyes don't even flutter as I say her name. Her pulse is slow and faint. I lift my head. There's no one else around but a skinny boy, and he stares at us dumbly. "Call an ambulance," I order him. He fumbles around in his pockets and I turn my attention back to Maggie. It looks like she's not breathing. I check her pulse again just to make sure she's still alive.

It takes five minutes for the ambulance to arrive, and when the paramedics burst around the corner and spot us, they put a mask over Maggie's face. They lift her up onto a stretcher, rattling off numbers and medical talk I don't understand. When they take yellow Maggie away, I follow them. No one stops me; the hall is full now.

"She's the girl that, like, doesn't eat, right?"

"No, she throws it all up, I thought."

My classmates' hushed, speculative chatter fills my ears. I follow the paramedics outside, and so does everyone else. I go as far as the edge of the parking lot and watch the men carry Maggie hurriedly toward the vehicle.

A moment later, movement out of the corner of my eye catches my attention and I turn to see Maggie's mom rushing toward me. "What happened?" she asks in a high, trembling voice. Her grip is so tight on her purse that her knuckles are white, and her hair is a wild mess.

"She collapsed." I'm not the only one staring at the commotion; the front steps are now littered with students. Their expressions are full of curiosity. Not concern.

"I was out in the car," she tells me with a twisted expression. Emotions shimmer into view and stand close to her. Guilt, Worry. I'm careful to keep my eyes on Maggie's mom. "I should never have let her come," she babbles on, "but she wanted to so much that I thought maybe—"

The paramedics slam the doors shut behind Maggie.

"I'd better go," her mom says, tearful. She touches my elbow before jogging toward her car. The lights of the ambulance, red and blue, swirl over the parking lot. I watch it pull out of the parking lot and squeal onto Main Street. Maggie's mom is close behind in her minivan. Before they're out of sight, I turn away. There's nothing I can do, after all.

I'm one of the first to head back to class.

THREE

I can feel Joshua Hayes staring at me again. I put my pencil down with a *click*, ignoring him. Our history teacher
prattles on about the Revolutionary War. "It was when the
outcome began to look worse for them that Washington
made his move…"

"Hey, freak."

Sophia Richardson pokes me, moving quickly so Mr.
Anderson doesn't see. I glance up from my notes. "Yes?"

She raises her brows in a mocking imitation of interest, resting her elbow on the back of her chair. "There's a
football game Friday night. Are you going?"

Unlike the others in my class, Sophia doesn't pretend I
don't exist. Her resentment shoves whatever instinct she has
to the back of her mind. Which is why she taunts me with
questions about football games and parties. Just like Fear,
she waits for my answer even though she already knows it. I

never go to social events. Not since Maggie stopped making me go.

"No, I don't think so," I tell her.

Satisfaction radiates from Sophia's tight smile. She plays with the ends of her straightened hair and says casually, "No one wants to hang out with you because you're—"

A crumpled-up piece of paper pops Sophia in the back of the head and she jerks, scowling. She reaches down to pick up the ball, scanning the room for the culprit. His head is bent down and he's studying his textbook intently, but I suspect Joshua Hayes isn't as innocent as he seems. Sophia must suspect it too, because she blanches. Tough as she may act, she's had a crush on him for years. A crush that's never been reciprocated. Then Sophia scowls, and when she turns her churning green eyes on me again, it's evident she somehow blames me for all of it.

Everyone has a motive behind their actions. Sophia's is based in pain and jealousy. I know a side of her she so desperately tries to hide. It's obvious she's tired today—she keeps rubbing her eyes and can't hold back her yawns. Rumors circulate all the time, but I don't need to listen to them; I know firsthand. Sophia's little sister, Morgan, is autistic. She has a babysitter who stays with her during the day, but since Mrs. Richardson works long hours, it often falls on Sophia's shoulders to look after her sister.

Once upon a time, Sophia considered me her best friend. I was over at her house a few times a week, playing dolls or whatever other game she invented for us. She tried to hide Morgan from me, deliberately dragging me to places that were as far from her as we could get. Until one day the babysitter brought Morgan outside for some fresh air and there was nowhere for Sophia to go, so I met the younger Richardson sister for the first time. And for some unfathomable reason, Morgan took to me like a drowning victim to a life jacket.

Things unraveled quickly. Morgan came in search of me every time she knew I was at her house, and she would scream if anyone tried to take her away. I didn't care, of course, but Sophia was another story. She watched the two of us with narrow eyes and a pinched mouth. Her thoughts were written in every line of her face, visible in every movement. Mrs. Richardson started calling me when Morgan was in one of her moods. She asked me if I was willing to take over as her babysitter—which earned me the money to buy my truck.

Then, one day, the phone calls stopped. The invitations halted. And Sophia began to spend her time with other girls at school. She'd finally had enough. I think some part of her hoped I would grovel, fight for our friendship. But, being me, I did the equations. It wouldn't work. So, since it would be fruitless to pursue anything, I went on my way.

Mr. Anderson has finally noticed the disturbance in his class and his piercing gaze shoots through Sophia, then me. I scoot down in my seat like a properly chastised student, and with one final glare, Sophia leaves me alone for the rest of the period.

The day passes quickly, and for a few hours everything is completely ordinary. I sit alone at lunch, I listen closely to the lectures, and I don't talk to anyone in my classes. It isn't until I'm back in my truck and heading home that I sense it again. That presence. I actually stop in the middle of the road, tasting it, tilting my head as I flip through my memories for a match to this essence. It's no one I've met before, I realize. Yet there's something so … oddly familiar about it. How can that be? And it isn't trying to hide itself from me; it's as if it's calling to me, hoping I'll try to find it. Is it an Emotion?

But Dad is expecting me home. The cows won't milk themselves. I also need to make a call to the hospital to see how Maggie is doing—the normal behavior of a friend. Shifting back into first gear, I continue on my way home.

The presence stays with me until I pull into the driveway; then it leaves, a silent mystery.

I know it will be back.

Everyone has a purpose. There are those who are unfortunate enough not to know what that purpose is, and there are those that are bound by it, thrive in it, know nothing else.

Unlike humanity, Fear and all the rest like him have no governors or presidents or kings. They're ruled by their own natures, which are hardwired into their every pore, vein, eyelash. And Emotions are not alone in their purpose. There is a design for every single thing. There is a being for Light, Song, Wind, Grass, Life, and Death. Winter, Spring, Fall. The Elements and the Seasons. They are part of our world and apart from it. They exist on another plane, spiritlike creatures that humans can't hear or see...unless they're strange, like me. There doesn't seem to be a limit on how many places they can be at once.

Some of these creatures I've met. Most I haven't. So every time I see an out-of-place being out in the fields, as I do now, I wonder who I'm looking at. It's dark out, and there's a thick mist. The figure walks with purpose through the crops, hands outspread. Fog again?

After a few moments, the stranger in the field vanishes, finished with whatever he or she set out to do. I pull my gaze from the window and try to focus on the conversation. Something about football, I think. Friday night. My brother is home for the weekend, as he usually is; he works at Fowler's Grocery in town until he goes back to college on Mondays. I'm quiet—I think my parents prefer it this way—and keep my head down, studying the patterns in the flowered tablecloth as I pick at my food. Corn and potatoes and pork. Yellow, white, pink.

"Liz, you haven't said a word all night," my brother says suddenly, and when I look up, his gaze is gentle, encouraging. Even though he probably thinks I'm weird, like the rest of the town, Charles is kind to me.

Something is off about him tonight, though. I sense it, and I probe Charles' expression. I suspect it has something to do with school; he told me he's been having trouble with his classes. I notice the way his hands shake slightly as he lifts his glass, the way his eyes dart to Dad and back to his plate again nervously. Apprehension is behind him, resting his hand on my brother's shoulder. The Emotion pays me no mind.

"I have nothing to say, thanks," I murmur. I've been watching the situation and I have no intention of taking part in it. If Charles has bad news, Tim—Dad—will need someone to take his anger out on later. Because Charles is the favorite child by far, I know it won't be him. Instinct urges me to be as invisible as possible until the inevitable storm hits.

"What about your friend Maggie? How is she doing?" Charles asks next.

"She's fine," I mumble to the table. To discourage more questions, I shove a forkful of potatoes into my mouth.

Dad says something about football again, and Charles dives back into that discussion. I shift my attention from him to Mom. She looks tired. There's a new bruise by her temple. She's doing her best to hide the pain, though. She butters a piece of bread as if it's her sole purpose in life.

"Sarah, my glass is empty," Dad mutters, and my mother doesn't hesitate; she gets up, a weary shadow. Charles says something about how good the pork is. There's no way to ignore what's happening, but he's always done his best. The three of us eat in stiff silence. The food is a tasteless lump on my tongue. Tim keeps his head down and Charles's knee bounces. My gaze strays to the window again. The mist rolls over the fields.

When Mom comes back from the kitchen, I see that Resentment is following her, touching her shoulder as she sets Dad's precious milk in front of him and sits down. The chair protests by uttering a long groan. The conversation doesn't continue. We're silent, a fragmented pretense of belonging, and we all know it.

When our eyes meet, Resentment nods in greeting. He's bald—even though they're immortal, Emotions resemble humans in appearance—and I've always thought he looks a lot like Mr. Clean minus the gold hoop earring. "How are you, little one?" he questions me. He's one of the few Emotions that enjoy talking to me. Then again, he enjoys talking to anyone. Resentment has always had a chatty tendency.

I give everyone an excuse and push my chair back, slipping into the kitchen with my glass in hand. Without looking, I know Resentment will follow. No one would appreciate me speaking to the air, so I'm careful to keep my voice low as I say, "I'm the same." I don't bother to tiptoe around his question. When dealing with anything other-worldly, I've learned to avoid playing the games they love so much. I twist the knob on the sink.

Water spills over the rim of the glass and splatters against the silver sink bottom. I don't even notice until I feel the cool splash on my fingers. I turn the knob back quickly. Resentment is appraising me. I move by him to stand in the door-way, watching the people I call family. The walls of the house creak, noticeable now because of the heavy silence.

Although Resentment has released his hold on my mother, his effect lingers. She will feel it for hours. And of course more will come to touch her during the course of the evening; it's the way of humanity to be consumed by Emotions. She hides Resentment's essence the same way she hides everything else. The only sign of her feelings toward Dad is the purse of her lips. Something no one else will notice but me.

"Fear has been looking for answers," the Emotion tells me now. "I actually caught him going through some newspaper archives the other day. I haven't seen him this intrigued about a mortal in over a decade."

"He won't find anything," I say flatly. For once, I don't have to pretend. "Fear only hunts because he's bored." No one in the dining room notices my scrutiny. Charles's knife clinks against his plate. Mom and Dad discuss the crops.

Resentment doesn't have a response to this, and we fall silent. As we stand there, it suddenly occurs to me that he might know about the presence I sensed earlier. For a few seconds I consider asking, but something holds my tongue.

Dad will notice if I stay away too long. Nodding a good-bye to Resentment, I rejoin them. Charles is saying something about Fowler's Grocery now. Sliding into my seat, I take another bite of my barely touched meal so no one will detect anything amiss.

"I have more summons to see to," Resentment tells me, his hairless head gleaming in the light of the chandelier. "Enjoy your time with these pathetic people."

I can't reply, and he vanishes. Resentment is a simple creature; he has his purpose, he is what he is, and there isn't much more to him. He's said before that he doesn't understand why I bother living among humanity, living a lie. The truth is, I hide my real nature because if I don't, my nothingness would consume me. I would become a wandering creature, with no connections and no soul. My life in Edson isn't perfect at all, but it is a life—the only one I'll ever have. So, even though I don't hold any feeling for my place in this family or this town, I will hold on to it because I can.

———————

After helping Mom with the dishes—or rather, trying to help and having her edge around me, avoiding so much as a look in my direction—I escape the house and make my way up to the loft of the barn. It's a serene place, silent except for the cows rustling below. Gentle shafts of the fading sun slip in through the cracks in the walls. Along each of these walls, set on top of bales of hay, are my paintings. Dad allows me to keep them up here; he doesn't use the loft because of the leaky roof. They don't get in his way.

The paintings are echoes of my dreams. Well, dreams and images that sometimes flit through my mind at random. I put them on canvas so that I can study and possibly learn from them.

One scene occurs over and over in the brush strokes, differing only in angles and colors. One place, one event: a beautiful girl I've never met before is crying out, cradling a limp boy in her arms. They look like they could be my age, or a little older. The boy's eyes are closed, his expression one of peace. There are trees all around, and out of the shadows, a hulking, faceless form emerges. No way to tell who or what it is, since it's surrounded by tendrils of darkness. It stands over the weeping girl, looking at the motionless boy she holds, but she doesn't seem to notice it. And there the dream is finished. An end of one thing and the beginning of something else, but of what I don't know.

There are other paintings besides these, though. My dreams have been consumed by more. More images, more mysterious flickers. A vague image of a stone house. The white fingers of the ocean. A pair of crinkled, smiling eyes. The long fingers of a woman, the flutter of a yellow skirt, the vibrant disorientation of parties and celebrations long finished.

Every time I look at these paintings, something inside me clenches. It's an odd sensation, as if I'm supposed to be feeling something but my wall of nothingness is blocking it.

Again my concentration returns to the boy and girl. Somehow, I believe, they're the key to all of this. In the painting, there she sits, weeping, torrents of tears streaming down her face. She's in the woods, wearing jeans and a long T-shirt. Surrounded by tree trunks, kneeling on the moss-covered ground. She's looking up at the sky—it must be sunset, like now, because the air around her is pink twilight—and she's screaming. The girl's teeth shine in the fading light. There is an agony in her face that I cannot even imagine experiencing. The boy she has her arms wrapped around is limp, lying on the ground. Once in a while I get a faint impression that there could have been blood surrounding the two.

Of course, these paintings explain nothing. They only raise more of the questions that I don't know the answers to. Who are these people? Who lived in the house? Is it real? Why do I dream of it? Common sense urges me to let it all go, but instinct orders me to solve this mystery.

Tonight there are more images crowding around inside

my head. The nothingness holds fast, though, a firm lock to the door that I'm trying to open. Over and over again, I see the shadow, the trees, the girl's open mouth and the silent scream.

You will forget everything.

It pops into my head, random and fresh. I sit up straighter from my perch in the barn window. This memory is new. The voice is unfamiliar—no way to tell whether it's male or female—but my intuition tells me I should know it. I reach out and grasp the sentence, tightening my hold, remembering it over and over again, trying, trying to place it. This might prove that there is outside involvement. Someone has done something to me, made me to be the way I am. *You will forget everything.*

Not everything, I think. There are holes in the wall, this I know. Where else would the dreams be coming from?

I look at all the angles, as I have so many times before. I have the ability to see the unseen. All these dreams, the nothingness—

"Elizabeth."

At the sound of the familiar voice, I turn. Fear stands in a dark corner, looking at me, one side of his mouth tipped up in a mischievous smile. I study him, blinking. I hadn't sensed him coming. "You don't usually come to see me this often," I say after a pause. "You found something."

A breeze drifts in through the open window, and Fear's white-blond hair ripples. Unaware, he raises his brows at me. "Something has happened here, I think. You looked like you were on a different planet when I came in. What is it, hmmm? Did *you* find something tucked away in that pretty head of yours?"

He's never seen my paintings before, and though I don't look at them, Fear glances away from my face and notices. He makes a sound of interest, striding from one to the next, doubtless memorizing them as clues to the mystery that is me. "You've never told me about your ... hobby before." He lingers in front of one, arms folded behind his back. He tilts his head, and that silky hair brushes against his jaw. "Your style is sloppy; there's no way of knowing who the girl is. All I can make out is her teeth and her dark hair." He reaches out and touches the curve of the girl's cheek in one painting. Phantom fingers brush my real cheek as he does so.

"Stop it," I say.

"Or what?" He spins to face me. "You don't care." When I don't reply, he sobers. "Tell me."

I shake my head. "You don't need to know."

He steps closer. I feel the air around us cool, and his essence clashes against me. When yet again I remain stoic, Fear sighs. I look up at him from where I sit.

"It's not boredom, or just the need to know," he informs me, eyes glittering. "I pity you, Elizabeth, and I want to help you."

Now I stand, and it brings me so close to him that our chests are almost touching. My wall of nothingness quivers at the proximity. It's an odd sensation. I just arch my neck back to meet his earnest gaze. "You don't pity me," I tell Fear. "You don't want to help me. You want to help yourself."

A scowl twists his beautiful face. He clenches his fists, checks himself, and forces himself to unclench them. A moment later his impish smile has returned. But underneath the charming façade his intent still lurks. "You do puzzle me, Elizabeth the Numb."

I turn my attention from him to the paintings. Shadows slant over them now as night sneaks in. "Whatever you think you found, Fear, is nothing. If someone did do this to me, they made sure that the trail to them would never be uncovered."

"Ah." He lifts a finger. "But that's not true. I found this." He reaches into his black overcoat and takes out a newspaper, yellowed with age. He hides its contents.

"What is it?" I ask, just as he wants me to.

Fear unfolds the paper, mocking me as he pretends to read it. I don't play the game by reaching for it. He sighs, relenting, and holds it out to me. "Oh, very well. Since you want it so badly."

I take it with both hands, noting my own picture on the front page. I'm about three or four—it's one of the pictures Mom has framed in our living room. It's the girl that I don't recognize as myself; her face glows with that inner life. *Girl Survives Car Accident*, the headline reads. But as I start to scan the words—I'm barely past the second sentence—the entire article fades away, the letters, the picture, everything, until I'm holding nothing but a blank paper.

"What is it?" Fear frowns when I hand it back to him. He takes in the empty page, brow furrowed in thought. "The plot thickens," he murmurs. "But now we know that there *is* someone behind this. Your immunity really could be a power of some sort in play."

"And how do you propose we find out?" I ask, sitting back down and looking out the window again. The hay pokes at the bottoms of my thighs. "I'm starting to think whatever happened to me was meant to make me forget something. I don't think it's just emotions that have been removed from me—there are memories missing, too." If that's what the dreams are. But are they my memories? Or ... someone else's? And why can't I remember when this change in me occurred?

I turn to face Fear again and see his gaze sharpen. "Maybe they did this to you to hide something. You could've seen something you weren't supposed to ... "

The sun has finally left, and the moon's faint outline begins to emerge from the other side of the sky. "Maybe," I say.

Before I can ask him about what the rest of the article contained, Fear tucks the blank newspaper back into his coat and bends down to me. "You're so distracting; I've lingered here too long. See you soon, Elizabeth," he whispers. His lips touch my ear and his arctic breath fans my face. It smells distinctly of strawberries.

The Emotion vanishes, and an instant later a man jumps from the shadows of the loft with a long knife, making as if to stab me in the stomach. He's wearing all black and his face is swathed in a ski mask. When I only stare at him, making no sound of alarm, the attacker disappears right when the blade is about to go into me.

"Fear?" I call.

"Just checking," he chuckles, his voice coming from the night sky.

F O U R

"You did this."

A whisper in my ear. The words are a hiss, meaningless to my groggy mind. But the strong sense of someone watching drives me completely awake. Fear? My eyes open to darkness and take a moment to adjust. The black becomes solid shapes. Dresser, mirror, chair. I'm alone; there's nothing but the furniture and the night. Yet there's a hint of power in the air. I sit up, frowning. It's raining outside, a light smattering against the glass of the window. It casts quivering shadows over everything. Something isn't right.

"You did this."

I turn. The voice comes from my left. Young, soft. I make out a human shape, standing in the dim corner, that wasn't there before. Slender. Not an Emotion, my senses tell me. Something else. "Who are you?" I ask. Thunder rumbles.

The strange visitor doesn't move. Doesn't speak. For what seems like hours we both remain frozen. Questions linger on the tip of my tongue. The storm intensifies, and a flash of lightning illuminates the room. And I'm able to make out his features.

It's impossible.

It's wrong.

When he continues to stare back at me with accusation in those familiar eyes, there are no plausible explanations. Because it's him. The boy who stars in all my paintings. The boy who never moves, never changes, never speaks. The one who the beautiful girl screams over with such anguish.

"You're dead," I tell him, clutching my blankets. Can't be, instinct keeps insisting. This is another one of Fear's games. Another illusion. My wall of nothingness stirs. I imagine a brick cracking, pieces of rubble showering down.

The boy doesn't acknowledge this. Now that the lightning has subsided, he's shrouded in oblivion again. For an instant I wonder if he's gone—disappeared back to the recesses of my mind—but then his voice emerges, drifts to me again: "You killed me," he whispers.

The storm bursts one more time, and I see that a stream of blood has slipped out from beneath his hairline to run down one side of his face.

———

My eyes fly open and I jerk upright, twisting instantly toward the corner where I know the boy won't be.

Because it was just a dream.

No whispers, no blood, nothing but the realities of this world.

How strange.

The rain is gentle outside, not as portentous as it was moments ago. Oblivious to my plight, the millions of drops fall to the earth with a symphony of wet sounds. I shove my blankets to the floor. *Hot, too hot in here.* I lie back again and invite sleep to return.

———————

I've known Joshua Hayes since we were small children, placed in the same kindergarten class. We've never been friends, exactly, but we're always aware of each other. Once in the fifth grade, when a group of boys gathered together and tried to make me cry by pinching my arms over and over, Joshua defended me, landing in detention with even more bruises than I had.

It wasn't until the beginning of high school that his feelings began to change. He watches me as if he sees more than what there is. He probably takes my silence as deep contemplation, takes my endurance of Sophia's vicious treatment as patience, sees my solitary state as a choice to stand apart from the others. Though he's right in his belief that I'm different from everyone else, he's wrong about the reason for this. I'm not special or an independent thinker. Yet I've never bothered to correct him in his beliefs because he's never approached me.

But he wants to. I see his desire growing each day, notice how the Emotions' visits to him at school are becoming more frequent. I watch and wait, knowing I'll have to put this fire out someday soon.

"I'm going to let you choose your partners for our first project," Mrs. Farmer says early Monday morning, toward the end of class. She tiredly brushes her hair out of her eyes.

"What's the project?" one of my classmates asks. Susie Yank, the tiny girl everyone has labeled *nerdy* and *know-it-all*. She's really just lonely, taking solace in knowledge rather than drowning in her friendless existence. I see Longing standing beside her, touching Susie's shoulder as the girl glances at Sophia, probably imagining what it would be like to be her best friend. Longing is a beautiful Emotion, with long sleek hair and slanted, exotic eyes.

Mrs. Farmer sighs. "I was getting to that. Your job, along with your partner's, is to make a portfolio of your own work. We're going to focus on creative writing for a while and take a break from the classics. I've given you partners because I know some of you struggle with writing. So you can help each other and feed off of each other's ideas."

"What does the portfolio—"

"Your portfolio"—Mrs. Farmer glares at Susie—"needs to have two poems and one short story, along with two peer reviews. This handout will have the details on what the reviews need to contain, as well as the specifics on the poems and story."

As she begins to distribute the assignment, I feel Joshua's gaze on me. I see that Longing has duplicated herself so she is also standing next to him—it's how the Emotions answer so many summons. It seems that Longing is fickle today; instead of touching Joshua's shoulder, she leans down and presses a long kiss onto his lips. Joshua can't see her, of course, but humans have instincts just like the rest of the living creatures of the world and he turns away from me, frowning, touching his mouth. He'll dismiss the sensation as nothing. Longing looks at me and winks.

"Poor baby," she croons to Joshua, addressing me. "You torment him so, dear. Why not give him a chance? I bet he's *delicious.*"

I don't respond. Longing pats Joshua's cheek, grins at me one more time, and disappears. She's also left Susie, so there are no other Emotions in the room at the moment. Only their influence.

"*Zombie.*" Sophia holds the handout in front of my face. She waves back and forth, fanning my face. "Hello, anyone in there?" I reach to take it from her, but Sophia jerks it away from my grasp, disgust etched in the lines of her face. "You're such a freak," she snaps. "What's wrong with you? Huh? *Answer me.*"

"Nothing I say will satisfy you," I say, glancing at Mrs. Farmer, who's staring at the clock now. Her glasses are crooked on her nose. I look at Sophia again. "Can I have the paper, please?" I know it's fruitless, but I try because it's what she expects, and what the kids around me listening expect. Sophia waves it in my face again.

"What are you going to do?" she hisses. "Try to take it from me. Come on, Elizabeth. Take it from me."

She holds it in front of my nose again, prepared to snatch it away. I don't move as I calculate. Mrs. Farmer hasn't noticed us yet, but if I defend myself it could get me in trouble with the office, and thus in trouble with

Tim. Sophia laughs at me, and a couple other kids do too, thinking I'm frozen because of Fear. But for once, he's far from here.

"*I'll* take it from you." Joshua moves so quickly that Sophia doesn't realize that the paper has slipped from her fingers until it's too late. She glares up at Joshua.

"N-nobody asked you to get involved," she says to him, her narrow face pinched with fury. She wants him to like her so badly, but she can't bring herself to be kind to me.

Joshua grins, a lazy, insolent curve of the lips. "'Course nobody asked. That's what makes it fun." He gives me the assignment, his eyes saying more than his words ever could. Joy and Courage stand by him, both touching his shoulders. Joshua's face is a mask of mischief, but the presence of the Emotions shows me the truth.

"Thank you," I tell him.

Sophia has turned around in her seat, but her stiff shoulders and Anger beside her are hints of future pain I can look forward to. Anger ignores my presence—he's never liked me, for some reason.

Mrs. Farmer has begun to talk again, so I pretend to pay attention to her.

"You're welcome," I hear Joshua say, which pulls my eyes back to him. Playing the part of the casual troublemaker, he grins at me, touches his temple as if to tip an invisible hat, and goes back to his desk. Joy has gone, but I know she's still with him from the spring in his step. Courage stays by me— one of the few Emotions I haven't met. I don't know how I recognize him, but I do.

The bell rings and suddenly the classroom is alive. Kids shoot to their feet and speed-walk to the door like their lives depend on it. Joshua gives me a last, lingering look as he leaves. "Make sure to pick your partners by tomorrow!" Mrs. Farmer raises her voice to be heard. She's following the throng into the hallway. Pretty soon I'm alone with Courage, who remains even though everyone is gone.

I stand and gather my books. "You're not as beautiful as your opposite," I inform him. "But you're not so restless."

Courage—brother and eternal enemy of Fear—looks down at me. He has a long nose, noble-looking, and his hair lodges against the back of his neck in tight black curls. "Of course not. I'm everything he isn't."

It's true. As dark as his brother is pale, Courage studies me. He's a formidable presence in the small, insignificant classroom. "You're an interesting one," he states, and there is a note of curiosity in his voice. "I had heard the stories of a mortal that we're unable to touch, but I hadn't given them much thought. Truly interesting. I can see why Fear is so captivated."

"He hates what he can't understand," I say.

Courage takes this in with a thoughtful expression. "You are very young to know so much. And knowledge in our world is dangerous. Remember that."

"You would encourage ignorance, then?" My tone is polite. His answer could be beneficial; it may aid in my survival.

The Emotion tilts his head, obviously distracted. Someone in the world is in need of a touch of bravery, no doubt.

His body twitches and shimmers just the tiniest bit, an indication that he's answering the summons by sending another copy of himself to the source. "What is that phrase you humans use?" he murmurs after a moment, focusing on me again. "Ah. Ignorance is bliss. Yes?"

Any second now he'll vanish. I release him from the discussion by saying, "I'll keep that in mind." When Courage doesn't move, I add, "Was there something else?"

He stands so close to me that I feel his heat, and it's an unusual sensation because Fear is so cold. Courage's voice is the slow smolder of lava as he tells me, "You should be kind to the boy who defended you."

"The other plane doesn't usually worry about human affairs," I observe.

Courage walks away. He's different from others; he's not flashy and quick to disappear. In the doorway he pauses, but he doesn't look at me again. "The other plane is changing. We're learning more about what it means to be mortal. Be kind to him," the Emotion repeats. "There is more than one among us who watches you; someone believes you will need that boy in the end."

Before I can ask any of the questions that this new development brings—*the end of what? Who watches? Why would I need Joshua?*—he leaves. I let him go. After all, even if he is different, he's still an Emotion, and they do love their riddles.

f I V E

The moment I slide out of the cab of my truck, gravel crunching beneath my tennis shoes, I know something is wrong. There's a heavy silence hanging in the air, a bad omen. The cows haven't been brought in for the milking. Dad's pickup is gone.

I walk toward the house, shouldering my bag. The quiet rings in my ears. I let the screen door slam shut behind me, to announce my presence as usual, but Mom isn't in the kitchen. Dropping my bag on the floor next to the table, I poke my head into every room, still sensing something... off. I climb the stairs, and just as I pass the bathroom a sob shatters the hovering gloom—Mom.

I recognize the situation immediately. My first instinct is to turn right around and hide, for the sake of self-preservation. My second instinct is stronger: *play the part*. A normal person—a normal daughter—wouldn't just walk away. On swift feet I go back down to the kitchen, grab a washcloth from the sink, wet it, and ascend the stairs again. Mom has locked the door. I run my fingers along the doorframe, looking for the small pick, and when I find it I stick it in the lock. Soon the knob twists in my hand.

"Go away," Mom cries when she sees that it's me coming in. Her mascara runs down her cheeks in black rivers, and there's blood flowing from a cut in her lip.

"Are you all right?" I ask, knowing she won't answer. And she doesn't. She clutches her knees and rocks back and forth. The back of her head keeps knocking against the wall, and I reach out to grasp her arm, stopping her. She cringes at my touch.

"Here." I hold out the washcloth; she won't let me near enough to clean the cut myself. And of course she doesn't take it. I'd guess that she's thinking about Tim, about whatever it was that caused this. "It isn't your fault," I murmur.

That gets a reaction. "Shut up!" my mother hisses, glaring at me through her tears. "You're not my child! You're unnatural, and I want you to *get out of my life!*"

I watch her for a moment. My presence is only upsetting her more, so I finally say, "I'll go." On my way to the door I pause by the window, noticing movement outside. I glance back at Mom. "Tim is coming back up the driveway. You probably should barricade yourself in the bedroom."

It's as if I haven't spoken. She just stares at me. "What are you?" Her voice is a broken whisper.

Tim's brakes squeal as he parks his pickup next to mine. I look back at Mom again. "Do you still want me to go?"

We both hear the screen door downstairs slam open,

accompanied by a belch and a colorful string of profanities immediately after. Tim is still drunk, then. And angry. Mom's breathing quickens. Fear materializes, kneeling down beside her to clasp her in his freezing embrace. Mom shivers, eyes glazing over.

"Help," she whimpers to me. One word, seemingly so simple, but it's so much more.

For just an instant, I catch a glimmer of true, undeniable compassion in Fear's fathomless pale eyes. He smiles at me bitterly. "Ah, mortality," he says. "Your kind is consumed by habits, traditions. The fact that she's married to him keeps her trapped here."

Mom is whispering something under her breath, over and over. I can't make out the words. Tim is stumbling his way through the kitchen. He knocks a chair to the floor. I think quickly, flatly. If I save my mother now, she'll feel as if she owes me, or that there's a possibility I might be normal, and she'll try to forget what's happened here. The pretense of our lives can continue until I find a way to feel. Then, maybe, I can be the normal girl everyone expects me to be, and I will survive.

Mom's whispers grow more intense as her agitation increases. "Stay up here," I tell her, and shut the bathroom door. I go back down the stairs. Stop in the kitchen doorway. Watch my father as he falls apart. He doesn't notice me there for a few minutes. He's mumbling to himself, opening every cupboard, hunting for something else to drink, probably. When I shift my feet, deliberately making my heel scrape the floor, he slams the fridge shut, twisting in my direction. His movements are sluggish.

"You," he slurs, red eyes latching onto me. "You're the reason all of this started."

"What do you mean?" I ask, unmoving, even when he walks toward me. But there are faint memories; I know exactly what he means. My strangeness drove my parents apart. First there were arguments, in low furious tones, over quickly. Then those evolved into loud matches that lasted hours. Tim began to drink and Mom sank into herself. Until our lives became what they are. So it's true; I did do this.

Tim keeps muttering, but his words are so jumbled I can't make any sense of them. He grabs my shoulder, slamming me against the wall. Pain slices up my spine. His breath is sour, his breathing labored.

"You're different," he mumbles in my face. Over his shoulder I see the shimmer of an Emotion that must be here for him. Guilt? Sorrow? I can't tell with Tim's red face in the way. "You used to be like Charles. You used to be a kid. Now you're not. You . . ." Tim loses his train of thought. "I need a drink," he mutters.

As they usually do around this point, my instincts come to life again, rational and cold. *Survive. Fight. Run*, they hiss. I can't release the mental image of my mother, though, so pathetic and alone up in that mint-green bathroom. So I ignore all the impulses and look up at Tim. My words are bullets, swift and calculated. "I think a drink is the last thing you need."

And as I expected, this infuriates him. "Don't tell me

what I need." He shakes me until my teeth ache. "You're just … just a freak!"

He isn't mad enough. If he calms down at all, he'll go looking for Mom. "Yes, I'm a freak," I concede, pasting an expression of false defiance on my face. "But at least I'm not a disgusting, abusive drunk."

His fist lashes out more quickly than I anticipated.

There's a swift intake of breath behind me. Someone watching. Fear. "Elizabeth!" I hear him snap. "Fight back!"

Slumped against the wall, I continue to shove aside those instincts and Fear's desperate insistence. I get to my feet and face Tim. I provoke him with taunts and names until stars dance before my eyes. Somehow I know it's guilt that makes my father sob. He doesn't even seem to be aware of his actions as he knocks me to the floor again. I never once try to defend myself. Those words Mom was chanting become a string of sound in my head, meaningless yet somehow relevant in this moment. *Save me, save me, save me …*

Just before the darkness takes over completely, I see Fear standing over me, that strange sympathy still haunting his expression.

"See you soon, little Elizabeth," he whispers.

———————

Word gets around fast in a small town. Since there's not much to talk about in the first place, everyone immediately grasps at the chance to gossip behind my back, their voices dramatic whispers that fill every corner of every room.

"I heard she let a guy beat her up as some kind of initiation for a gang."

"Sophia Richardson kicked her ass after school yesterday. Didn't you hear about their big fight in English?"

"She works on a farm—maybe a cow kicked her in the face or something."

The stories and theories go on throughout the day. It's strange how no one gets near the real story. Are people so eager to deny the obvious? Or do they really believe what they say? It's times like these that I realize I don't understand human nature as well as I'd thought.

It's Tuesday. As the last bell rings, releasing everyone, I walk to my locker slowly, contemplating the excuses I can give Maggie for not being able to visit her. She can't see the bruises on my face; she'll only worry, and that can't be any kind of advantage in her fight against the disease eating away at her body.

Someone slams into my shoulder, making me stumble. "Have fun doing nothing tonight, freak," Sophia singsongs, a friend giggling at her side. In a whirl of perfume and labels the pair hurries away, swerving around a man. He catches my attention just as I'm about to face my locker again, and I pause to study him. He stands farther down the hall, right in the center of the tiled floor, legs apart. He's staring at me. It's hard to make out the features of his face because the double doors are right behind him and sunlight streams through the glass. *Wrong*, my instincts whisper. He's not moving, and he's clearly out of place in this high school. A bizarre blend of tastes fills my mouth.

Before I can dissect this further, the man turns his back. Hands shoved in his pockets so casually, he walks away. *Thud. Thud. Thud.* His long shadow stalks him. There's a fresh flood of light as he pushes the doors open, and then he's gone.

Curious. I dismiss the voice of warning in my head—I haven't been getting too much sleep lately, what with all the dreams and faceless condemning whispers—and slam my locker shut, planning on using the phone to call Maggie. It's become more of a habit than anything. But just as I shoulder my bag and aim for the office, I crash into Joshua Hayes. He grunts in surprise as he sprawls onto the floor. I look down at him.

"Sorry."

He recovers quickly and grins up at me. His red hair is too long for a boy. It hangs in his face and splays over his jacket collar. "If you want to talk to me, you could have just said 'hey,'" he says. Belying the boy's cocky façade, Apprehension kneels down beside him, a soundless presence. Again, he doesn't bother to acknowledge me.

Opening my mouth, I prepare to say a quick goodbye, but Courage's words echo through my mind: *someone believes you will need that boy in the end.* I think swiftly and decide to follow the Emotion's advice—there was something about Courage that assured me he'd spoken the truth when he said he doesn't play games.

Silently, I extend my hand to Joshua, who hesitates for just an instant before taking it and allowing me to help him to his feet. His palm is damp, and when I let go, Joshua tries to discreetly wipe it dry on his pants.

"So…" He grins at me some more, shyness overtaking him now. "In a hurry to get somewhere?"

"No," I answer. "Just going home." The office is only a few yards down the hall. I start toward it.

Joshua walks beside me without an invitation. He wants to know me, and he's not about to let this opportunity slip through his fingers. At my words he chews his lip. "Oh." He hides behind his hair as he thinks. "I'm going home too. Lots of chores," he adds lamely.

"Yes." I halt outside the door marked *OFFICE*. A memory nudges at me, and for some reason I voice it. "I remember my mom taking me to your house once when we were little. She was bringing your father casserole."

He's nodding, features tight and shadowed. His current emotions swiftly dissipate and evolve into something darker. Sorrow and Anger. They hound him like merciless spirits and I'm careful to keep my gaze away. "Yeah," he says with a tightness in his voice. "I remember that, too. A lot of people brought casseroles after Mom died."

"I'm sorry for your loss." I meet his gaze and picture Courage as I make the words sincere. "Even though you know it's not her fault, you must struggle not to be angry with her sometimes, for leaving."

At this Joshua studies my bruises, and he isn't trying to be subtle. He's frowning fiercely, like maybe he's thinking about saying something. But in the end all he says is, "You talk like you've lost someone before."

"I haven't," I reply, deliberately curt. I sense the questions hovering on his tongue; I can't encourage this. Joshua is the kind of person to take action if he thinks he hears a cry for help. But the statement—*you talk like you've lost someone*—brings back images of the girl in the woods, screaming up at the sky. The boy in her arms. That house by the ocean, the woman's smile.

You killed me.

Knowing now is not the time to think about any of it, I put my hand on the doorknob as a hint that I'm finished with the conversation.

"Wait," Joshua says quickly. I wait. He hesitates once more, looking down at his shoes. Then he takes a deep breath and lifts his head. "Can I ... call you sometime?"

It's taken him years to ask me, and here it is. Again, the words whisper through my mind: *someone believes you will need that boy in the end.* What end, I wonder once more.

Joshua is still holding that single breath, preparing himself for my rejection. I force a smile at him, pretending interest. "That sounds great." I rattle off my number. Before he has a chance to stumble over a response, I duck into the office, already thinking about my phone call to Maggie.

S I X

Charles finally tells Dad about college—I was right in thinking he was having problems. He dropped out, in fact. I'm up in my room, listening to Tim shout at my brother about responsibility, money, growing up. It doesn't escape me that Tim is much more restrained with Charles than he is with me or Mom.

Afterwards, when Tim has stormed out of the house, leaving a menacing stillness in his place, Charles climbs the stairs. He comes into my room without knocking and flops face-down on my bed beside me. The bedsprings squeal from the added weight. Charles groans, but even after all of this, the only Emotion near him is Relief. Charles has had an easy life. Relief is stiff, younger-looking. He takes his purpose seriously; he doesn't acknowledge me.

"What are you going to do now?" I ask my brother, staring up at the ceiling. The smooth expanse of white makes me think of the dream-girl's skin in the moonlight.

Charles doesn't seem to notice my distraction. He also doesn't answer my question. Not because he doesn't want to, but because he has no idea. I know him. All he has is his job at Fowler's Grocery, and yet he isn't afraid of the empty prospects his future holds. Such is my brother's nature.

"You should decorate this room," he murmurs after a time. "It's depressing in here."

"I didn't know white was depressing," I say.

He rolls over to face me, serious for once. He can't ignore the bruises on my face anymore. "Has it been hard for you, while I was gone?" Relief vanishes at the question.

Mulling over the best response, I ponder the white walls, imagining them covered in posters or paint. It's strange— they've been white for so long, empty, like me, that it's difficult to picture it. "Nothing is ever hard for me," I tell Charles, making my tone sincere. "And Mom is tougher than you think."

Charles sighs, his fingers gentle as they skim the yellow bruise beneath my eye. "I-I'm sorry I haven't... I'm sorry I never..." A new Emotion appears—Guilt. She places her hand on my brother's cheek, in the same place his fingers rest on my own face. Unable to confront these truths and feelings, Charles abruptly switches course. Now he rolls to his back, arm under his head, and gazes up at the ceiling. "College wasn't for me, Liz," he murmurs. "You know I've never liked school."

I nudge him with my shoulder, playing the part of the little sister well. "You've never liked school as much as you like parties and alcohol, that is."

"Hey!" he protests, grinning ruefully. "I'm weak, okay? I tried to stay away. Really."

He's lying, but I don't call him on it. With one last grin, Charles leaves me. The floor creaks, and then the door is clicking shut. Silence. Soon I'm closing my eyes, my muscles relaxing. Just as I'm hovering between reality and dreaming, I sense that odd familiar-unfamiliar presence from the road, lurking nearby. Watching, waiting, for what?

Sleep has too firm a hold on me to break. This mysterious visitor isn't even close to being finished with me, though. Somehow, I'm certain of this. I will find out what it wants one way or another.

For now, I dream.

––––––––––

I'm standing at the edge of a clearing. The grass is knee-high; it ripples in the breeze. The skies above roll with fluffy clouds that make me think of the inside of a cupcake. Not sunrise or sunset, just a space in time that feels frozen, content.

Across the wide space, sitting with his back to a tree, sits the boy from my dreams.

His head is bent. He studies the pages of a book with intensity, his brow furrowed. In the daylight, even from this distance, I can see his features better than ever before. He's . . . delicate. His hair falls over his brow in a dark, silk curtain. His face is oval-shaped, his lips a thin line of contemplation. He's wearing a button-down shirt and jeans. No shoes.

Without my realizing it, I've started walking toward him.

The boy doesn't so much as twitch at the sound of my approach. The tips of the grass tickle the palms of my hands and a light material brushes against my knees. Glancing down, I notice that I'm wearing a dress I've never seen before. It's a summery creation, all yellow and beaming. Something I would never own.

Once I'm just a few feet away from the boy I halt. Wait. He's more slender than I realized, his fingers long and tapered as they grip the corner of the book. "Where is she?" he asks without looking up. His voice is calm this time, so feather-light it could be a lullaby. When I don't answer, his gaze meets mine, wide, innocent, chocolate-brown. Such a contrast to the black hatred that burned in his eyes that night in my room. A fly buzzes past my ear. Now he's the one waiting.

"Where is who?" I ask, just an instant before it occurs to me. Who else could he possibly be talking about? The one connection I can make to him, the other person in my dreams. She screams and weeps and rocks, forever imprinted in my mind as a broken thing.

Tears pool in the boy's eyes suddenly. "What did you do to her?" he demands, clutching the book so tight that his knuckles go white. Now his tone and expression are as harsh as Tim's backhand. I open my mouth but no sound comes out. What answer can I give?

The book falls to the ground and the pages flutter. Mindless, the boy presses his forehead to his knees and his shoulders shake. His shirt catches in one of the grooves of the tree bark behind him but he doesn't bother to pull free. He's drowning in grief just as his companion is in my other dreams. But who is really dead? What is this place? Where do I belong?

49

Somehow, none of it matters. A bizarre instinct consumes me to reach out, to touch him. Maybe just to prove to myself that none of this is real, or that he's real. I don't know. "She's alive," I tell him. It just pops out. I have no proof, I have no knowledge, but something inside of me clenches and releases when the boy comes alive. He stands, his red-rimmed eyes suddenly fierce, and seizes my shoulders. The movement is so quick; one moment he's on the ground and the next he's too close, with all his heat and passion.

"Where? Where?" he demands.

I shake my head. This infuriates him. I can see it in the way a muscle twitches in his jaw . . . but there are no Emotions. What does it mean?

There's no time to analyze. "You owe me," the boy says through his teeth. Suddenly the beauty of this place roils and changes. The sky darkens to an orange hue, and a sound fills the air, something akin to television static. "You did this. You ruined everything. We were happy. We were safe. You need to tell me the truth. Tell me the truth."

An ironic statement, though he doesn't know how ironic. It's impossible to get the truth from someone who doesn't know it. Pretending not to notice the rumbling world around us, I tell him point-blank without any façade of regret or empathy, "I don't know where she is."

An insect lands on my arm and I experience a brief flare of pain as it stings me. I shake it off, and my gaze shifts from the boy's face. For the first time I notice the dark cloud surrounding us like millions of grains of pepper. A swarm. Bloodthirsty, incensed. It grows louder and louder, a hungry hum. No way to escape.

"This isn't real," I say, turning my focus back to the boy. Before I can ask him questions of my own, attempt to understand the strangeness of all this, the boy's eyes turn red. Not just pink from tears, but a violent, ruby red. His pupils disappear and his lip curls in a snarl. "Lying," he hisses. His fingers bite into me. Not him, my instincts whisper.

His body quivers and stretches. Those eyes switch back and forth between brown, red, brown, red. Monster, boy. I look up at him. "Who are you?"

The words echo: Are you ... are you ... Time stops.

And then, just as quickly as it began, the changes retract, swift as claws. The violent swarm dissipates, the sky brightens to the happy blue, and the powerful creature is a simple boy again. Sitting against the tree once more with the book back in his hands, he turns a page as if it's the most fascinating text he's ever encountered. As if none of it happened.

I take a step toward him, prepared to demand everything and anything.

I wake up.

SEVEN

"Elizabeth?"

It's Thursday morning. English class. Lost in thought, I lift my head to meet Mrs. Farmer's gaze. "You've been called down to the office. Someone wants to talk to you," the teacher says. She doesn't offer specifics, but we both know that the school counselor is the one waiting for me. My bruises need to be addressed, no matter what the stories say the cause of them are.

I nod, gathering my things as quickly as I can. I feel Joshua staring at me. When I pass her, Sophia sticks her foot out in an attempt to trip me. I sidestep her neatly. She scowls. There are more dark smudges beneath her eyes. Morgan keeping her up again?

I push the door open with my back. Kids in the class study my face anew, probably coming up with fresh theories. Avoiding Joshua's gaze—he's too perceptive for his own good—I exit the room as fast as I can.

My footsteps echo in the empty hall. This won't be the first time I've been to see Sally Morrison, the school counselor. She doesn't believe the gossip and she never accepts my explanations, which consist of various accounts of clumsiness. This doesn't happen often, truthfully, but it occurs often enough that she's gotten more direct.

"Hi, Elizabeth," she greets me when I appear in her office doorway. The main office behind me is busy, the secretary talking loudly on the phone, the fax machine spitting out papers in the corner. "You can shut it," Sally tells me, pointing at the door with her pen. As I move to comply, I notice that she's added yet another plant to her shelves. That makes eight now.

"So what's the story this time?" Sally asks without preamble. No more small talk during our meetings, then. I sit down, waiting for that creak that always happens when I rest my full weight on the chair; we've developed a routine.

I run through my options before answering. Sally has no power unless I give it to her; she can't make any calls or get involved in my life unless I give her information she can use. Information I have no intention of giving.

"I was milking our cow. She kicked me in the face. She gets touchy like that sometimes." I shrug, as if to say, *What can you do?*

Sally sighs, tapping her pen over and over. Her features are too strong to be considered pretty, with her square chin and thin lips, but she seems to try to make up for this in style. As her pen continues to *tap, tap, tap* I study her silk blouse, silver necklace, black slacks.

"Okay, Elizabeth," she says, returning my attention to the conversation. "We both know this game. We've been playing it for a couple of years now. And by now you should know that all I want is to help you."

Games. Her words make me think of the Emotions. And with the thought of them come thoughts of my nothingness, of my paintings, of my dreams. Sally waits for me to respond, and I try to empty my mind; I'm not usually so easily distracted. I force myself to the task at hand and give her a fixed smile that will hopefully confuse her. "I know how this looks, but honestly, I really am just that clumsy and stupid."

"You're not stupid," the counselor says automatically, brushing back mousy, chin-length hair. Emotions appear behind her: Frustration and Worry. They don't linger. "But I do think you're keeping something from me. Elizabeth, if you're afraid, *I can help*. I won't let anyone hurt you. Are you sure you don't have anything to tell me?"

From the expression in her eyes, I know she really does mean what she says. In a way, Sally reminds me of Maggie, of Joshua; they all look at me and see more than there is. They all care, no matter what their instincts probably whisper. I smile at her, as if I'm amused by all of this. "Really, I'm doing fine. Thanks for asking."

She's frowning, but she lets me go reluctantly. She has to. No one can be helped if they don't want it.

———

This time Fear doesn't catch me by surprise. He approaches

from the west, quick as a shooting star—I feel the wall of nothingness stir, hear the cows' sounds of unease begin. I sit in the loft of the barn, my hands lying limply in my lap, staring at one of the paintings. My attention keeps going to the boy, and the last dream replays over and over again in my head: those words, the red eyes, the hungry insects.

There are just a few minutes of sunset left. The weakening light leaks into the loft, warming my skin. I close my eyes.

"You never did explain the newspaper to me," I say.

Fear sits down beside me, his dark coat billowing around us, sending cool air flowing in all directions. I shiver, keeping my eyes on the brush strokes. Fear reaches out and brushes my hair over my shoulder. His finger touches my neck in doing so, and where any other person would scream, I only look at him. He pushes images into my mind that might drive someone else insane. Blood. Rape. Glinting knives and torture devices lying on a table, then a moment later being delved deep into flesh. Even more, which I only observe, a detached spectator.

"You've lived a long life," I say. "Some might say too long."

"And others may say too short," he counters, pulling away. "I am what I am."

"Do you ever get tired of it?" I ask, because I wonder if anyone is really capable of change. Or are we only lying to ourselves, believing in something different, something more? Perhaps change is equivalent to believing in Santa Claus or the tooth fairy.

Fear scoffs at the question, stretching out his long legs

before him. "What a strange idea—getting tired of instilling terror in humanity when it's what I exist to do."

"Your brother said something along the same lines, I think." I'm not paying attention to the words coming out of my mouth; my mind wanders, contemplating the dreams again. Never once has the girl or the boy said a name. And those red eyes... my instincts still want to point at someone. Or some*thing*. For some reason, the image of that menacing shadow chooses to push itself at me at that moment. The one in the painting I'm looking at now, standing over the girl. Just watching.

"You met Courage?" Fear's voice is sharp and it brings me back to reality. His white-blond hair is wild, unpredictable. The beautiful layers are alive with light. He can be a pleasure to look at, and I understand how some other humans love to experience his essence. We can sense beauty, even if we can't see it.

It's colder now that the sun is slipping away. Pulling my knees close to me and clasping my arms around them, I look down at the floor as I answer. "Yes. He was visiting someone in my class."

"And what did you think of my counterpart?" Bitterness twists Fear's voice, his agitation making the hay around our feet stir. Some cows below sense his unrest and begin to bay uneasily.

"Calm, Fear," I say, resting my hand on his arm. He stills at the touch, looking at my hand with a combination of bewilderment and wonderment.

"No mortal has ever touched me so willingly," he murmurs. The silken quality to the words causes my wall of nothingness to quiver again. Instinct takes hold, but just as I start to pull away, Fear moves in a blur, snatching hold of me. His fingers interlace with mine, and his power wars with my emptiness for the umpteenth time. But on some deeper level, I do sense a connection to Fear. Not to his essence, of course... to something else. Something far more substantial. But I can't name it.

As the quiet wraps around us, I bend my head toward Fear's and examine the touch. Our hands are odd together— my skin is dark from hours working beneath the sun, and his is pale, smooth, perfect. Not human.

At the thought, I pull away. "I'm just not like most mortals." I smile blandly at Fear.

Surprisingly enough, he doesn't react. "I've been watching you your entire life," he says instead, directing his attention to the beams in the ceiling. "The first time we met you were... four? Maybe five. That scum swung his fist at your mom, and my touch didn't affect you. You were just standing in a corner watching it all. You looked right at me. You were wise enough even at that time not to speak out loud. You're wrong when you say I'm here because I'm bored. I've been looking for answers since that day."

The screen door to the house slams in the distance. Probably Tim coming in from the fields. I turn my head to look at Fear. He doesn't notice; he's staring at the painting straight across from us. His brow is furrowed. He'll never quit trying to figure me out, not even for a second.

"How did you entertain yourself before you found me?" I ask him absently, just filling an empty space with words.

Fear goes against my expectations by actually answering.

And it's strange, because his tone is similar to mine: detached, blank, inconsequential. Like he doesn't want to care. "Before you, there was another girl," he murmurs. He shifts, restless, and I see a pain in his eyes that he can't hide. He's never spoken of this before, and I speculate the reasons behind this. "Not like you, of course." He doesn't smirk or grin. "She was...she felt everything. She danced with so much abandon that everyone would stop just to watch. She was impassioned by just about anything. Her family, her home." He falters, very unlike his normal behavior.

"And you loved her," I say simply. Why does the insight cause my wall to twinge? Even more bizarre is that I ignore the usual impulses and refrain from exploring this.

There's a pause. Then Fear swallows. "Yes, I did. I loved her."

Nothing more. I don't bother asking where she is now, since it's obvious the girl is dead. I find myself trying to calculate what marked her and made her stand out to Fear. We have nothing in common; he said so himself. Do I look like her? Was she surrounded by mystery as well? I don't voice any of the questions, because Fear's posture is stiff and I know he's reached his limit for truths tonight. But maybe I don't know him as well as I thought.

We fall silent again, each buried in our own pasts and unsatisfactory circumstances. It's not like the silence yesterday with Charles, a stillness where we didn't speak because there was no need to say anything. No, this silence with Fear is laden with a thousand words, meanings, hints, inclinations.

The sun is gone entirely, sunken down into the other side of the world. Somehow it always happens without my noticing. The only source of light now—the moon is smothered by clouds—is an old, flickering light bulb dangling from the ceiling. As one, Fear and I look at it.

What a peculiar pair we must make, I think. I see it from the outside: surrounded by strange paintings, a seemingly ordinary human girl sits, face devoid of all expression, looking as if she belongs among the wood and the hay. Beside her, lounging against the wall with so many expressions on his face that you could never hope to catch and define just one, is a lovely, changeless being, whose very name evokes shivers down the spine. He looks so out of place in the barn that anyone else would keep blinking, thinking he would vanish in another instant.

"You never answered my question," I say when the hush is broken by a cow moaning in its stall below.

Fear shifts his position a bit, enough so that his shoulder is pressed to mine. He can't resist. For once I stay where I am. Maybe it'll make him cooperate. "What question?" he inquires. I raise my brows at him. Fear smiles, knowing that he hasn't fooled me. "I answered you as best I could." He runs his finger down my cheek before I can evade the touch.

"No, you didn't. I asked you if you ever get tired of it all, and you sidestepped it pretty skillfully."

"But it *is* my only purpose," he points out logically.

A breeze has picked up strength, slipping through the cracks in the walls. It stirs my hair, cooling my skin. The air and Fear's closeness make me shiver again. He notices. In a blur he's crossed the room, picked up a horse blanket I brought up for cold nights like this, and draped it around my shoulders. I don't thank him; showing gratitude would be unwise.

"You're tired," Fear says suddenly, sounding surprised.

I tighten the blanket, huddling into its warmth. A screaming flash hits me, an image of the boy's shrinking pupils. I pull the blanket tighter. "I haven't slept well, is all."

Fear hesitates. "I . . ." The hay begins to tremble again as he, again, becomes edgy. He plunges. "I could help you sleep."

He means he could use his power. But his offer isn't what's out of the ordinary—it's the motive behind it. In the strength of his uncertainty, his carefully constructed expression of arrogance has weakened, melting away to vulnerability, and I see that he isn't thinking of himself or personal gain. His only thought is of me.

I don't comment on my discovery. "No. I'll manage on my own."

Fear's expression closes, and he nods. The distance he's put between us is slight but palpable. "Perhaps I should leave you to your rest, then." Deliberately formal.

I watch him stand, feeling the pierce of shovels inside me, digging the hole of inhumanity deeper, deeper. "Okay."

The air around him practically crackles. I've hurt Fear's ego by rejecting his offer of help.

"You really do feel nothing," he says to me, voice colder than a Wisconsin blizzard. "I thought you had to feel *something*, even just a little. Sometimes when I touched you, or watched you, I thought I saw a glimmer of humanity."

"I've never lied to you, Fear," I murmur. "I'm good at pretending, is all."

"Apparently." His eyes burn. I remain seated on the bale

of hay, considering my next words. Suddenly Mom's voice slices through the tense air, distracting Fear.

"Elizabeth, there's a phone call for you!"

She sounds as if she doesn't expect a response—really, she doesn't want one—but I raise my voice. "Coming."

"Who's calling you?" Fear demands as I brush past him to the loft's stairs. He vanishes and reappears in front of me, blocking my way. "You have no friends."

I walk around him, the stairs squeaking beneath my feet. "That's not true. Maggie is my friend."

"Not for much longer," he retorts, following me. His presence disturbs the cows once more; they start to bawl frantically. Fear's coat flares around his feet as he stalks me to the house.

Choosing not to acknowledge this, I lower my voice as I tell him, "You should go. My mom isn't feeling well right now." And I don't want her feeling any more uncomfortable around me than she already does—if I can't live here, I'll have nowhere else. Fear doesn't reply, and when I turn, I see he's gone. A lingering sense of hurt fills the air.

As I enter the kitchen Mom does her best to appear preoccupied, avoiding me. The phone lies on a table and the cord dangles across the floor from its base on the wall. I step over it and pick the phone up. "Hello?"

"Hi, Elizabeth. It's ... it's Joshua."

"Hello." I notice Mom listening; besides Maggie, no one has ever called me before, much less a boy. When Joshua says nothing in response, I add, "How are you?"

He clears his throat. "Fine. Good. You?"

"Good."

Joshua pauses a second time, then says with a nervous waver in his voice, "So, listen—" Something in the background clatters, and I imagine him tripping over a chair. He coughs, probably in an attempt to cover the sound. "I just wanted to let you know that today in Mrs. Farmer's class, uh, after you left, everyone chose their partners for the project. And you and me are the only ones left."

It wouldn't be sensible to encourage this, to begin another friendship—not when that person is as observant as Joshua, and I've been so distracted lately. But then there's Courage's advice; he'd been so frank, and for once I find myself inclined to trust an Emotion.

"That's great," I say, trying to sound young and just as shy as Joshua.

If he's surprised, he does well hiding it. "Okay, neat. I mean, cool. You've probably already looked at the handout, but the poems and story have to have a theme to them, I guess, and I was thinking we could—"

"I've looked at the handout," I interrupt, hearing Tim's heavy tread outside. "We can talk about it more at school. Okay?"

Joshua doesn't ask questions or try to stay on the line. "Okay. See you."

"Bye." I hang up. Mom is still looking at me curiously, but I don't offer any explanations. Tim's opening the door, the hinges groaning. I'm gone before he sets one foot into the house.

EIGHT

It didn't escape me, during his last visit, that Fear never gave me an answer when it came to the newspaper. Clearly the article disappearing changed things for him, and he intends to pursue this on his own. Although Fear is an excellent liar—he's had centuries, millennia, to perfect the art—he can't seem to hide the truth from me. As if some part of him wants me to know. And I will know; I'm good at research.

During lunch, rather than sitting in a corner by myself like every other day, I go to the school library. The librarian, Mrs. Marble, nods when she notices me slip into the room. I move quietly to the back corner, slipping in and out of shadows between the bookshelves.

I can't rely on Fear to find answers; as soon as those words vanished right in front of me, I'd made the decision to search for my own copy of it. Though there shouldn't be anything strange about a story like surviving a car accident, the fact that the article faded right as I was reading it makes one fact obvious: there's something in it worth hiding. And I've tried, but I can't recollect ever hearing about the incident from my parents or anyone else—why wouldn't they tell me?

The school archives are limited at best, but it's the only library in Edson, so if a copy of the paper is anywhere, it'll be here. Mrs. Marble leaves me to my search and I bury myself in the dusty corner where all the records are kept, sneezing once in a while. No one has been back here in ages.

I start by looking at dates. If I was three or four at the time of the accident, the paper should have been published in 1999 or 2000. Many of the newspapers are missing, but I look anyway.

There isn't much excitement in this area. I see headlines like *Crops Bad this Year* and *School Teacher Fired for Drug Use.* Articles range from reports of small crimes to business spats and school events. But nothing about a little girl surviving any kind of car accident partway through 1999.

There's no time to keep delving through the year—the bell rings overhead. My next class is U.S. History. I make sure to put away the mess; Mrs. Marble is known to hunt kids down and stand over them as they clean up their clutter in her library.

Joshua is waiting for me when I enter the classroom. Holding my book to my chest, I make my way to a desk in the back, as usual. At the sight of me Joshua pastes that same lazy grin on his face. I can't tell what he's really thinking—his eyes are hidden by his long hair. I smile in greeting, appearing friendly. He pulls himself clumsily to his feet and approaches. He reminds me of a newborn colt, but he's doing better at concealing his anxiety and excitement.

"So about the project," he begins without preamble, sitting on the edge of my desk. I've never noticed what he's wearing before, but now I do glance at the ripped and worn jeans, stained white T-shirt, and scuffed boots. Working on a farm all of his life has benefited Joshua; his arms aren't scrawny as I'd first assumed, but sinewy. His body isn't gangly, just lean.

"…okay with it, right?"

I blink at Joshua. "Excuse me?"

He frowns, his expression becoming worried. The Emotion manifests next to him, touches him briefly before vanishing again. "Do you have a problem with it? Because I can talk to Mrs. Farmer if you want. I thought—"

Oh. The assigned partners. "It's fine," I say to Joshua, cutting his anxious tirade short. "I'm sorry; I was thinking about something."

"Oh yeah?" Joshua raises his brows at me. "Care to share?"

"People, people, find your seats and zip your lips, please. Get your pencils and notebooks out and prepare yourselves—lots of notes today. Your wrists are going to love you by the time we get out!" Collective groans as Mr. Anderson strides to his desk followed by the bouncy figure of Excitement, a female Emotion with spiky hair and a slight frame. Mr. Anderson really does love teaching us. Joshua grins at me, shrugging, and goes back to his own desk.

Sophia is gone for once, and I know that if I had the

ability, I would be grateful. I settle on the hard desk seat and put the whole of my concentration into taking notes.

Joshua tries not to look at me for the rest of the class period, yet the boy can't help glancing back at me under his lashes. I can practically hear the thoughts buzzing around the inside of his busy brain. It serves to be a little distracting.

But not nearly as distracting as my own thoughts.

————

Two days pass without event. Dad keeps me busy on the farm, and he's pleased with the progress we've made on the harvest. His good mood affects Mom; she treats me less as a frightening stranger at supper and more like a distant relative coming to stay for a while. "Pass the peas, please, Elizabeth?" she asks politely.

Charles, of course, pretends everything is good and happy. He has a new plan to get out of Edson: drag racing. He's bought an old run-down car from the junkyard. Old Tom gave him a deal. Every night while I paint, Charles is in the garage, tinkering away at the thing. He's also been going to a small track in Chippewa Falls. "To check out the competition," he tells me. "I think once I get my baby all fixed up, I can take 'em." I agree, because it's what he wants.

By Thursday, my bruises are faded enough to be covered by makeup. The result is adequate, and I make arrangements to see Maggie. It's been too long since my last visit— over two weeks—and I feel the insistent nudge to maintain appearances. Charles agrees to cover the milking and make an excuse if Dad notices I'm gone.

After school I get into my truck with my plan in place. The parking lot thrives with the sound of engines coming to life and kids shouting "Bye!" and "See you tomorrow!" Just as I jam the keys into the ignition, though, something caught in the windshield wiper catches my eye. I open the door and pull the object free. A piece of paper. Blue ink. There's the curve of a *Y* visible. I smooth it out against the steering wheel to read the rest.

ARE YOU HER?

The handwriting is neat, elegant curves and loops. Frowning in thought, I hold it to my nose and inhale. The smell of something fresh, dark, and cold clings to the paper. Odd. It's either a prank or something else, and I have no idea what that could be. Best to dwell on it later. Pocketing the piece of paper, I start the engine and head to Eau Claire, about a forty-minute drive.

The trip offers the same scenery: the rolling hills of Wisconsin all around. The minutes and miles pass by in a blur. I find myself thinking yet again about the dreams.

Finally the silver arches of the hospital appear on my left, a huge building jutting up in front of the horizon. I find a parking space, reading the words over the doorway: *Sacred Heart Hospital.* The staff here knows me well. The curly haired nurse at the front desk nods at me when I walk through the automatic doors and I go to the elevator, pressing 9 for Maggie's floor. The button glows red. A small *ding* sounds each time it goes up a floor and I focus all my attention on that sound, mentally preparing myself for the visit. My expressions, my reactions, my voice and gestures—all smoothed into the caring, concerned friend.

Maggie is asleep when I walk through the door, the tiles squeaking beneath my shoes. I stop, standing in a shaft of sunlight that slips in through the window. Her parents aren't here, and I don't know how long she'll sleep. Every second that passes is a second that Tim will notice my absence, so I move to leave again.

"You aren't even going to leave a note?" she whispers. I turn around and watch her eyes flutter open. She's weakened considerably since the last time I saw her. Her face is almost as pale as the pillow she's leaning against. She's not wearing a wig today—wisps of hair stick up in forlorn tufts—and someone must have made her remove the lip ring. But in typical Maggie fashion, she's rebelled by wearing a necklace with a skull pendant and painting her fingernails black. I approach once more, sitting down in the uncomfortable pink chair by her bedside. Maggie watches me, smiling sleepily.

"I was dreaming about the ocean," she tells me. "Did you know I've never been to the ocean?"

"Yes, you've told me."

Maggie tosses her head restlessly, a thin hand going up to touch the remaining strands of her once-shining red hair. "Just once, I'd like to put my feet in," she says. "See those colorful fish I've heard about, take pictures of the coral reefs."

"I know," I reply softly. "And you will one day."

"No, I won't. And we both know it." Maggie faces me,

forcing herself to smile again. It looks unnatural, as if that smile wants to shrivel and crawl away to a dark corner to weep. Out of the corner of my eye I notice that an Emotion now accompanies us—Sorrow, who huddles near Maggie with a glistening tear on his cheek. His dark hair hides the rest of his face. I act as if he isn't there and lean toward Maggie. Even though she contradicts me, I know she wants more lies. So I give them to her.

"We'll put on skimpy bathing suits and run down the beach," I tell her, touching her hand. She clings to my fingers and my hold tightens automatically. "Boys will look at you and want you. Girls will be so jealous of you. We'll have our cameras, and we'll take thousands of pictures. We'll buy corn dogs from the beach vendors, we'll wear those ridiculous big hats you see in the magazines"—Maggie snorts here—"and maybe we'll even swim with some dolphins. What the hell."

My friend sighs, her smile bittersweet now, but real. "I don't know if it's these meds they have me on, but you look so strange in the sunlight. Beautiful, really. As if you're absorbing all the light and it's shining from you instead of the sky."

"Could be the meds, or maybe it's just you," I tease.

Suddenly Maggie doesn't want any more jokes. Her mood swings in another direction—the doctors once said her medications would make this happen—and she makes a sound of impatience. "Forget all of this. Fuck it. I'm tired of talking about me. I'm sick of listening to the doctors and the nurses and my parents. Distract me, Liz. Give me all the dirty gossip from school. Or better yet, let's blow this Popsicle stand! You drove here—let's go find a party!" Her eyes glitter, and Sorrow fades, swiftly replaced by Desperation. So many Emotions. It's almost dizzying.

It's my turn to force a smile, meant to comfort. "Why don't we just stick to the gossip?" I suggest. Maggie deflates and sinks back against the pillows. Desperation abandons her, already looking for his next victim. "Let's see…" I think. "The Dorseth brothers were arrested again. For stealing from Hal's hardware store, I think. Oh, and I heard Joshua Hayes turned down Sophia Richardson when she asked him to go to the homecoming dance with her."

"What?" Maggie squeals, struggling to sit up. I put a restraining hand on her shoulder and she leans back again, but her eyes are still wide with glee. "Where did you hear this? Tell me *everything*."

For an hour I regale her with stories. Maggie eats it all up, intent, and for a bit I do manage to make her forget. But at some point she begins to lose focus, and more Emotions blur into existence, all touching the sick girl. Envy, Loneliness, Longing. Dark skin, skin pale as my bedroom walls, frizzy hair, sleek hair, dismissal and interest. Maggie half-listens to me now, nodding to keep me talking, but I'd guess she's thinking of all she's lost, all she'll miss, everything she wants and will never have. I focus on this so I don't give away the presence of all the Emotions.

Finally I glance at the clock on the wall: 5:46. I'll only be able to stay for a few more minutes. My gaze flicks back to Maggie and traces the outlines of her hollow cheeks, the sprinkling of freckles across her delicate nose. She's so tiny, a fragile bird that will forever be in the nest and never know what it's like to spread its wings and feel the wind and the radiance.

I've gone quiet. Maggie turns her face to the window. Orange-yellow light spills across her blanket. She closes her eyes, and I watch her long lashes brush against her skin. "Elizabeth," Maggie says. There is so much put into that one word, my name, that I know she feels enough for the both of us.

"Yes?"

Maggie swallows. "I was thinking...you know I joke about death"—the word makes her cringe—"and I brush it off. Hell, I dress like it." She sniffs, attempts to harden, but it doesn't work. Not now. Shuddering, she meets my gaze squarely. She's decided something. "We're all pretending, all the time. But now it's different. I feel different. I think I need to face the fact that I'm going to die, and I need to hear someone say it."

There's no going back, and she seems to finally accept it, so I don't attempt to help her with the pretense anymore. "I know, Maggie."

She grins weakly. "You do, don't you? You've always seemed to know things. But I wasn't bothered by it like everyone else. You made me feel...safe. I used to get jealous. You're so strong, so certain in who you are. I wanted more. I wanted to be beautiful, like Sophia Richardson, popular, loved, perfect. Since that wasn't possible, I tried to be special by being the school Goth. And look at me now. I'm special now, aren't I?" Maggie utters a bitter laugh.

"This isn't—"

"I know. I know, okay? I don't need to hear the speech

again. I didn't do anything to deserve this, bad things happen, it's out of our control. I know, I know, I *know*. But *why*? Why me, why now? You know so much, Liz, then tell me. *Why did this have to happen to me?*"

I've been expecting this, anticipating this moment. No human can look into the face of death and not cower or panic. But I don't have any words to calm Maggie, because the answer she's looking for doesn't exist. There's no rhyme or reason for pain and suffering, for those beings that live to distribute it—these things just are. I could give her all the pretty lies, but it won't hide the truth this time, and there's no going back to our old ways.

"I'm here," I tell her, so simple. There's nothing else. Well, nothing but one more truth. And she's waiting for me to say it. She needs me to say it. So I do. With all the reality of how empty I am. "You're going to die, Maggie."

She stares at me, the girl in the bed with the wet, white cheeks and the bleeding heart. Emotions are crowding close, reaching out for her like weeds in water. My nothingness swallows me whole. I stand. As if on cue, I hear Maggie's parents down the hall, talking in lowered, worried murmurs. "I'll see you soon, okay?" I say, standing.

"I love you, Liz," Maggie whispers to my back. I pause, consider offering another false sentiment in return, but for some reason, I don't. I walk out the door and don't look back.

NINE

"So when did you want to do this?"

I squint up at Joshua, lifting a tired hand to shade my eyes. The drawing I'm working on lies half-finished in my lap, an image of hands braiding long hair. Quickly I unfold the cover of the notebook and close it. "Do what?" I ask. I'm slow this morning; more dreams and unanswered questions plagued me throughout the night.

Joshua shifts from foot to foot, debates for a moment, then plops down on the ground beside me. "We need to work on the portfolio. So, well, we could decide who should do what and work separately, but I'm not exactly creative, so..."

"It's not due for almost two weeks," I remind him.

He plays with a rubber band around his wrist, staring out at the street. "Yeah, but I like to be prepared," he answers.

We're sitting on the front steps of the school. It's quiet; no need to pretend, no risk of making a mistake.

Joshua moves restlessly. I can see that he's one of those

people who never stays still, probably not even when he's sleeping. "Do you want to meet somewhere after school, maybe later this week?" I finally ask him.

A group of our classmates crosses the street, approaching the school. Their voices startle Joshua. The crowd is followed by two Emotions: Apprehension and Desperation. It's so important to these kids to fit in, to belong. Joshua watches everyone clattering up the steps for a moment and then he looks back at me. There's no way to know what he's thinking from his expression. I note how neither of the Emotions stops to touch Joshua.

Then the front doors open, and the others are gone. Silence hovers around us again.

He realizes I'm waiting for an answer, and red spreads along his neck and cheeks. "Yeah, that'd be great," he says, grinning at me sheepishly. "How about Thursday night? I can probably be done with my chores a little early and we can meet at my house."

I lift an eyebrow. "Why not my house?"

His lingering glance at the hidden bruises on my face says more than words could. "I just thought you might like to have an excuse to … to get out for a while," he tells me, his tone careful, gentle, as if I'm glass and he's handling me in his callused palms.

"Fine. I'll be there at six."

Joshua grins, and his crooked smile brightens the sky. I arch my neck to keep my gaze on him as he stands, studying that unpractical hair of his, the strong jawline. There's something … different about Joshua Hayes. My body reacts to him; I note the clenching sensation in my stomach where there should be none. It's similar to how I feel when I'm working on my paintings or an Emotion is near: like I should be feeling something. Like I would if it weren't for the wall. This has also happened with Fear.

It isn't until Joshua's smile fades that I comprehend I've said some of my thoughts out loud. "You're different too, Elizabeth." His voice is soft and he touches my shoulder, not an instant of hesitation in the movement, before turning and going back up the steps. "Bell's going to ring," he calls over his shoulder. "You already have too many tardies. Get up."

I don't move, just watch him disappear through the front doors. *Danger*, my mind whispers. *Stay far away from him.* I should. I really should. This can't end well.

But I know I'm not going to.

――――――

I'm lying on my back on my bed, staring up at the ceiling. It's dark out, and the single lamp on my dresser makes soft light spill out down the floor and over my bedspread. Charles' words come back to me: *You should decorate this room. It's depressing in here.*

I sit up, touch the eggshell-colored wall. An idea comes to me. I gaze around, seeing the potential. No one besides Charles ever comes into my room; my parents won't protest against what they don't know about.

Making plans for tomorrow, I sit back against the headboard of my bed, hugging my knees to myself. Images dance before me, all my paintings and waking dreams. Trees, darkness, the spray of the ocean, screams. *You will forget everything. You did this.*

Suddenly, disregarding it all for a moment, I jerk upright. After a moment I jump up and go to my door, opening it just a crack. I poke my head out into the hallway. Tim is downstairs on the couch, and he lets out a long belch as he watches TV. Mom is at her sewing machine in the corner—the steady hum of the needles drifts to my ears.

But this isn't what makes me so alert, so attentive. The wall inside me is moving again; there's someone near. Someone with power. A haze at the edge of my consciousness confirms it: the presence from the road is back. Not in the house. Outside.

I close the door and go to my bedroom window. But then I pause, reconsider, walk back to my nightstand, and dig a flashlight out of the drawer. Then, as quietly as possible, I return to the window and slide the glass pane open. Flashlight clamped in my mouth, I straddle the sill and grasp the trunk of the tree that's only a foot away from the house, positioned slightly on the right. It's easy to climb down and drop to the ground. Leaves crackle under my weight and I look around. The fields stretch out and I know that the stranger is in there, waiting for me. The power is strong. Without hesitation, I plunge into the dark depths. I wait to switch the light on until the house is out of view.

The air is cool tonight. Ignoring the discomfort of going barefoot, I move stealthily through the corn stalks and focus on the being moving in the trees beyond. I know it's there because its presence is still an insistent poke in my mind. After a few more yards, I reach the edge of the woods. I start to run, light on my feet. I do make some noise, but the visitor doesn't disappear at the sound of my approach. Pain suddenly pierces through my heel—I've stepped on one of those weeds with prickles decorating its leaves—and I stop, hissing as I exhale. But I attempt to ignore the ache and continue through the trees. The nothingness is thrumming inside me. My mysterious visitor is closer than ever.

When I know for certain that it's just a couple yards away from me, I halt at the edge of a clearing, tilting my head to listen. My flashlight sweeps the tree line. The presence is still palpable, still nearby, but I see nothing. Is it taunting me? I wait for a sign of its location, gazing around silently, alert. My heel is throbbing.

Finally there's the sound of a twig snapping—it's on purpose. This creature wants me to find it. I jerk the flashlight toward the noise, my entire body poised, ready for anything. I finally spot my visitor, a dark shape standing behind a tree just a few feet away from where I am.

"Who are you?" I call. "What do you want?"

For a time there's no reply, but the stranger is still there. Is it testing me, somehow? I don't address it again; that's what it wants. The woods around us thrive with life, time itself seeming to speed up and slow down.

Finally there's more movement. My senses are at their best, intent only on survival. The stranger finally steps out from behind the tree and into the circle of light. Still tensed, I take in her appearance—and it's female, without a doubt;

even though her sweatpants are baggy and a hooded sweat-shirt covers her body and face, the form is willowy. Definitely not male.

"Are you going to answer my questions?" I ask flatly. At this proximity, her essence sweeps over me more than ever before, and I can't put my finger on it. Is she an Emotion or an Element?

She keeps her head down, using the darkness as a cover. I lower the flashlight to my side so I don't spook her. "I came here to warn you," she says. Her voice is rich and deep, but I get the sense that she's young. Again, there's an ongoing sense of recognition. Before I can prod for more, she continues. "He's found you, and you need to try harder to remember." The words are halting, as if she's speaking past a pain in her gut.

"Remember what?"

An owl hoots somewhere above, a deceiving sound of normalcy. "What *we* started," the stranger replies, taking a step back. She's nervous. She's angry. She's … scared. As if she's reading my thoughts, she takes another step away from me. Under her long sleeves I suspect she's clenching her fists.

"You can't tell me more?" I ask, not bothering to pursue her. If this woman wants to evade, she's proven that she can do it.

"Don't ask stupid questions," she snaps. She takes a third step. A fourth. "You already know. *Remember*, for both our sakes. And don't trust … anyone."

With that, she spins and runs, melting and becoming part of the black beyond. Her tread is almost completely silent, and soon not even the rays of my flashlight can touch her. I wait until I know she's gone to start for the house.

I've only taken a few steps when I see another movement out of the corner of my eye. I stop, every muscle in my body taut, and then I realize that it's only a deer, standing by a bush. Its ears flick back and forth and its nostrils flare, probably smelling me. I turn my back on this place and its quiet lure. I have more to think about.

And I need to pull the thorns out of my foot.

———————

"No," she sobs, clutching the boy tight to her chest. Her shirt and skin are saturated with bright red blood. She glares up at the sky, tears of rage and anguish pouring down her cheeks in skinny rivers. She starts to scream at the innocent stars.

When her throat has gone hoarse, she rocks the two of them back and forth, back and forth, sobbing some more, jagged rasps of sound. "No, please. Please, come back," she whispers, stroking a bright head of blood-smeared hair. "Don't leave me alone. Please, please, come back. Come back…" She rests her cheek on the boy's head, whimpering.

There is no answer, no reply. Not from the boy, at least. "We need to go," a voice says, somewhere in the trees. The girl doesn't bother replying, just keeps rocking. She digs her fingers into the boy as if she'll never let go. She murmurs something—his name—and kisses his forehead. When she pulls away, her lips drip with blood.

"It's not safe here. We need to—"

"Leave me alone!" the girl shrieks. Her eyes blaze. Just an

instant later, though, she's a moaning hole of pain again. "You can't leave me all alone. Please, please, please," she chants. "Come back…"

But he never will.

————————

My eyes flutter open to embrace the stark and colorless walls of my room, and the first thing I'm aware of is the fact that I can't move. Pain rips through me, shrieking. I glance down and note the fact that my wrists and ankles are duct-taped to the four posts of the bed. There are numerous cuts on my body—legs, arms, stomach—some deep and still bleeding. Tim stands in a corner, watching me, holding a long, glinting knife in one hand. It still drips with my blood.

I lift my nose and sniff the air. Power fills the room. "I can't be late for school," I say, unable to see him, but of course he's here. I make the mistake of shifting a bit, to get a cramp out of my leg, and wince at the second rush of pain.

"You already have more tardies than everyone else," Fear says, appearing at my side. "One more isn't going to hurt." He sits down and cool air rushes into my face. He smells of dew and sunlight and horror. "Why is that, by the way?" he adds, small wrinkles appearing in his otherwise-smooth forehead. "You're a robot in every other aspect, but you can never seem to make it to class on time."

Struggling is pointless, so I try to find a more comfortable position, hurting myself in the process. Fear only watches me; he's still angry. I've injured his pride, and he won't be able to forget that easily. "Could you at least get rid of part of the illusion?" I ask, nodding to my limbs and torso, where the cuts continue to bleed.

Fear smiles faintly, but it's not a real smile. "No," he replies. "I want answers."

I give up, going completely still. "What could I possibly know?" I ask.

In answer, Fear reaches down and picks up one of my paintings. He must have brought it over from the loft. It's the one of the house by the ocean. Foam shoots into the air, reaching up the cliff side with white fingers. "You create these," he says. "You dream. And I know you think about it constantly. I want you to tell me everything you know. Who are these people? What happened? Ah..." He holds up one long, pale finger. "And *don't* lie to me. I'm afraid I don't have the patience for it today."

"As you said, I dream and paint," I say after a moment. I'm weakening from all the blood I'm losing. I wonder how long Fear will let the charade go on. "I know next to nothing; I've never seen the girl before. She screams and weeps, and she begs the boy to come back. There isn't much more than that."

Fear grimaces, leaning closer, his hands clasped loosely between his knees. "You're keeping something from me, Elizabeth. I need to know. Please, just tell me."

The wall within me trembles. For an instant, I see the depth of his desperation, his desire, before his mask falls back into place and he's the cocky, arrogant, self-assured Emotion that I know. The pain is almost gone now; my body has gone numb. I turn my head away from him to look out the window. Morning light is always the most gentle, most serene.

"I have a theory," Fear says, disrupting the silence. "About you. See, I don't really believe that you feel absolutely *nothing*. There's too much to indicate otherwise."

"Such as?" I prompt. The sooner this ends, the sooner I can get my normal world back and get to school. I've never skipped once in my life; I do everything I can to avoid the school making phone calls to my house.

"You do care, Elizabeth." Fear touches my cheek, tenderness suddenly filling his gaze. "You care about your friend Maggie, you care about your mom, you care about hurting that boy's feelings at school. You may not feel in an overwhelming way; you're subtle about it."

"Wishful thinking, Fear. You want to understand, and you want to able to put me in a category. But the reality is we'll probably never know the truth about what happened to me."

"I can't believe that," he says, and once again he seems unable to resist touching me when I'm so near. His fingers trail down my neck and he makes little designs on my chest. His fingers are cool, and his essence battles with my immunity. Images of war and pain and terror sweep through my mind.

The ball of fire in the sky has risen even higher into the endless expanse, and the light inches into my room. It catches the icy blue of Fear's eyes. "You watched me grow up," I say. "Wouldn't a child cry when her parents ignored her? Wouldn't a girl care when her father hit her? Wouldn't the way Sophia treats me bother me? And wouldn't seeing Maggie—"

"Why are you so insistent?" Fear challenges. "You're so

adamant that you're right and I'm wrong. Isn't *that* feeling something?"

Arguing with him is pointless. I glance at the clock by my bed. "Fear, I do need to go. Would you please release me?"

He sits back, sighing, roughing up his hair in frustration. "Not yet." He follows my gaze to the window. He shifts restlessly, a wild thing, a creature no one can tame or understand, not completely. He makes me think of a pale, pale lion. Beautiful and feral and always on the hunt.

"Everything has a purpose," I remind him, my voice soft. "And yours isn't to solve me. If you're ever going to be happy, you need to move on."

He laughs quietly. "See? Right there. Why would you say something like that unless you really do care?"

I lift one shoulder in a mild shrug, ignoring the pain the movement costs me. "I have instincts, Fear. But I don't have all the answers. So, please, let me go to school."

He sighs yet again, waving his hand. Suddenly I'm back in my real room and Tim is gone, as are the cuts and blood on my body. "I'm sorry," Fear says. I don't know if he's apologizing for the pain or the rest of it.

"It's fine." I slide my feet to the side of the bed, standing. Fear watches me, longing in his eyes. I don't have time to shower now, so I move to my closet, pulling out jeans and a T-shirt—what I wear every day.

"You'd look beautiful in a dress," Fear says, so quietly that I almost don't hear him. I don't bother asking him to leave— he never listens to me, anyway—so I turn my back to him and take off the shirt I slept in. I hear him suck in a breath, but when I turn again to speak, he's gone.

TEN

After a day of Sophia making snide comments every time she shoulders by me in the halls, and Joshua doing his best not to stare at me, I pull out of the school parking lot. Instead of going home, I head to town.

Hal, the owner of the hardware store, waves at me when I pass him. Nodding in return, I go directly to aisle eight. I study the selection carefully, though it's very limited. There are exactly three shades of green: lime, emerald, and myrtle. Debating for a moment, I decide to take them all. As an afterthought, I also grab cans of gray and black and white.

"Do you need help carrying those to your truck?" Hal asks as he takes my money.

I stack the paint cans and lean them against my chest, shaking my head at him. "No thanks." I start for the door.

"No, don't touch anything!"

A display of vitamins topples over. The same female voice curses, and a woman appears in the aisle. Her hair is streaked with blond and her acrylic nails glint in the light. With a cell phone pressed to her ear, she bends and begins to stack the bottles. "I told you to keep your hands to yourself!" the woman snarls. Her glare is directed at someone blocked by the display. "No, I'm fine," she says into the phone now, still stacking. "Morgan is just being a pain."

She has to mean Morgan Richardson. Sophia's little sister. This must be her babysitter.

The clock over her head catches my attention, and I hurry outside.

I drive over the speed limit to get home; Tim will start bringing the cows in from the pasture, and Charles won't be around to cover for me when it comes time for milking. Once I've pulled into the driveway, I park beside Tim's truck and leave the paint cans, heading straight to the barn. Mora pokes her head over the edge of a stall at the sound of my approach—I'm even later than I realized—and I immediately move to the milking supplies.

"Where have you been?"

I should have seen him when I first came in; he's standing by the shelf of bottles, holding a halter in his hands. He must have just finished taking the cows in. "I had school," I answer carefully, trying to get an idea of what I can expect. My father glares at me.

"I know you had school, Elizabeth. You usually get home at three. It's twenty after. So I'm going to ask one more time: where have you been?"

He's forcing himself to be calm, but danger lurks beneath his scruffy exterior. I won't tell the truth; he'll find a reason to let his fury loose. "I was working on a school project with a partner," I say. "For English class." If he thinks I'm being responsible, he might let me go another night without bruises.

Tim fiddles with the halter some more, his expression becoming thoughtful. "Who's your partner, sweetheart?"

I hesitate, assessing the situation from every angle, trying to figure out which one will let me off with the least pain. "Joshua Hayes." I pause. No reaction from Tim. "He lives on a farm across town with his dad. His mom—"

"I know who he is, Elizabeth." Tim finally sets the halter down on his workbench and I notice for the first time how his beefy fists are clenched. His knuckles are white. "Funny thing…" My father takes a step toward me. I don't move. "Joshua Hayes just called the house ten minutes ago, left a message with your mom. Said something's come up and he can't work on your 'project' tomorrow. Weren't you with him ten minutes ago?" Tim moves even closer, until he's backed me up against a wall.

I look up at him, blinking. *Fight or flight* fills my being. And for some reason I find myself choosing to hold my ground. "Where do you think I was?" I question.

He studies me, expression still unfathomable. "You know, I didn't notice at first. It took me a while to make any connections. But the least I can figure, you changed after that car accident. The kid I knew was just gone. I don't know what happened to you, but the doctor said you were fine, we were just worrying too much. I don't think so," he repeats.

Clearly, I'm not going to be able to get any more out of

him. I try to look afraid. "I could try harder to be that person you knew. I will try."

"If I've learned anything in this godforsaken world, it's that people don't change. Look at me." He laughs softly, and I smell the faint tang of alcohol on his breath. "I tried to be a good husband, I tried to be a good dad. When I couldn't do that, I tried to be a good farmer. Nope, people sure don't change!"

His words strike a chord somewhere inside me. He's wrong; people can change. They can. Now is not the time for argument, however. Now is the time to appeal to his humanity. "Dad—"

The word coming from my lips seems to anger him even further. "You're just like your mother," he says, grabbing my shoulder quicker than I can jump out of his reach. "Always lying!"

I shove him without thinking, and my resistance infuriates him further. Swift as a snake, he bangs my head against the wall. Reflex tears spring to my eyes. More instincts shriek at me. *Run, claw, reason.*

" . . . would you lie to me about where you've been unless you were with a guy?" Tim is demanding. "Did you sleep with him? How long has this been going on? What if you get pregnant, slut? Huh? Do you expect your mother and me to clean up the messes you make?" The questions come at me relentlessly, each one punctuated with a head slam. My vision blurs, the first sign that I'm going to lose consciousness. Impulse takes over again, and my fist lashes out before I can stop it, connects with flesh. Tim stumbles back, bellowing.

"I wasn't with anyone," I attempt to say. But the words are lost when Tim utters another cry of rage. He seizes my arm and throws me to the floor. I start to scramble up but he steps on my hand with his heavy boot, and we both hear something crunch. I let out a scream of pain, and I can tell that the sound gratifies him. He bends, lifting me by my throat. With my good hand I reach to scratch his eyes out, but he jerks away just in time. Kicking is pointless, but I try anyway.

"You're part of this family," he says through his teeth, shaking me. "I take you to church every Sunday. Where did I go wrong? Why am I cursed with a daughter like you?"

I couldn't say anything even if I wanted to—Tim's grip is too tight. I see now that I shouldn't have said anything. I should have taken his abuse, endured the hits, the insults, his revolting breath and sweaty palms.

No. *Fight or flight.* Once again I gravitate to fight. Is it really instinct that urges me to it? Has to be. Before I comprehend what's happening, my nails are digging into Tim's hand. He releases me, making yet another animal-like sound that's part grunt, part growl. I tumble to the dirt, scraping my knees and the heels of my hands, jarring my injury. The pain nearly consumes me. *No*, I think again. Quickly I glance around for a weapon, something to deter him. The manure shovel—

Tim comes at me from behind. Then his fist is in my hair and he's yanking me back. Out of the corner of my eye, I see Fear materialize—he must've been coming for one of his visits. His white beauty makes the ugly scene almost surreal. His expression is thunderous and ... torn.

"It won't last long," he says to me. "He's going to pass out soon."

I know this. It doesn't lessen the physical pain any. I try to crawl away, but Tim kicks me and I slump against the wall. A groan slips past my lips. "Get up!" he orders. "Get up, whore!"

Fear stands close, so close that I can feel his cool presence gently flowing over me. I touch the edge of his coat. There's blood on my fingers I didn't know was there. Fear kneels down, his icy eyes lovely and anxious. "I can't interfere," he murmurs. "It's one of the few rules my kind has. You know I would help if I could."

"Doesn't matter," I manage to say.

"What's that?" Tim sneers. "What did you say?" He reaches down, hauls me up by my shoulders. Yet another slam. *I'm going to have some bruises tomorrow,* I think insipidly. Fear touches my cheek before standing back.

Then, suddenly sagging, Tim stumbles into me so that I'm crushed between him and the wall. My hand shrieks and I struggle to escape, but Tim is dead weight. His breathing becomes more labored as he hangs onto me, as if he's really the child. "Well?" he mumbles, the words muffled and watery now. "Answer me." He sobs, a gurgled, ruined sound.

I stare straight ahead. Blood runs down my temple. "I have no answers that will satisfy you."

My father laughs, more of a bark, really. "You're so … strange. I hear people in town calling you a freak. Yeah, a freak. That's what you are … " I still can't move, and I scan the area around us again for anything to use as a weapon.

Fear is still watching from a corner, his jaw clenched, and our eyes meet. Tim groans, distracting me. As I pull my attention away from Fear, another puff of Tim's foul breath assaults my senses. "I'm so sorry," he mumbles tearfully, mindless. "You know I don't mean it, don't you? Sarah won't even look at me, you know. She doesn't love me. It's my fault. I was the one who was supposed to be watching you that day…"

I grow more alert at this. Is he talking about the accident?

But Tim is too far gone to answer any questions. He makes another sound deep in his throat and stumbles against me, trying to stand. I'm forced to shift to the side and lose my balance. Tim continues to sob as I fall…

…right into a pitchfork.

I let out another cry of pain, instinctively dropping and rolling to my back. The end of the tool clinks against the ground but doesn't fall out. The tines should be easy to extract, yet the agony is already blazing through me, making it impossible to move. *Should I pull it out?* I think distantly, lying in some moldy hay. Tim is blubbering, moaning more apologies and woes. I pull my hand away from my side and gaze down at the red on my fingers. *Too much*, a voice in my head whispers. Black begins to cloud my vision. "Fear," I say without thinking. I don't know why.

And that's all it takes. One strangled word, his name, his essence, and Fear is there, a gust of frozen fury. Yet the hands that cup my face are gentle, and it's as if I'm made of something more breakable than glass. As if I'm infinitely precious. "This is going to hurt," he warns. Before I can tell him that

I already hurt the burning intensifies, and I arch my back and scream. Somehow the pitchfork is gone, and the holes in my middle close. One, two, three, four. When it's done I pant, blinking through sweat. The wall of nothingness quivers, then becomes firm once again.

Fear smooths damp hair away from my face, still kneeling there. His palms are so cold. "Are you all right?" he asks.

"I didn't mean to!" Tim chooses that moment to whimper. Forgetting me, Fear jerks upright, eyes wide, nostrils flaring. He vanishes in a burst of smoky tendrils, and Tim is across the room before I realize what's happening. Fear bends over my father, his clothes a fluid, dark waterfall that obscure my view.

"You're not going to touch her again," he snarls, and blood sprays against the barn door.

"Fear, stop," I say, struggling to my feet. Fear pounds Tim's face, over and over, with all his unrestrained strength, and he doesn't stop until I touch his back. My hand jars him out of his wild stupor, and he lets Tim slump to the ground.

"Fear," I say again. He whips around, staring at me.

I stare back. There's a tight sensation in my stomach. "You're going to pay a price for helping me," I tell him quietly. He already knows, of course, but I say it anyway. Although Emotions and Elements have no sovereign, any of the few rules they break are brought to balance by some unknown force. Maybe sooner, maybe later. Years ago, when I was learning more about the other plane and those that dwell there, Fear informed me that Disgust had killed a human once. Ten years later, Disgust's lover was murdered.

Coincidence? None of the beings from the other plane seem to think so.

What will be Fear's consequence?

My hand—still unhealed—throbs as Fear makes a sound of contempt. "Doesn't matter," he says, imitating me. And then he smiles, a slow, gentle smile. I feel my nothingness twinge, harden itself. For a reason I can't fathom, I think of that night in the loft when he held my hand. Offered to help me sleep. As Fear looks at me, that same expression of unexpected vulnerability crosses his beautiful face. My body aches all over, but I owe him this. Stepping forward, as if I'm moving through water, I slowly place my arms around him, rewarding him because I pay my dues.

He hesitates only an instant before embracing me in return. He buries his face in my hair, inhaling. Tim had done the same thing just moments ago, but it's vastly different with Fear. There's that sensation again, of something within me moving. His touch brings on images of panting terror and horrific experiences of people around the globe, but I ignore them all.

Fear heaves a sigh, arms tightening around me like he never wants to let go. "I have summons," he murmurs reluctantly. "Better get back to work." I don't respond. Smiling again, Fear bends and brushes a soft kiss on my lips. Once, twice, three times, as if I'm a drug and he's a drowning addict. He shudders in my hands, this timeless, powerful Emotion. Being with me really does change him, affect him.

"Don't." I pull away. An odd instinct doesn't like the distance between us, but I chalk it up to my mind striving for safety. Right now, Fear represents safety. Yet Tim isn't a threat anymore. He lies there with his back to a stall, a lump of regrets. Above him, the cows watch us curiously. "You'll only get hurt."

Fear winks at me, buoyed by the kisses. "We'll see, won't we?"

He disappears from my sight, and I turn to see how much damage he's done to Tim. It's not encouraging when my father coughs up blood, hay sticking to his pummeled face.

"Oh, dear," I murmur, feeling my own injuries twinge, demanding attention.

"Since I'm already breaking the rules..." I hear Fear's voice say in my ear. A moment later my cuts and bruises close up; my skin becomes smooth and unbroken as if none of it ever happened. The burning pain in my hand is gone, too.

"More interfering," I say.

Fear doesn't bother with a reply, leaving me alone to figure out what to do with Tim Caldwell. After much debate, I decide that the best course of action is to do nothing at all. I milk the cows and shut up the barn for the night, leaving one door open.

ELEVEN

The next day, there are two abnormalities. Joshua isn't at school, and when I get home, Sheriff Owen is in our kitchen. He's taking statements from Mom and Tim, who refuses to go to the hospital.

The story is simple: Tim woke up alone in the barn last night without a memory of how he was beaten or who did it. Standing there with his calm expression, Sheriff Owen waits for my statement, pen poised over a notepad. I focus on his sandy-brown mustache and tell him in simple terms that I came home late yesterday, milked the cows, and went into the house for supper and homework. No, I didn't see Tim in the barn. I went to bed around ten. No, I didn't see anyone suspicious around the farm.

"One of the doors was wide open, and you found Tim lying a few feet away in his current condition, correct?" Owen asks my mom. Lips trembling, she nods.

The sheriff frowns, rereading his notes. "Well, the way

I see it, Tim, you must've been working in the barn and someone came at you from behind. It explains your lack of memory. Are you sure there's no one angry with you that would have a motive to do this?"

Holding an ice pack to his head, Tim just scowls and shakes his head.

Owen sighs, pocketing the notepad. "I'll ask a few questions around town and see what I can find out."

Mom shows him to his car. There's the sound of an engine revving as Sheriff Owen leaves. Mom comes back inside and goes right to her dishes. Tim lumbers upstairs to lie down.

I wait until he's gone—I can hear him moving around above us, a water faucet turning, the bedsprings squeaking—and then sit down at the kitchen table. Mom doesn't notice me at first. She sighs in her isolation, shoulders slumped. I notice the grooves in her soap-covered hands, the natural downturn of her mouth. I shift, making the chair creak deliberately. Mom gasps, whirling around. When she sees it's just me, her expression tightens.

"Elizabeth," she mutters unhappily. The name sounds reluctant on her tongue. "Did you want something?"

"I'd like some answers," I say, and it occurs to me how much I sound like Fear. "I won't take long."

She turns her back to me, resuming the dishes. "What is it?"

I fold my hands on the surface of the table and decide to be direct. "Will you tell me about the car accident?"

She stiffens, facing me again. Her gaze is sharp. "Who told you about that?"

I smile wryly, acting real for her benefit. "People talk, Mom."

Her face twists up. She's so many things. Disgusted, sorrowful, wistful, angry. Suddenly we're not alone—my gaze flicks briefly to Resentment, where he stands among the others. He winks at me. "…call me that," Mom is saying. "A mother knows. You're not my child. I may not know how or why, but you're not her. My baby *laughed*. My baby threw tantrums when I wouldn't let her wear a princess dress all day, every day." Mom's fists clench in front of her, and there's a desperate darkness in her voice. "The doctor said you were catatonic because of the shock, but I knew. I *knew*."

Guilt also appears beside Mom, rubbing her shoulders. Even though Guilt is a big, lumbering Emotion, there's something slimy and sly about her. She fills the room with her aura.

"Hello, odd one," she greets me. I don't take my eyes off my mom.

"She's too good to talk to the likes of you," Resentment tells her, smirking. The other Emotions have gone.

Mom is silently crying. Despite the evidence and the impossibility of it, she wants to believe her real daughter is out there somewhere, waiting to be found. She wants to believe that her child isn't the cold person beside her. I need to fix this. I have to fix this. "It's not your fault," I say to her as I ignore the two guests sharing the space in the kitchen. "Whatever you think happened. The accident—"

"The accident." Mom sniffs. She shakes her head, wiping away some sweat on her forehead with the back of her arm. Is the incident with Tim what's rattled her? Or is it this conversation, here, now? "That's when it all started. You never found out about it because we never talked about it. For Tim it was a matter of pride. He didn't want to think about our four-year-old daughter wandering all the way out to the road without our knowing and getting hit by a car."

"How long was I in the hospital?" I ask next.

Trying to regain her composure, my mom starts on the dishes yet again. Resentment leaves but Guilt remains. "Just a day," Mom replies. "The doctor said it was a miracle. You got away with just a few scrapes and bruises. They only kept you overnight for observation." She laughs softly, her shoulders shaking. "Since the driver that hit you was the one to call 9-1-1, Tim and I got to the hospital later. As soon as I walked into your room and you turned ... that was the moment I realized you'd changed. You looked at me like you didn't even know me."

I stand, moving to the counter to help her dry. She doesn't object. "It really could just have been shock."

Mom shakes her head so adamantly that some of her hair comes loose from her ponytail. She's going to cling to her delusions. "No. No. I rocked my daughter to sleep every night, I sang her songs, I dressed her, I fed her, I played with her, I carried her inside of me for nine months. She knew me, and I knew her." She scrubs a dish so hard that she slips a bit and dishwater splashes over the edge of the sink. I think, not for the first time, of how different we are, yet it's her I look like the most. Both of us tall, slender, blond and blue-eyed.

"I should have done more," Mom murmurs, pulling me back to the present. "Said more. I should have fought for my daughter, tooth and nail, looked for her until my last breath. But I stood here in this kitchen, doing dishes, pretending that everything was all right."

I should have expected this; it's the way of humanity, after all, to deny. To hope when there is none. I study the shine of a glass in my hand as I ask, "What do you think happened, then?"

Mom just shakes her head. Really, she has no idea what she believes.

People are so complex. They want to hear the truth, but they want you to lie to them. I choose silence rather than making another mistake with my mother. I dry each dish meticulously, concentrating on the plates and silverware and pans as if they're the reason for my existence. I become aware that Mom has stopped washing and is watching my hands, her eyes wondering, worrying.

"You can ask me anything you want," I tell her. She shudders, probably because I've guessed her thoughts. She doesn't move away, though, or snap at me. I watch her toy with her wedding ring. It slips easily off her wet finger, and she puts it back on little by little.

"Who are you?" Mom asks finally, her voice a broken whisper. "*What* are you?"

My hand towel goes around and around on a plate. "I'm your daughter, no matter what you believe." Around, around.

Following my example, Mom starts scrubbing again. "Just the way you're so controlled ... " She purses her lips. "Even when you were little, you didn't crack a smile."

"I could try harder—"

"No." Mom ducks her head and hair falls forward, hiding her haggard face. She grips the edges of the sink. Knuckles white. I can see her heart breaking all over again. Guilt is still there, answering her summons solemnly, her spindly fingers tight on Mom's shoulder, and she's joined by others again. Sorrow, Anger, Hope. As the seconds tick by the air begins to tremble with expectation. Tension and pressure builds in the room and I know something's coming. Something that won't be easy for her. Finally, her chin trembling, my mother plunges. "Do you know where my daughter is?"

I meet her sad, sad eyes. And in this moment I realize that she'll always deny me, never accept me. I'll never be her child. But I can't release her. If I let her sink into these impossible despairs, there will be no place for me. So I tell her, in the same hard way Tim speaks, "*I'm* your daughter. And you owe it to me to believe that, no matter how much I've changed."

Silence. The soap in the sink bubbles. After another minute she nods, pursing her lips. She turns away. And thus ends the first meaningful, sincere conversation I've ever had with my mother.

———

This time there's no disorientation. I know, the moment I open my eyes and find myself in an unfamiliar room, that this is another dream. The walls are blue, the furniture all mismatching. There's a narrow bed in one corner with messy sheets, all wrinkled and tossed. There's a stereo on the dresser. But what makes this square place remarkable, individualistic, is the books. Dozens upon dozens of them are stacked up, covering every surface, every possible spot. Some are open, some are bookmarked, some look ancient, and others have yet to have their spines cracked for the first time. Titles and words fly at me: THE GREAT GATSBY. THE GRAPES OF WRATH. THE ASSASSINATION OF JOHN F. KENNEDY.

I'm standing in a corner, gazing at it all. Through the window to my left I see that it's morning. The sun is just awakening and fingers of orange and pink stretch out over the world. There's a distant roar, something mighty and older than time. My mind recognizes it after a moment. The ocean.

The realization hits me then: I'm in the house. The one that I see sometimes in my dreams. The one by the cliff side.

"...almost time to eat," a woman says from down the hall. And then the door opens and the boy enters. I remain where I am, expecting him to lift his gaze and see me. But he doesn't. I might as well be invisible. He just strides to the cluttered desk and rifles through some papers in a drawer. His mouth is puckered and his movements are graceful, thoughtless. He's just showered; his hair is wet and he smells of sharp soap. He finds what he's looking for—a notebook and a textbook along with it— and he pulls them free of the pile, tucks them under his arm, and leaves again. Without hesitation, I follow.

We walk into a kitchen. The house is small; it only takes five steps. Everything is clean and orderly in contrast to the boy's room. Though the furniture is worn and there's only one very old TV as entertainment, someone has worked very hard to make this place a home. The rugs are colorful and there are pictures on the walls, framed images of a smiling family of three: the boy, the mysterious girl who always weeps in my dreams, and an older woman with crinkling eyes. Grief doesn't exist. These pictures ... these pictures are genuine. The Caldwell mark is nowhere to be seen—no shadows in their gazes, no tight smiles, no distance between shoulders.

I pull my attention away from the pictures and examine the room. A woman has her head half-inside a refrigerator. As the boy circles her and approaches the table I see that she's sniffing milk. "You're going to be late," the boy says.

The woman sets the milk down in front of him, telling him, "I'll be fine. Oh, and I did pick up an extra shift, so I'm going to be little late tonight. Make sure you tell your sister, okay?" Of course she's his mother; the knowledge is there in the way she brushes his bangs back, the way she moves around the kitchen with such purpose. This is her purpose. He is her purpose. It must be so fulfilling, to have a design.

The boy pops the mouth of the milk carton and tilts it. The sound of the milk streaming into a glass is the only sound for a second. It's strange for me, the silence. There are no ticking clocks or thudding boots coming into the house.

"Where is she?" the boy asks his mom after a moment. I lift my head at this—it's the same thing he asked me in that clearing. Before the churning skies and bloodthirsty swarms.

This time he receives an answer. The dark-haired woman sighs. "She went out to the woods again. She didn't hear me when I tried to call her back."

He watches her. "Don't worry. She'll be back. She always comes back."

It doesn't soothe her, but she hides her expression. When she turns back to her son, she raises her brows. "Are you sure you want her to? You wouldn't have to share that damn bathroom anymore."

He smiles faintly, holding his fork tight. She smiles too, a sad curve of the lips. They're entwined together through loyalty, not obligation. This is what family is supposed to be.

The boy bends his head again, back to his food, and hair falls into his eyes. Just like Joshua. I lift my hand to push it out of his—

Suddenly the scene is rushing away. Cold air and streaks of black and blue shoot by. A dizzying sensation makes my head swim, and I lower to my knees to maintain balance.

Everything goes still again. It's not gradual. One moment I'm on a speeding, burning train, and the next I'm at a stop, and the whistle announcing my arrival is an abrupt silence. I lift my head ... and see.

He lies there. He's just a foot away, so close I could reach out and touch him. Where any other person would recoil or cover her mouth in horror, I just stay right there on my hands and knees, gazing down at him. My wall of nothingness twitches a little.

This time the girl is nowhere to be seen. There's no cradling, no screaming. Just the absoluteness of death. The moon gazes down at us with its white face. It's chilly. Dew coats the grass and soaks through my dress. I hardly notice. Blood seeps into the earth. I study the scene for a long, long time. No matter what other theories I've had up until this point, I now know one thing for certain: this was no accident.

The isolation wraps itself around me. Briefly I wonder why there are no crickets. I continue to sit there by the body, trapped in this place. For some reason, I seem unable to tear away from the sight.

"You did this," his voice whispers in my ear. The boy himself doesn't open his eyes or move. But it's true. I feel it to the marrow in my bones. Because of me, somehow, someway, all of this is ended. No more breakfasts, no more laughter, no more studying. Never again will that beautiful boy turn the page of a book or squint at a sentence. Never again will he share a joke with his mother or wait for his sister to return.

I should care. This dream, this memory, whatever the correct term for it is, clearly is meant to serve a purpose of its own. To help me remember? To cause an Emotion, any Emotion? Or maybe the intent is something far more basic. Maybe this is just a dream, a random story tucked away in the back of my mind like all those paintings.

Do you really believe that? an inner voice asks me.

It would be easier if I did. It would be beneficial. The truth is looking less and less appealing as this winding path brings me deeper into dark wilderness.

But I might be more human than Fear or I thought, because I can't sink into oblivion. This boy means something to me. He's part of my past. And he's not just some random story.

He's my story.

TWELVE

Friday morning Joshua is back in class. He looks normal but tired. Worry touches his shoulder. Sophia's sister and my penchant for bruises aren't the only subjects Edson High has to talk about. There's been some speculation about the Hayes farm, about how their crops have been failing the past few years. Is that why he missed school yesterday? To help his dad?

When the bell rings, I approach Joshua slowly, treating him like I would a hurting animal. He looks up, sees me. Kids shuffle past us—Sophia slams by, and I stumble a bit—but Joshua and I stay where we are, two unmoving stones in a wild tide. His eyes narrow at Sophia as she passes and she falters, her cheeks heating. She regains her composure, however, and whisks through the door as if she doesn't care what he thinks of her.

"How are you?" Joshua asks, shifting his gaze to me. All that hair hangs in his eyes.

He really is odd; his weariness and anxiety are evident, and he's asking about me. "I'm fine," I answer. "What are you doing after school?"

Joshua blinks, taken aback. "Uh . . . nothing."

I nod, brisk, because I believe it's what he needs: someone to take control, someone to offer him a distraction. *Why are you doing this?* that voice in the back of my head asks. *Courage said I would need him,* logic points out.

What is your excuse for indulging Fear? it asks next.

I ignore this.

"Come over to my house," I say. "There's something I need help with."

He's curious. "What?"

"You'll see." I hug my books against my chest and pivot on my heel, walking to the door.

He says my name, softly, uncertainly. "Elizabeth?" I turn. Standing up, Joshua clears his throat. He blushes a little and tries to cover it up by sounding confident, casual. "Why would you want to hang out with me?"

Teasing him, keeping up the pretense, I raise a brow. "It's just a project, Joshua."

He straightens, grinning. "Yeah, but you're a girl, and you're you."

I study him some more, taking in the plaid shirt that hugs his thin torso, the stained jeans, the old work boots that I suspect belong to his father; they're too big. "Because I think I should get to know you," I answer honestly. *You will need that boy in the end.*

"Why?" he asks again.

We're going to be late, and I still need to take a trip to my locker. I turn my back to his questions. "Meet me on the front steps after the last bell. You can follow me home."

Before he has a chance to open his mouth and ask anything more, I vanish through the door, throwing myself into the sea of kids. My senses are consumed by their chatter, the sound of sneakers on the floor, laughter. These people are always in motion, always full of a life I lack, no matter how much I pretend.

———————

There's little danger in bringing Joshua home; Tim is asleep upstairs, under the heavy spell of alcohol and pain killers. He hasn't moved for two days.

The door to Joshua's beat-up car squeals loudly as he opens it and gets out. He shuts it, looking around. The farm isn't much different from his, but the boy looks at everything like he's never seen a farm before. I try to see through his eyes, and appraise the chipping white paint on the house, the way the barn roof sags, the rusty tractor abandoned on the lawn.

"So this is where you live," Joshua says, so quietly he probably doesn't mean for me to hear.

I shoulder my bag, inclining my head. "Come on. My room is upstairs."

Joshua follows me inside. The screen door slamming announces my arrival to Mom. She doesn't look up from her position behind the counter, where she's breaking up some broccoli in a bowl. It isn't until she hears the heavier thumps of Joshua's shoes in the entry that her head snaps around. "Oh." With wide eyes, she sizes Joshua up. She recognizes him; Edson is tiny and it would be impossible not to. Mom wipes her hands on a towel, turning. She glances at me once, and I know she's surprised I've finally brought someone home. "You've grown," she says to Joshua after a moment, taking a couple steps to extend her hand.

He shakes it quickly, shifting from foot to foot. "That's right; you brought some food over once, after … "

Displaying a sensitivity I wasn't aware my mother had, she smiles at him, smoothly directing her next words elsewhere. "I suppose you and Elizabeth are going to work on your project." She chews some skin from her lip, a nervous habit.

There's no way to miss how she doesn't address me, avoids it, really. I hadn't mentioned working on the English project tonight, but Joshua isn't stupid. He knows something is off. "Yeah, we are," he tells Mom. He brushes some of that long hair out of his eyes. "Thanks for letting us do it here."

Mom flaps a hand dismissively, smiling at him some more. She's probably thinking about how nice it is to finally have someone normal around, someone who isn't her family. "Are you hungry?" she asks. "I could—"

"We don't have much time," I interject, giving her a warning look. There's a possibility Tim could wake up soon. She understands and shuts her mouth. "Thanks, though. We'll be upstairs if you need us."

Mom nods, returning her attention to the broccoli. I take my shoes off, indicating that Joshua should do the same.

He does so, trying to hide how dirty his socks are. I pretend not to notice and lead him upstairs.

It is an odd sensation, having a warm presence at my back.

I shut my bedroom door behind us. Joshua looks around curiously, eagerly, as if the room will tell him everything about me, add more pieces to the puzzle. He eyes the blank emptiness, the scant furniture, with interest. He says nothing. Just studies it all.

"It's white," I state, making a motion to the paint cans in the corner. While Tim was sleeping last night I'd gone and fetched them from my truck. "We're going to change it."

He takes this in with a bemused expression. "You want me to help you paint? That's your project?"

"What did you think it was?" I've already moved the furniture to the center of the room, so all there is left to do is spread the tarps out on the floor to keep the wood from getting splattered.

Joshua doesn't answer. "So . . . " He begins to roll up his sleeves. "What do you want to do here? I see a lot of . . . green." He eyes the paint cans, his mouth curving with amusement. "Guess we're going for a forest."

I raise my brows at him. "Exactly. A mural, of sorts."

Nodding a second time, Joshua faces the wall. His lips twist. Seconds tick by and I know he's imagining the possibilities as he squints at all the white. Twist, squint, twist, squint. Then he turns back to me. "I told you, I'm not very creative," he sighs. "So you're just going to have to tell me what to do. You don't have a problem with that, right?" He actually attempts a wink. When I smile, he flushes, a bright red that crawls up his neck and face.

To ease his discomfort, I begin spreading out the tarp. He jumps in to help, the material crackling between us. "Let's start on this wall first," I direct, and once we have the tarp laid out, I tape it down to the floor. I stand back, thinking. "I'll outline the trees with pencil, and I'll let you do whatever you want with them."

"What?" Joshua scoffs. "Are you serious? You really want to endanger your mural like that?"

His laughter is loud, boisterous, and I listen carefully for movement in the hallway, alert to any stirring in Tim's room. He snores on in his drunken stupor. Relaxing a little, I turn my attention back to Joshua. "I trust you," I say with an easy shrug. The simple words startle him; his eyes widen. For a moment he doesn't seem to know what to say. Before he can read more into it, though, I slap a paintbrush into his hand. I step away quickly. "We don't have much time today," I repeat. "I'll get started."

Joshua just watches me. After another moment, he slowly turns away. As I draw the outlines, instinct is pushing at me again, insistent, loud, demanding. I already have one Sophia making things more complicated. I already have one Maggie to pretend for. I already have one mother who sees how I don't belong. *Don't encourage the boy,* it says. *Don't be friends with him. End this before it's too late.*

And I consider this. But then there is Courage, his dark loveliness before me, solemn and chilling in his truth: *You will need that boy in the end.*

I draw.

"It's going to storm," Joshua murmurs. He stands by my window, staring out at the fields. Gray skies and strong winds frown and swirl on the other side of the glass. The paintbrush drips in Joshua's hand, green paint staining the floor, but I don't mention it.

"You should leave soon," I say, stepping away from the wall to eye it. I've drawn trees on two of the walls, a small stone house and the edge of a cliff on a third, and on the fourth . . .

"What's that?" Joshua appears beside me, frowning at the scene before us. When I don't answer, he steps carefully around my bed. The pencil markings hold all his attention. "It's sad. Beautiful, but I don't think I'd want to fall asleep every night with that looking over me."

I reach out to touch the boy at the same time Joshua does. Our hands brush, and he jumps. Neither of us move. I observe the girl's silent scream for the millionth time.

"Where did you come up with this?" Joshua asks, his voice husky. I don't answer, preoccupied with the curve of the girl's cheek, the way her fingers curl over the boy's shoulder.

Where is she?

You killed me.

Joshua fidgets—his thumb taps his thigh and his foot makes a beat on the floor—proving my theory that he can't stand still for even a moment. "I didn't know you could draw so well," he adds. Again I say nothing. "Elizabeth?" He sounds worried now; I've been silent too long.

"I'm not that good. And I made this up," I reply. I toss my pencil on the bed, glancing out the window, where rain has begun to patter against the pane. "Thank you for helping me. I'll walk you out to your car."

He follows me mutely. So strange. I'm used to demanding questions, impossible expectations. I've never known anyone like him. But when we're going down the stairs, his silence suddenly makes sense. Sorrow stands in the shadows, waiting for Joshua. The boy shudders when Sorrow reaches out, as if he can sense the Emotion's presence. My mural must have spurred it on—I can guess what sprang to Joshua's mind, to make Sorrow pay a visit.

Mom isn't in the kitchen on our way out the door. The house is holding its breath. I don't think Joshua is aware of much else besides his soundless pain. The screen door begins to close, but Joshua turns back quickly, catching it before it slams. Sorrow looks at me while Joshua is distracted, those constant tears streaking down his white, white cheek. His black hair thrashes in the wind and his essence clashes against me. I see death, sobs, emptiness.

"Are you all right?" Joshua's staring at me. I keep walking, gravel crunching beneath my feet. Pressure pounds on all sides; the storm is approaching fast.

When we reach Joshua's car, I ask him, "What made you think of your mother?" A leaf blows and tangles in my ponytail. I pull it out and hold it by its stem.

Joshua toys with his keys, flipping them back and forth, pursing his lips. They jangle and the silver flashes. "How did you know I was thinking about her?"

I shrug. "A guess."

He scowls. Roughly, he shoves those bangs out of the way to glare at me. Sorrow remains close by, but Anger joins us. He says nothing, just grasps Joshua's shoulder and pointedly ignores me. "You know what I realized?" Joshua snaps. "You lie a lot, Elizabeth. I'm not stupid."

"What do you think I'm lying about?"

He makes an abrupt gesture toward the house, my room. "You didn't make that drawing up. No one can *make up* that kind of pain. It was real, even if I don't know what it's all about."

Clouds gather above us, and thunder rumbles, warning us that it's coming. There's just a light sprinkle now, but I know it'll get worse. The leaf is delicate in my fingers. Joshua doesn't even notice the drizzle. He keeps glaring at me, waiting for me to speak.

Finally I just shrug again, as hollow inside as ever. "You want the truth? Fine. I don't know why I drew that. I dream about it. But I'm not like you; I'm not sad, or suffering. I don't feel anything."

His eyes become dark shades of disappointment; he thinks I'm still lying. It's the way humanity is; give them what they want, and it turns out it's not what they wanted after all.

"Whoever that person is," Joshua says, his voice thick, "you care about him. I saw it on your face when you touched him. I watch you in class sometimes," he adds suddenly. My mind scrambles to adapt to the subject change. "I've never seen anyone so sad. It's why I was interested, at first. I thought you were the only person that could understand. But then I saw something more." The sky opens up and the rain comes down without restraint. Joshua reaches down to unlock the car door, swiping at his nose with his sleeve. He avoids looking at me now and the rain plasters his hair to his head.

"What more did you see?" I prompt, when it's apparent that he doesn't intend to say more.

Surrounded by Emotions, Joshua opens the door and plops down into the driver's seat. The engine starts with a sputter and a cough. "I saw you," he says simply. Then he slams the door in my face, putting the car in reverse. The Emotions dissipate one by one.

I stand alone and quiet as he leaves. His words play like a record in my head, again and again. They hold no meaning; he can't be right.

His red taillights turn at the end of the driveway, and then he's gone. Soaking and cold, I turn to go back into the house. Just before I slip inside, I remember the leaf and let go of it. It flies away, snatched out of my fingers by the greedy wind. I watch it soar over the corn stalks until I can't see it anymore.

THIRTEEN

Four days without seeing Fear. Four days without his games, his tests, his watchful presence. This is what I'm thinking about as Mrs. Farmer drones on about the different kinds of poetry there are. I keep thinking of Fear. There have been stretches of time over the years he's stayed away, of course, but recently he's been a constant presence. The fact that he's gone pokes at something within me. Speculation fills my head. *He's up to something. He's found something.* And the most insistent possibility: *something happened to him.* He did break the rules by healing me. Could he be out there somewhere, dying, helpless, alone?

You don't care, my little voice reminds me. To affirm this, my numb wall stretches taller.

"There's free verse, as well, which has become more popular in modern times…"

Sophia, her head bent down in concentration—the picture of a model student—is writing a note. Her pencil scribbles across the paper furiously. As I watch, I suddenly recall the piece of paper I found on my windshield. *ARE YOU HER?* Was Sophia the one who put it there? Judging from the tense line of her shoulders, whatever she's writing right now is intended for me. She looks exhausted again. I know her mom works nights at the clinic and her dad left them when they were small. Besides the babysitter, Sophia has no one to help her watch Morgan during those long hours.

When Mrs. Farmer isn't looking, Sophia is quick, tossing a crumpled-up ball over her shoulder. It lands on my desk with a soft rustle. I debate whether or not to open it at all, but I figure it'll appease Sophia for a time if she thinks she's hurt me.

I unfurl the lined mess. *You're not normal,* she's written. *They should lock you up and throw away the key.*

Maybe.

The handwriting doesn't match the other note.

Sophia and one of her friends laugh softly under their breath. They glance back at me, expecting a reaction. I sniffle for effect, and this pleases them. The two girls turn their backs, whispering to each other about nothing that interests me. Humans are cruel. Sometimes worse than the Emotions and the Elements.

It strikes me how I'm thinking like I'm not human, myself. Like I'm not one of them.

"For those of you who've forgotten, your portfolios are due this Friday. Make sure you finish, guys. They're a big part of your grade!" Mrs. Farmer calls. I glance at Joshua, who's hiding behind his hair.

Joshua. He hasn't spoken to me since he left my house, so angry and sad and suspicious, but throughout the lecture he's struggled not to glance over his shoulder. He wants me to think he's not affected by what happened yesterday, but in truth, he blazes with yearning. He yearns to understand, he yearns to know me. In many ways, Joshua reminds me of Fear.

When the bell rings and it comes time for lunch, he catches up with me in the hall, giving in to his desires. "We need to work on the portfolio," he says sharply. He's still irritated. He knows I'm hiding something.

I nod, spinning the combination on my locker. "I know. I don't have time today; my dad wants me home right after school. But we can start talking about it at lunch tomorrow if you want."

"What's wrong with lunch today?" he counters, challenging me. He brushes his hair out of his face. I wonder why he doesn't just cut it.

We walk again. "I'm going to the library to do research."

"Research for what?"

He steps in front of me, stopping our progress in the middle of the hall. Kids part around us like a wave, some bumping into us, changing and evolving to the disturbance without thinking about it.

I arch my neck to look up at Joshua, studying his resolute expression. His scent drifts to my nose, a mixture of pine and hay and soap. "My past," I say.

Joshua absorbs this for a moment, pursing his full lips.

"Okay." He nods. "I'll go with you. We have to stop at my locker first, though."

Where's the timid boy I've known most of my life? He disappeared so quickly, and the Emotions that used to always surround him are now absent in this new assurance he's found. "I never said I wanted company," I inform him with raised brows.

Now he reddens. So a part of that shy boy is still there, I see. He's a strange combination of grins and blushes and silent contemplation. "If you want to be alone . . . " he begins to say, stopping in relief when I shake my head.

"It's fine. Let's go, then. We have twenty minutes."

———

Browsing through the papers every day during lunch hasn't given me any of the answers I've been looking for. I'm halfway through the year 2000 and I still haven't been able to find a copy of the newspaper Fear showed me.

"You know," Joshua says as we rifle through the yellowed documents, "it seems like I'm always helping you with your projects and we never actually work on the project we're getting graded on." His lunch rests by his elbow, and as he turns a page he sinks his teeth into an apple. *Crunch*.

My eyes scan an April edition, the front headline reading, *Child Drowns in River*. "We'll get to the portfolio," I mutter. I set the paper aside and reach for the next one. But before I can, Joshua stops me, his palm warm on the back of my hand. My fingers curl on the tabletop, and I absorb the sensation of his skin against mine. No human has ever touched me so willingly...

Fear said the exact same thing, about me.

The thought is jarring, and I lift my eyes to Joshua, gauging his expression. Again, he doesn't give me time to study the angles of this moment. "I'm sorry about how I acted last week," he says sincerely. "I was...frustrated. But that doesn't give me an excuse to call you a liar. If you don't want to share something, that's your business."

I can smell the sweetness of the apple on his breath. I pull my hand out from under his. It reminds me of Fear, and his obsession, and one Fear is enough. *Is that really why you're pulling away?* my mental voice challenges. *What other reason would there be?* I ask placidly. In answer, an image of Fear's tender kisses bursts and vanishes like the flash of a camera.

Realizing that Joshua is still waiting for a response, I shrug and say in a neutral tone, "You didn't call me a liar, exactly. You just said I lie a lot. Which is true."

Joshua shakes his head, smiling faintly. "You're so weird, you know that?"

I smile in return, finding for the first time that the pretending isn't so hard. "I could say the same about you."

We sit in compatible silence for a time. The only sounds in the room are the papers crinkling in our hands and a pair of girls whispering to each other at the computer desk. I close my ears to it and concentrate on my search, but just as I accomplish complete isolation to the world all around, Worry appears next to the table, a twitching, distracted Emotion with frizzy curls and stick-thin legs. I set a paper down, examining the top of Joshua's head. He got his red hair from his mother. I don't know why that random thought pops into my head.

"How are things on the farm?" I ask, my tone gentle. If I'm going to be able to focus, he needs a steadying hand.

My words startle him; his head jerks up. He brushes that wild hair away, frowning at me. "What?" He heard me, though. I just sit, waiting.

Joshua squints at me, resigned but bewildered. "Sometimes you know things you shouldn't. You say things. I don't suppose you'll tell me how that is?"

I shake my head. "For now, it's better you don't know."

His gaze sharpens. "But you might tell me one day." It isn't a question.

It would be wise to crush his hope. It would be sensible to staunch his questions. "Maybe," I say. *You will need that boy in the end.*

"Dad and I worked for hours yesterday, since we can't afford to get the new parts our harvester needs," Joshua answers abruptly. "Of course he's too proud to ask anyone for help." He takes a bite of his sandwich. He probably realizes that he won't get any further in his own quest for truths. "The rotations aren't doing any good. Planting the crops late didn't change anything. The land is just tired."

My stomach growls as he says this, and I realize I haven't eaten anything today. I forgot to grab breakfast this morning; I slept through the alarm once again—more dreams.

Courage's words are pressing in, growing louder and louder each day.

Joshua hears my stomach and grins, mindless of my inner struggle. "Want half of my sandwich?"

Oddly enough, his offer gives me that strange sensation again—my nothingness quivering, hardening, fighting against any and all urges to feel something. I wonder what I would be feeling for Joshua at this moment, if I had the ability. Even odder, I don't have the faintest idea.

I could help you sleep.

His voice comes out of nowhere, but it reminds me that Joshua isn't the only one who's offered something to me. Fear... why am I thinking of him so often lately?

As I make an effort not to lose myself in theories, the boy doesn't wait for me to reply. He bends his head once more, flipping over some newspapers, looking for any stories about me, as I'd instructed him to. He's genuine in his desire to help me. I'm beginning to realize that Joshua Hayes is a paradox; he's simple yet complex, direct yet thoughtful, eager yet patient. Just when I believe I have him labeled and put into a box, he says or does something that forces me to reconsider.

For what seems the hundredth time, I study Joshua's face, the familiar features. It's a good way to occupy my mind. I've never really stared at him before, noted each and every detail. Behind that long, dark-red hair, his lashes are extensive and gold, his eyes a gentle amber. His nose is long, slightly dusted with freckles. His mouth is generous and naturally upturned at the corners, as if he's always ready to smile. *All in all*, I think, *he's quite nice to look at.* Beautiful, really. Not in the way the Emotions or the Elements are, but in a real way. I know when I look at him that there's nothing otherworldly about his loveliness; it's just him.

If I were normal, if circumstances were entirely different and beings like Fear had no place in my life, Joshua could be someone to me.

He glances up, feeling my eyes. He smiles in question. I look down at the paper in front of me, copying him. The nothingness is harder than it's ever been. The sensation in my stomach is almost painful now, and I grimace in response.

"Are you all right?" Joshua asks.

I nod quickly, and as if on cue, the bell rings above. I stand, almost tipping over the chair in my haste. Clumsiness is unlike me.

"Elizabeth?" Joshua is worried now. He follows, leaving our mess behind. Mrs. Marble won't be happy with either of us when she discovers the papers littering the table in the back. I don't let Joshua catch up; I'm much faster, and it's all too easy to dart out the door and leave him. But even when I've disappeared from his sight, he calls my name.

———

"I miss you. This place is hell on earth. Have you been busy over in good ol' Edson?"

I hold the phone close to my ear, straining to catch Maggie's faint rasp. I put a note of cheer into my voice. "Yeah, busy with all the boring stuff. Chores, homework. You're not missing out on anything."

She laughs, but there's not a drop of mirth in the sound.

She's gotten worse, not just in the sickness but in her spirit. "Wrong, Liz. I'm missing out on life."

Tim's loud whistling disturbs the silence, and I lean backward to see out the window. The corn stalks crackle as he shoves them aside. Mom's making supper and Charles will be home soon. "Maggie, I have to go."

She doesn't respond for a few seconds and I stare at the wall, seeing her face drawn on the plaster: thin, pale, hopeless. "I'm going to visit again soon," I add, knowing the words are empty for her. But I give them to her nonetheless, because besides her parents, I'm all she has.

Finally, she sighs. The sound is broken. "Okay. Goodbye, Liz."

Her tone is infinitely sad, resigned, like this is the last time we'll ever speak.

Standing in the middle of my room, hardly noticing the mess of splattered paint and tarps, I study the partially finished mural. The green and the smell permeate everything. These images mean something for me, they have to. But where's the connection? What is the timeline here, who are all the players?

You ruined everything.

He's found you.

Please come back, please…

The sound of music pierces the silence—it's coming from Charles's room. Some kind of rock, the singer screaming rather than attempting something remotely melodious.

Outside, the wind howls and pushes at the glass panes of my window. Ignoring it all, I trace one of the tree trunks in the mural with the tip of my finger, thinking, attempting to remember what may have been erased. Around and around like a chaotic carousel.

You will forget everything.

You're completely human—I'd know if you were anything else. You haven't been sought out, collected, or studied.

I rocked my daughter to sleep every night, I sang her songs, I dressed her, I fed her, I played with her, I carried her inside of me for nine months. She knew me, and I knew her.

Sometimes you know things you shouldn't. You say things.

You're not normal. They should lock you up and throw away the key.

"Liz?" An impatient tap on the door. I turn away from the mural, sensing Emotions on the other side of that door. Emotions and Charles. He's upset. I open the door a crack and slip out into the hall before he can see the walls of my room. In his present state, I'm not sure how he would react. "What is it?" I ask, acting concerned.

There are no lights on. My brother is a dark shadow as he rubs the back of his neck in an agitated manner, but I see the Emotion standing beside him is Guilt. Something must have happened with Mom and Dad. Charles sighs, taking my attention away from them. "Listen, would you do me a favor?" Without waiting for me to answer he goes on, "I need you to cover for me tomorrow night. I know it's my turn to do the chores, but me and some guys are going to do test runs on the track. I just finished some more tweaks on my car and I want to see how she does."

"It's fine," I say. He's not going to tell me what's bothering him, and I won't ask. Guilt stares at me with a half-smile, her hand tight on Charles, eyes luminous in the dim lighting.

He nods, hesitating. "Okay, then."

Just as my brother turns to go, I say, "Charles?" He turns, and I notice how much he looks like our mother, too. I study his face. "Do you remember what I was like as a baby?"

If he's surprised by the question, he doesn't show it. The Emotion fades as Charles smiles at me, probably thinking about how odd I am. "Sure, Liz. You were annoying as hell."

"What do you mean?"

Charles sighs and fidgets—he's working the night shift at Fowler's soon—but he indulges me. "You were a handful, Liz. You were always wandering off, exploring. And you never stopped talking. Ever."

"Do you love me as much as you did then?" I don't know why I ask; there's no motive behind the question. No purpose to the knowing. What's come over me?

Now Charles lets his impatience show. He doesn't have time for dumb questions from his little sister. "Yeah, of course, Liz. I got to go, okay?" The words aren't real, and he avoids my gaze as he swings around—the sounds of his footsteps bounce off the walls and echo in my head like a heartbeat. *Thump, thump, thump.* He leaves me there in the darkness.

———

"Elizabeth? Are you even listening?"

I raise my eyes to Joshua's. "Hmmm? Oh. Yeah, I'm listening." My voice carries through the stacks, and Mrs. Marble lifts her head, giving me a look. I wave at her in apology.

Joshua pushes a list into the side of my hand, where it's laid flat on the table in front of me. "Since you and I never seem to get anything done, I did this at home by myself," he tells me. "It's the project, divvied up between us. All you have is a poem and a peer review. You can just give me what you've done on Thursday. Oh, and since Mrs. Farmer wants the poems and the story to have a sort of theme going to them, I just picked one out..." His eyes meet mine. "Hiding."

"Interesting theme," I say dryly. "What was your inspiration?"

The boy shoves his hair out of the way, leaning forward. His eyes glow as he picks up the list and looks it over. "I was thinking about high school and how typical it is, you know? But then I started thinking about the small things, like..." Joshua's gaze lingers on where my bruises once were, then he hurries on. "I just realized that there are so many things I don't know about the kids I see every day. How many of them have secrets they keep from the rest of the world? How many of them wear masks everywhere they go? We're anything but typical," he finishes, serious.

There's a window beside our table with an odd metal grate over it, and the sunlight casts intricate shadows across Joshua's face. I sit back, away from his body heat, mulling this over, absorbing his words.

Then other words drift back to me, demanding and subtle at the same time. Driven on by *secrets* and *masks* and *hiding*.

And you loved her.

Yes, I loved her.

Why those words? Why now? Attempting to ignore the memory, I force a smile at Joshua. "And you said you weren't creative."

He blushes—I realize he hasn't blushed in front of me in a while. I remember when he once used to trip and stutter over his words when he talked to me, and now... I watch the way his long lashes flutter, gold flecks in his eyes that I never noticed before flashing in the weak light. Almost as brilliant as Fear's.

Fear.

In my mind's eye, I see his cocky grin, the way he looks at me and believes so blissfully in my potential to be more. It's been a week.

My eyes go to the newspapers a few aisles away from us, drawing my own thoughts away from this unethical territory. From all of the unethical territory my brain seems inclined to travel to lately. The newspapers beckon, a sure distraction. There's still a lot of 2000 to go through; I should do some more searching today.

Joshua sees where I'm looking. He sighs, waving the list through the air as if he thinks it's a lost cause. "Just take it and do your part," he orders, grasping my wrist to lift it, putting the list on the table, and setting my hand back down on top. But when he's done, he doesn't pull away. Instead, his hand slides down. Hesitantly, afraid I'll protest, Joshua interlaces his fingers in the spaces between mine.

I don't move.

I look at him, and he looks at me. It's so unusual, this sense of being the only two people in the world, when really, we're never alone. It's him—his innocence, his belief that everything really is just so simple. Joshua's skin is so eager, alive, clashing with the detachment of my own. He has to notice the difference, but he doesn't say anything. Joy appears behind Joshua's chair, beaming at me. Her hair is even redder than Joshua's, almost orange, and she's one of the more heavyset Emotions. "You make him so happy!" she chirps, hugging him. The fat in her arms jiggles. "I'm so glad, because I haven't seen too much of this one since, well, you know. It's really interesting that you're the one who brought me here, isn't it?" She giggles.

Her chatter fades as my examination of this situation intensifies. I should pull away. I should tell Joshua how useless it all is. I should warn him, I should tell him the lies I tell everyone else, tell Fear. Should, should, should. The truth is, I don't. He represents what I need to be, and my instincts are drawn to this.

"Well, well."

It's as if thinking of him has brought him, because it's Fear's voice slicing through the stillness. "I'm gone for a few days and what's this? I come back to a little high school romance. Interesting pair, really. The girl who can feel nothing and the boy who feels too much."

Joshua senses that something's changed, even before I

take my hand back and put it under the table, safe from his tenderness. "Elizabeth?" He stays where he is, and both he and his Emotion stare up at me when I stand. For once, Joy is jolted into silence. Because of Fear's presence, of course. I lift my bag from where it's dangling off the back of my chair, studiously keeping my eyes off of them all.

"See you in class," I murmur, turning my back to Joshua. He looks like a lost little boy now, his hair tousled and his expression one of warring hurt and confusion as I abandon him and his joy. For once, he doesn't follow me.

Fear does, though. He doesn't speak again until we're out in the hall. It's empty at the moment; everyone is at lunch. I stop in front of a poster that says, *QUIT SMOKING. IT KILLS*. The picture is of a person lying on a metal table, covered by a sheet. I stare at it, waiting for the inevitable.

The silence drags on too long; now it's my voice shattering the air, and it sprinkles over our heads like shards of glass. "I don't belong to you." I say it because it must be said. No matter what other components there are in the equation, this is the most prominent.

Fear stands behind me, and there's a gust of wind where there shouldn't be one. The lights flicker. He's so close to my back that his coat flaps against me. I can hear screams, sobs, moans of people all over the world, trapped in Fear's shadow.

"For the first time in your life, you act without thinking," Fear finally says, his voice a growl. "Nothing good can come of this."

I face him, arching my neck back. His beautiful eyes blaze and his mouth is set in a thin line. His long hair whips at his cheeks. He can't ever know about how often he invades my thoughts; by just doing nothing, I've encouraged him, and for both our sakes, this has to end. "Do you care for my benefit, or for yours?" I ask.

My words displease him greatly. He's tolerated my oddity and insolence up until now, but in his world, mortals obey and tremble when confronted by those from the other plane.

"This boy has disrupted everything," Fear snaps, grasping me by the arms. His hold is so tight that I wince. "You've stopped looking for the truth. What do you think can happen from here? You grow up, marry him, live a normal life? No. Whatever you think, you can't live a life like this. Eventually he will want to tear away your façade, and when he realizes there's nothing behind it, everything you think you have will be destroyed. It's all pretense, Elizabeth. You especially should know this."

The feeling goes out of my arms, and instinct shrieks to succumb to Fear, but I don't. I know what I need to do to pierce him, drive him away. Even Fear wouldn't want to remain if it seems I'm drawn to another. "What if it's not?" I whisper. The statement is quiet, helpless, a fragile thing, but Fear's eyes widen as if I've sprouted seven heads and stuck out a forked tongue at him.

"Have you changed?" His voice is hoarse, and he's even paler than normal. "Do you feel?" He leans closer, inhaling my scent. When that's not enough, he presses his cold, cold lips to mine. I close my eyes, seeing terror in the darkness of my eyelids. Fear pulls back, breathing heavily. "No, you're the same. But…" He shakes his head. "This boy," he repeats, fingers tightening even more like I'm about to float away and he's all that anchors me to the earth. "Stay away from him. He's a danger to you." Fear is earnest in this; I see the desperation in the depths of his gaze. But again, it's for his own purposes that he says it.

The bell is seconds away from ringing; I hear doors slamming open, a loud laugh breaking out. Sophia calls out to a girl about her birthday party this weekend. "There are people heading this way," I tell him. "I need to go."

He only jerks me closer. "You can't love *him*," he whispers. "I've waited so long. Why the boy? Why is it he that pounded a hole through the wall?"

Finally he lets me pull away, watching me go with wild eyes. And even though it causes an alien sensation in my wall to say it, I do, because this is not the way things should be. "Maybe it's because he wasn't trying to."

F O U R T E E N

This time, when I walk into Maggie's dark hospital room, she's really asleep. I falter. It would be smart to turn around and head straight back home before Tim notices I'm gone. But after a moment I find myself walking to the chair by her bed and sitting down, looking at her. Light slants across the floor from the hall.

She's steadily getting worse. The evidence is there in the lines of her face—lines that shouldn't be there—and it's there in the way she frowns even as she dreams. Her eyelashes brush gently against her sallow cheeks. There's no black eyeliner, no skull necklace, no black wig. Just a sad, dying little girl. She breathes evenly, and my gaze slides down to the IV in her wrist, the pulse-oximeter clamped down on her finger, up to the glowing machines with the green lines that prove her heart is still beating.

Maggie doesn't have much time left.

I lean my head against my hand and lift my gaze to the

dim outline of the window. Outside, day is dying. The curtains are drawn and there's no way to see the sunset. Quietly, I stand and stride over to the glass. I pull the curtains open just a little. Sit down again. The chair creaks beneath me. Maggie sleeps on. Hues of pink and orange fall over her face. In that instant, it's almost easy to pretend she's like any other teenage girl, sleeping. Something inside of me twitches, like an electric shock.

Maggie's fingers curl suddenly, as if she senses me, or maybe she's finally traveled to a better place. *I was dreaming about the ocean.* I start to reach forward, reacting to an odd instinct to smooth those straggles of hair out of her face. But then I lean back, clenching my hand into a fist to stop myself. It would be cruel to wake her up.

Silence trembles around us. The darkness isn't a menace now, but an understanding friend. There's a clock somewhere in the hall, ticking a warning to me. I should go. I will go. Just as soon as the sun sets. For this moment—just this moment—I lay my head down on Maggie's bed and close my eyes.

This time I have no place in the dream. I'm only an observer.

"Damn it, answer me!" The woman with the strong chin and crinkled eyes stands on the front step of the stone house, hands on her hips. She glares out at the trees as if they'll shrink from her and reveal something. "I'm not joking!"

Suddenly there they are, two teenagers emerging from the green shadows. Their clothing—simple shorts and T-shirts—

is dirty. The woman watches them approach, unmoving even when the boy wraps his arm around her shoulders. They're both smiling as they greet her. She's angry. "Where have you been?" she demands. For the first time, I notice that there are streaks of gray through her hair.

The question kills the boy's mirth and he shrugs, averting his gaze. When it's obvious he refuses to answer the woman turns to the girl. Unlike her sibling, her eyes sparkle. "We were just in the woods," she informs their mother. Her smile is still secretive. "We were dancing."

At this, the woman's frown deepens. "Were you alone?" There is suddenly fear in her voice. "Tell me you were alone," she orders when neither of them responds.

The girl looks out to the trees, as if even now she's drawn to them. "We were alone, Mom," she parrots. "I'm sorry." She embraces her, trying to placate, but she doesn't look away from those quivering shadows.

"We're fine," the boy says.

Glancing around warily, like something else might come out—something far less welcome—the woman ushers them into the house. "No more going to out there without asking me first," she instructs. "And no more dancing. All right?"

The boy agrees, but the girl glances over her shoulder one more time as she follows her family inside. She pauses in the doorway, mouths something—a name—and an Emotion shimmers into view behind her. The Emotion is achingly lovely, and she grasps the girl's shoulder hard. The girl doesn't even flinch. Her expression is soft and dreamy. All her focus is on someone in those woods, someone who is watching her just as intently. His

*face is hidden in shadows, but he lifts a hand in a wave. The
girl blows a kiss.*

"Honey, what are you doing?"

*Slowly, reluctantly, the girl turns her back on the woods and
goes inside, closing the door behind her. The Emotion visiting
her vanishes.*

She is Love.

————————

Mora looks at me with her big, brown, dewy eyes. "What
do you think?" I ask the cow, her teats warm in my hands.
Swish, swish. The sound of milk squirting into the pail is
familiar, rhythmic, and my muscles relax. Mora shifts and
huffs through her nose, taking no interest in my dream.
She focuses on the hay in front of her.

The barn is still. The cows chew slowly, their jaws going
around and around. Suddenly, though, the peace is disrupted. My senses sharpen and my nostrils flare, recognizing the scent. It's the presence I encountered on the way to
school, the one I followed out into the woods that night—the
hooded woman.

A breeze rustles my hair. I've been expecting this visit,
and this time, I'm ready.

"It's almost time," a low voice says behind me.

I turn, unsurprised. "Time for what?" Playing the game
even though all my instincts go against it.

She's hunched over, like being near me is causing her
physical pain. Once again she's hidden in layers of clothing—

the same black sweat pants, black boots, and black hoodie as before—and all I can see of her face is the tip of her nose. "You'll see, won't you?" my visitor says through her teeth. There's an underlying waver to the words; she sounds exasperated, worried, scared. But there are no Emotions. Proof that she's not human, if I needed more than I already do.

I concentrate on the motions of my hands. "Why is it that you answer my questions without giving me any real answers?"

Of course the stranger doesn't answer this, either. She stands there and watches while I finish. Eventually I get to my feet, the small stool scraping across the dirt. "You haven't given me enough information," I tell her, locking Mora in her stall with one hand and clutching a bucket of milk in the other. "If you really want me to…remember, or feel again, then I need more."

Now she sighs. "Oh, you'll get answers. Of that, we can be sure." Her hood flutters and I get a whiff of forest. Her essence is so strong. Without giving me a chance to define it, she walks away. The doors to the barn are open—they weren't before. She wants me to follow again. Quickly I go put the pail in the cooler.

I trail her outside, unwilling to give up just yet. "What's your name?" We slosh through the mud—it's raining.

"Later," she dismisses me. I knew she wouldn't tell me. But she'll make a mistake eventually, and when she does, I won't miss it.

She's leading me into the fields, toward the trees, like last time. Mom and Tim are in the house for the night, both lost in their own existences; they won't notice I'm gone. I know that if I let this woman slip away again, I may be losing my last and only chance to find the missing pieces to the puzzle.

She mutters as we walk. "The power hasn't faded yet. You're beginning to break through it, though. It's almost t-time." Why does she sound as if she's in pain?

A moment later her words register. *Almost time.* This is more than she gave me the last time we spoke. I don't press for more. The corn stalks brush my shoulders on either side as I follow. My visitor moves at a steady speed, but I stay on her heels. She isn't trying to run from me. She must want to show me something.

We abandon the cover of the crops and plunge into the darkness of the woods. We hike in silence, save for the sound of the wind in my ears. We've left the farm behind, and she's taking me east of Edson. The wall of nothingness hardens; Emotions are nearby. There are Elements, as well. I sense Greed and Hope and Rain and Curiosity weaving through the trees, answering their summons as they were made to do.

"You have a purpose," I venture after a brief silence. "But I don't know it. Have we ever met before?"

She sighs, an irritated sound. Then she starts to run, and I quicken my own pace to keep up. Our surroundings speed by in blurs of green and black. She swerves around a tree trunk. She's careful to keep her back to me, keep her face concealed in that hood.

We're slowing down. I move quickly to avoid a fallen tree hanging over our path; it's caught in a V between two others. At first I continue, following my mysterious visitor, but then

I process the trees, stop, jerk around, and study the V formation again. It's getting dark out, and the trees' outline stands out in the orange twilight.

"So you do recognize it." Her voice sounds somewhere behind me. "I wondered if you would."

I barely hear her; my attention is fastened on the V ... the trees ... the shadows ...

Something inside of me clicks, and my nothingness cinches painfully tight when I realize the truth. *This is the place.* This is the clearing. Those are the same trees that surrounded them; those are the same dark shadows, the same grass, the same leaves. This is the place that haunts my dreams.

This is where he died.

I don't have to close my eyes to see the image. I've painted it dozens of times, drawn it, seen it in my sleep, in my daydreams. It's permanently embedded into my brain, an enigmatic tattoo. There is the beautiful girl, her face twisted in anguish, the blood spilling out onto the grass I see now, and the boy she holds in her arms ...

The stranger steps into my peripheral vision, staring at the scene with me. The air around her shimmers with power. "Understand that this is not the actual place where it happened," she tells me. "I recreated it to test the p-power on you." As she says this—her voice still holding that odd, tight note of discomfort—the V formation melts away and becomes nothing but erect, unfamiliar trees. I hardly notice this, though, because the stranger is doubled over. I take a step toward her, but her hand flies out to keep me away and her face is turned in the opposite direction. It's obviously important I never see her or learn who she is.

This is the first time one of my theories has been confirmed as fact; this was done to me. It was not something of my doing. Is this being admitting that she's the one who placed it? And not only that, but she seems to know the story that appears in my dreams and memories. *Remember for both our sakes.* My awareness and instincts sharpen, but all I say is, "Why did you bring me here?"

It's darker now. She's unable to reply for a moment, but then she chokes, "I told you. You need to break it, you need to face..." It's like there's a lump in her throat that prevents her from saying anything more—she swallows and halts mid-sentence. But she goes against my expectations by managing to spit, "I came back because it's not safe."

It's random. There's nothing to bring on the sudden realization. But I stare at this powerful being and wonder how I didn't see it before. "You're the girl, aren't you?" I ask softly. The girl in all my dreams. Who smiles and weeps and loves.

Yet again she doesn't answer. Is it because she can't... or she won't?

It's so obvious. They're the same size. The voices may be a little different, but that's easy to alter. The question comes from all sides, a relentless drum. *Where is she? Where is she? Where is she? Here,* I tell the boy silently. Not dead after all. But secrecy surrounds her like a shroud, this girl who haunts me in both dreams and sleep now.

"What are you hiding from?" I press, thinking of the shadow in the dreams. "How do I fit into all this?" She only shakes her head and backs away, head bent toward the ground.

In the distance, I hear a stick snap. Yet another unknown presence teases my senses—are there *two* beings stalking me? This bizarre girl and ... someone else? *Something* else? I whip around quickly, narrowing my eyes to better see into the brush. The girl is right about one thing; it isn't safe out here. My instincts are singing. "We'll continue this later," I tell her, abandoning the clearing. My fingers brush the ribs of a tree trunk as I pass it, and I start to sprint.

Somehow the girl gets ahead of me. "One more thing before you go," she rasps, her baggy pants billowing in the breeze. With all her shadows and facelessness, she almost looks like a ghost.

I dart around her. "Yes?" The wind rushes past, a roar in my ears.

She deliberately falls behind, but I don't stop. Her tone is a mixture of determination and worry and real warning as it floats to my ears: "Do not, under any circumstances, go to Sophia Richardson's birthday party."

I don't bother asking any questions.

F I F T E E N

The blank page stares up at me, mocking, beckoning. I stare back down at it. Thinking. My pencil taps against the kitchen table. *Tap. Tap. Tap.* A poem about hiding. I'm not a writer—if it weren't for the dreams, I wouldn't be a painter, either. Joshua thinks I'm creative; I should've corrected him. Maybe then I wouldn't be distracted by this.

Not only do the words not come, but my mind buzzes with more theories. The woman said it's almost time. That someone—*he*—has found me. And I need to remember. What does all this have to do with the car accident? How do the dreams fit in?

"You never work in here."

I glance up at Mom, who's standing by the kitchen table and staring at me with an indiscernible expression on her face. She's tired; her shoulders sag, and there are lines under her eyes. For some reason, as I look at her, all I can think is that I should have tried harder to be the daughter she once tucked into bed every night.

She stops waiting for me to say something. I watch her walk to the sink. It seems there are always dishes to do, no matter how often I try to do them when she's not around. Once in a while I'll also do a load of laundry for her, clean out the fridge. If she notices the small gestures, she doesn't allude to it.

"Sally Morrison called, by the way," Mom suddenly informs me. "The school counselor? She wanted to know how you're doing." As Mom speaks her voice is low, careful. She doesn't look at me. "When I asked her for a number, she said you would know where to find her."

I know she's wondering what I've told Sally. But I also know she doesn't want me to acknowledge what goes on in this house. Sometimes Mom and Charles are alike that way. So all I say is, "Thank you for taking the message." I tap my pencil some more, my eyes on the white paper spreading miles before me.

"Would you say I hide from you?" I ask abruptly. Mom starts, faces me. Wisps of hair falls into her eyes, and she brushes them away. The house is so silent that I can hear a clock ticking. I mark each second as it passes.

"What do you mean?" Mom finally asks.

"I'm writing a poem about . . . hiding," I say, weighing my answer. "As a person. I suppose pretending is the same thing as hiding, isn't it?"

"You're asking my opinion?" Disbelief colors her voice. She wipes a plate clean, clearing her throat. She takes her time to answer, mulling over it as I had. Then, "Yes, I guess pretending can be similar to hiding. Hiding doesn't seem like the right word to use, though. I would say that when someone is pretending to be something, or hiding who they are or what they believe, they're really more ... protecting themselves." My mother—no, I shouldn't say that anymore, for really, she won't ever accept it—sighs. Regret fills the empty space beside her. Regret is a rather plain Emotion and she pays me no mind, intent on her summons. Her eyes are wide and muddy, her hair dull and limp.

"I'd like to think that it's never too late to change the way things are," I say casually. Sarah—that's her name—looks at me again.

"What do you mean?" she repeats.

I give up on the poem, sitting back in my chair. It's time to go to school soon anyway. "Just that nothing is set in stone." I bend down to grab my bag. "The past may be the past, but everything else is changeable. You can adjust the path you're on, right?"

Sarah doesn't answer now, but I see that her brow is furrowed and Regret is gone. I walk to the door, smile back at her once. Caught off guard, Sarah smiles back. It's tiny, and it's hesitant, but it's a smile.

———

"I'm going to Sophia Richardson's birthday party."

Joshua jumps a little at the sound of my voice. He glances at me as he slams his locker shut. His eyes behind that red hair are wary. "Assuming," he begins tiredly, "that you also got an invitation to that horrible event—no offense, but I doubt it—why would you want to go? I sure as hell don't plan to."

I shrug, hold my books to my chest. "There's ... something there I want to see." The girl—that Emotion, Element, whatever she is—either wants to stop an event from happening at that party or wants to stop me from discovering something. And if it's so important that she would advise me against going, then it's definitely something worth seeing.

Joshua eyes me skeptically. "What on earth would you possibly want to see at Sophia Richardson's birthday party? The Dorseth brothers getting so drunk they can't even walk? Sophia bullying her friends or forcing me to dance? Spin the bottle, truth-or-dare? What could *you* find interesting there?"

Nothing I say will be a good enough reason for him, so I just shrug again. "I thought you might want to come with me."

He starts walking to class. I don't have this one with him, and mine's in the opposite direction, but I catch up anyway. He doesn't speak for a moment, and somehow I know he's thinking about the last time we were together, in the library. The way I ran away, how limp my fingers were when entwined with his.

"Tell me something," Joshua says. He flips that hair out of the way for the millionth time and I resist a peculiar urge to tell him to cut it. "Why do you want me to come?"

If I answer right away, he'll know I'm lying. If I don't answer, he'll walk away and never look back, no matter how much he likes me. I've pushed Fear away, Maggie is dying, and my brother is a coward, so technically, Joshua is the only person in the world who gives a damn about my fate. I think about it for a moment, and then realize I don't *want* to think about it. This in itself is strange, unsettling, dangerous.

"If you don't want to come, I understand," I manage to say. My nothingness is weakening, because even though it tries to dig a deeper hole inside of me, I feel just the tiniest bit of... vulnerability. Completely unaware of anything else, I stop in the middle of the hallway, grasping at the scrap of Emotion. There is no other feeling except for this, and the taste of it is so unfamiliar. My knowledge and experience have not prepared me for it. More than ever before I realize that I do not understand humanity nearly as well as I'd once thought. My breathing quickens, and even though the floodgate is barely open, a painful fist of Emotion buries itself in my stomach.

Grief.

Why?

"Elizabeth? Are you all right?" A hand cups my elbow. Joshua looks down at me with concerned eyes.

"Elizabeth?" Sally Morrison stands in the doorway of the office, gazing at me worriedly, her forehead all scrunched and wrinkled.

Please come back, please...

You killed me.

Then, inexplicably, I envision that shadow standing over the girl and the dead body of the boy. The red eyes, the fog of beetles. Coming after me. Now the breath hitches in my throat.

"Your terror tastes just as I imagined, Elizabeth," Fear whispers into my ear. The sweet scent of strawberries wafts past my senses. He's pressed to my back, and for the first time his touch affects me! My heart hammers, and past the dread I'm seized by a fierce desire to turn, press my palm to his chest, and experience his lips against mine again—

And just like that, a brick slams into place and the wall is whole again. The power is stronger than ever. The fragile memory of feeling is gone. Black ink drips through my soul, the nothingness darting every which way to swallow me whole. Fear sighs with both satisfaction and disappointment, stepping back to observe. "It must be the boy," he mutters to himself.

I pull away from Joshua, regarding him thoroughly. Was he really the one to bring on the tide of Emotions? No— the strange girl said it was almost time. So this connection with Joshua Hayes is no longer logical. He takes up time and effort, and the very idea of him enrages Fear. Not to mention Tim. Courage may have believed I would need this boy, but unlike the hooded girl, Courage is not particularly powerful. It's unbeneficial for me to listen to him.

"I'm fine, thank you," I say to Joshua, and Fear makes another satisfied sound in his throat. "If I don't leave now, I'll be late for class." I look at Sally. "I'm fine," I repeat, smiling for good measure.

"What about the project? The poem? Did you finish?" Joshua calls after me. "They're due tomorrow, you know!"

Fear walks beside me. I ignore Joshua and pick up my pace to make it to Chemistry class. Fear is quiet; unusual for him. At the doorway, I pause. No one else is around, save for a tall boy hurrying to his own class farther down the hall.

"You won't ever taste me again," I tell Fear in my flat way. "I hope you savored it." Mildly, I wonder why there had been that sudden impulse to kiss him.

Surprisingly, given his nature, he is not smug or quick to react. He touches my cheek, leans in, and inhales me. "I should be glad you've decided to break all ties with the boy," he murmurs. He runs his hand down my arm. "But in a way, he was good for you. I think, little by little, he was breaking through."

"No one can break through," I lie. Yet again I think, *the girl did say it was only a matter of time...*

Fear picks up on the false note in the words, and it isn't until he raises his pale brows at me that I comprehend I've said that last part out loud. "You've discovered something," he states with interest. "And you're not going to tell me." It wouldn't be sensible to have Fear hunting the girl down; she won't tell him anything. I open my mouth to give him more excuses, but the Chemistry teacher notices me standing outside the door and glares.

The bell is going to ring any second. Turning aside so my teacher won't see me talking to myself, I say out of the corner of my mouth, "I'll tell you what I know if you do something for me."

Fear is intrigued. He tilts his head in question.

I wave at the teacher in reassurance, then face Fear again. "I want you to come with me to a birthday party Saturday night. I don't know what I'll find there, and I might need pro-tection."

The lovely Emotion smirks. "What can be so danger-ous about a human's birthday party?"

I open the classroom door, thinking, *We'll see, won't we?*

————

When I get home, Mom is locked in the upstairs bathroom again. Standing in the hall, I can hear her quiet, dry sobs. But I don't try to comfort her; it didn't go over so well last time. Instead, I shut myself in my room and work a little more on the mural covering the walls. I study the V formation once again, the two figures on the ground that represent everything and nothing to me.

And just like that, I'm sucked into another memory that's sprouted from a corner of my mind I thought was empty.

"I'm bored. Let's gather the others and dance again."

The girl waits for her companion to respond, standing eagerly in her dirty clothes and tangled hair. He glances up at her from where he's sitting with a book, his back against a tree. His dark hair curls over his neck. "You promised Mom we wouldn't," is all the boy will say. He turns a page, tracing the words with the tip of his finger.

The girl pouts. She stoops. There's a wilting flower at her bare feet, turning brown. She touches it, and suddenly the flower straightens on a stem that's newly green and strong. The petals streak with fresh shades of pink. "It's been so long," she wheedles. "Please? Just one last time?"

Wavering, the boy looks at her with uncertainty in his eyes. There's another dead flower by his leg, and as she waits for an answer he touches it. Just like with the girl's touch, the flower grows at the contact, stretched full of life. Green and pink, no more brown. The boy frowns in contemplation. He wants to please her. He wants to dance again, too. He opens his mouth to answer, maybe give in, but before he can utter a word there's a crackle nearby. The pair jump and whirl.

"Who's there?" the boy calls out, failing to sound brave. The book falls to the ground, unheeded. The girl frowns and tugs at her brother's arm.

"Landon, it's nothing. You know we don't have anything to be scared of out here..." As she speaks, though, a figure emerges from the green shadows. The boy shifts so he's in front of the girl, and he glares at the man.

"You don't belong here," he snaps. There's recognition in his eyes.

The intruder stares at them with an odd little smile curving his lips. He's older, though there's no way to guess his age. He's out of place in the woods; his clothing is impeccable, pressed and dark. He wears slacks and a white dress shirt. "I'm sorry if I scared you," he says, folding his hands behind his back. "I was answering a summons, just north of here." His tone is friendly. "I heard you and thought I would drop by to say hello. What are you two doing all the way out here? It's not safe." His smile is too bright. The girl glares at him. When neither of them answers the man takes a step closer, tilting his head. "Where are your parents?" he asks. "Your mom... and your dad?"

Landon opens his mouth to speak again, but the girl beats

him to it. "Leave," she snarls, and in her agitation, the leaves in the tree actually tremble. "You have no summons here, and you're not welcome."

"Rebecca," her brother hisses. "Stop it!"

Their visitor, surprisingly enough, is already backing away. He's still smiling. "Better get home," he advises as he reaches the tree line. "Don't want to be out here after dark. You never know what could be roaming these parts."

And then he's gone.

I slowly withdraw my hand away from the dead boy in the mural, my lips pursed in contemplation. The man … How do I know him? He looked familiar, somehow. I struggle, searching all my memories for a placement. But there's nothing. No, not nothing. Whatever else I don't know, I now know this.

The siblings in my dreams were something more than human.

And their names were Rebecca and Landon.

———

The phone rings through the empty house. It's the only sound besides the clock in the hall. My eyelids slide open, listening to the harmony. *Ring. Tick. Ring. Tick.* Tim snores on, oblivious. Since Mom and Charles don't creak out into the hall, they must not hear it, either.

No one ever calls this late.

The phone stops ringing for less than a minute before beginning again. It's almost like an abrasive slap in the sacred silence of the night. I set my covers aside and get out of bed, padding downstairs on silent feet. I pick the phone up on its third ring.

"Hello?"

"Elizabeth? Is that you?" a tearful voice asks.

Still affected by remaining dregs of sleep, I don't identify it right away. The person on the line asks if I'm there, and it slowly clicks. Maggie's mom. I lick my dry lips, unable to make my voice properly concerned as I ask, "Yes, what is it? Is Maggie all right?"

My friend's mother sobs once, tries to smother it. "I'm sorry to call so late," she chokes. "But Maggie's been asking for you. I thought you might want to see her one last time … the doctor says she won't be with us much longer. Until tomorrow night, at the latest."

I don't respond for a moment, and just listen to her cry. It's a wet, desolate series of noises. Whimper, snort, hiccup, exhale. "Elizabeth? Are you still there?" she asks when I've been quiet for too long.

"Yes. Let me think."

"I'm sorry," she repeats. "It's just … Maggie is barely holding on as it is. You're so important to her, and I just thought …"

It wouldn't be prudent for me to see Maggie, even now. Tim would find out if I skipped school, and the portfolio for Mrs. Farmer's class is due. I still haven't written a poem or a peer review. I shouldn't encourage these connections—not until I know the truth about myself and the influence over me has been broken.

"Elizabeth?" My name has never sounded so bleak on another person's lips. I clutch the phone tight, holding it away from my ear slightly as if it could sting me. Maggie's mother sniffles one last time, and I decide to pretend again despite the consequences. After all, Maggie *will* be dead in a matter of hours, and no one would understand if I were to go on like nothing is wrong.

"I'll see you soon."

Maggie's mom sounds so relieved and grateful as she says goodbye. After I've hung up, I stand in the kitchen for a couple minutes, thinking, remembering. An idea forms in my mind. A few more minutes pass, and then I quietly exit the house. I go into the barn, up into the loft, and don't leave until morning.

———

The air in the hospital is brittle this time, grim, as if everyone knows about the girl on the ninth floor. The nurse at the front desk doesn't smile at me, and after I've stepped off the elevator, the anguish hits me like a wave. Walking up to her room, I see Maggie's dad, John, sitting in a chair in the hallway, bent over his knees, eyes in the heels of his hands. Sorrow is beside him, his white palm resting on John's bowed head. As usual, the Emotion doesn't speak when he sees me.

At the sound of my approach, John glances up. Recognizing me, he attempts a smile. "She'll be glad you came," he murmurs. His eyes are red-rimmed and he looks like he hasn't slept in days. This man watched us grow up. He drove me and Maggie to the park. He took us out for ice cream.

"Is she asleep?" I ask.

John shrugs as if the weight of the world rests on his shoulders. Maybe it does. "It's off and on. Her mother is in there with her now, and it's quiet, so probably."

I nod. Maggie's dad focuses, and he finally notices the wrapped package in my arms. Sorrow also notices. "What's that?" John asks lifelessly. I look down at it.

"Something I made for Maggie."

He tries to smile again, fails. Sorrow is unrelenting. "Why don't you just go in? You can wait by her bed. She'll be so surprised when she wakes up and you're there."

I glance at the door. "Are you sure?" John waves me in, and I walk past him. The air in Maggie's room is warmer, still dark. Slumped in the chair by the bed, Maggie's mom startles when she sees me, then relaxes.

"Oh, Elizabeth," she sighs. She's in no better condition than John. "Thank you so much for coming."

"Elizabeth?" Maggie's voice is a rasp, a croak, really. It sounds like it hurts just to say my name. I approach the bed, clenching the package close to me as if it's a defense against her. Realizing this, I release my grip.

"Hi."

Silently, Maggie's mom gets up from her chair and leaves us. She gently touches my arm as she passes. I stand there over my best friend. Her chest rises and falls rapidly as she struggles to breathe. She manages to smile up at me, something neither of her parents was able to do. I don't know this person. She's just a shriveled, waning thing lying in that bed. There's no expression, no light, just bones and skin and organs that are fast losing their purpose. How odd, for something to lose its purpose.

I sit down in the chair by her bed, making my expression serene. "I brought you something," I tell her. I watch Maggie's eyes go to the square package in my arms, see the question in them. I scoot closer and unwrap it quickly. She takes in the painting I've done for her, and suddenly Emotions surround the bed. Joy, Sorrow, Anger, Confusion. None of them address me, since it's Maggie that takes up the whole of their attention. She seems to love the painting, but I'd guess she's also thinking that it's the last one of mine she will ever see. She looks glad that I've come, but she's also probably wondering why this had to happen to her.

"Since you can't go to the ocean," I say softly, "I thought I would bring it to you."

She's still smiling so softly, and a bubble of spit appears at the corner of her mouth. I reach out and wipe it away, and she moves her fingers a bit. They're limp in her lap, and, focusing on our hands, I reach down and lace them together.

"Thank you, Elizabeth," Maggie whispers. Raw.

I look at her face again, and she's studying our hands, too. "You're welcome."

Maggie lifts her gaze to meet mine. Suddenly she coughs, and her body racks. "Hurts..." she rasps. My grip tightens, as if I hold on tight enough she won't drift away in this current, as if I hold on tight enough she won't hurt so much.

Courage appears at my side, among the rest of the watching Emotions. Though he's not as handsome as most of them, he's more ethereal in appearance. He looks at me. "You've done well with this human," he says. His voice is gravelly and smooth at the same time, ancient in its wisdom and kindness.

"I haven't done anything," I say to him without thinking.

"Who are you talking to?" Maggie follows my gaze.

I focus on her quickly. "Oh, just…talking to myself. Sorry."

"You've always been so different from everyone else," she mumbles with another half-smile.

I lean closer to hear better, still pretending. "And yet you stuck with me. I may be different, but I think you might be a little crazy." My tone is teasing.

My friend tries to laugh, but the sound breaks off into more vicious coughing. I can only watch. My nothingness is as strong as ever, but I sense it hardening, slamming more bricks into the wall.

"It's a little cliché, isn't it?" Maggie wheezes. "The dramatic last speech, the cancer. I don't want to be a cliché."

Even now, I feel nothing. It shouldn't be unexpected, but still, it seems…wrong. I should be able to mourn my only friend. The hooded stranger seemed to say that the power on me would eventually fade. Wouldn't now be a good time? Isn't grief one of the strongest Emotions, overwhelming enough to shatter the hardest of hearts?

Disregarding the question for now, I touch Maggie's cheek and slowly shake my head. "You could never be a cliché."

She just tosses her own head restlessly—the movement costs her, and she winces—and I stand to set the painting on a ledge by her bed, where she can see it anytime she wants. I'm careful to keep my face away from the light; I worked on the painting all night up in the loft, and it would be unfortunate if Maggie notices the smudges under my eyes. I sit back down. The chair creaks. I hold Maggie's hand again and she squeezes weakly.

"Can I tell you a secret?" she asks. I nod. Her lips tremble, and she abruptly changes the subject. "You don't show it all the time, but I know you care. That's what kept me going, sometimes. When you weren't around...when I didn't hear from you...I knew it was just because it's hard. It can't be easy s-seeing me like this." She swallows painfully, closing her eyes for a moment.

This girl really is an extraordinary being. Lying in this hospital bed, shrinking away before my eyes, she thinks about how hard this is for *me*. I blink, pursing my lips, unsure how to respond to such sentiment. "What's the secret you wanted to tell me?" I finally say.

She turns her head again to look out the window. It's a cloudy day out; no rain, but no sun either. Unfair that on a day like this there shouldn't be brilliance for her.

Maggie swallows several times before admitting, "I'm afraid." Her breathing becomes more frantic, and I do the first thing my instincts tell me to do: I lean over and I hug her. She hugs me back, desperate for comfort, for someone to tell her everything's going to be okay. Now Fear is there, among the others, but for the first time I barely notice him.

"Everything's going to be okay," I whisper in Maggie's ear. "You're going to be all right. You'll see. You'll see." Empty words from an empty person.

She lets out a ragged breath in my ear, and I know that even as gentle as I'm trying to be, I'm causing her pain. I pull away, and Maggie lets me go reluctantly.

"It just wasn't supposed to end like this." She looks at me with red-rimmed eyes and yellow skin. Colors should be a good thing, but now, they're marks, omens of bad tidings. "I was supposed to grow up, go to college, get a job," she continues in that gut-clenching croak. "Meet my dream guy, marry, have k-kids. You were going to live next door and we would grow old in the same nursing home. Chuck oatmeal at each other and watch soap operas all day in our rocking chairs. That was my daydream. My perfect life. I don't want to keep asking myself why until the end, but…" A lone tear trails down her sunken cheek. This time I don't reach out to wipe the water away; I let it go. Down, down, until it drips off the side of her jaw. This is humanity. This is life and death in one room.

Time is running out. I feel the air drawing closer, sense the Element we all meet once in a lifetime coming this way. I cup Maggie's bald head in my hand, leaning close a third time to offer her a sweet story. Truth or not, I don't know, but I won't send her on her way afraid.

"There's a place"—my voice is a whisper again—"that everyone goes when they die. It's beautiful, so perfect it seems unreal. There's always sunlight, and when it rains the water is warm and glittering, so that you can dance in the storm without having to worry about sickness or danger. Your friends and family are waiting there for you, they're so excited to see you. All those babies your mother didn't get to have are there, all your brothers and sisters. In this place you can have that perfect life you want. There are gorgeous cities and everything is so easy there. Time passes much more quickly, so that by the time I get there you won't even realize it's been a while."

Something dark moves out of the corner of my eye, and the room chills. When I glance over, I see Death, watching us patiently. He's so hard to look at. He's everything and nothing. Beautiful and ugly, terrible and wonderful. His eyes are black waters that are too easy to drown in. I can't even look at what he's wearing; it's impossible to look away from that face. He doesn't spare me a glance—Maggie is who he's come for.

I move to get her parents, but she stops me. "Elizabeth?" Maggie's eyes have begun to flutter, and since my hand is on her wrist I feel her heart accelerate and slow down at the same time. "Don't stop talking. Your voice is so pretty... like bells..."

"I'm right here," I say, tearing my gaze away from Death. I act like he's not there at all, act like the dozens of Emotions in the room aren't there. "I'm not going to leave you."

"How long until I see you again?" She's fading fast now. I should go get her parents. But I don't move. It would seem like a betrayal to her, somehow.

I press my hand to her forehead, her cheek, her hand. "Soon. Don't wait up for me, okay?"

Death doesn't move, but his power is a gentle, unstoppable force. She doesn't even get a chance to answer me, because Maggie Stone is gone. When I look to Death again, he's gone, too. All that's left of my best friend is the shell in the bed. Quiet, empty, nothing.

SIXTEEN

I sit on the front steps of the school during lunch hour. I stare down at the sidewalk, waiting for the bell to ring so I can go inside and get back to class. A shadow falls over me, but I don't bother glancing up. Only one person would make the effort to seek me out.

Joshua doesn't try to say anything. He just stands there. After a while he sits down. Silence. A bird calls. A car goes by. Joshua chews the inside of his lip, and I know what he's thinking: he's debating over the right words, how to comfort me. He can't begin to comprehend that none of it matters, that no comfort is needed. I let him flounder.

He finally chooses to say what thousands, millions before him have said. "I'm sorry."

Feeling his gaze on me, I just count the lines in that side-walk. I expected something different from him, somehow.

When I don't respond, Joshua clears his throat. "I know people around here aren't making that big a deal out of it, but it's because none of them knew Maggie. I knew her, though. She was in one of my art classes, once. She made fun of my tree." He laughs at the memory. I can imagine the scene, and it's classic Maggie. Decked out in all her black and skulls, she's pointing at his sketchpad and laughing.

Joshua knows he isn't doing this right. He's probably remembering how he felt when his mom died.

I decide to change the subject. "I'm sorry I never gave you my part of the portfolio. It was irresponsible of me."

He stares at me in disbelief. "I'm not worried about it, Elizabeth. Mrs. Farmer isn't, either. She knows about Maggie."

I squint up at the sky. Irony of ironies, it's sunny today. "I shouldn't be given special treatment. I'll finish my part of the homework and hand it in."

Joshua processes this. He probably decides it's is my way of dealing with the grief. "Look, I know this must be hard for you. So if you ever need to talk, well, I'm not a counselor or anything, but I am a friend. You can call me anytime."

I turn my head to meet his gaze, cold. "Joshua, I don't care that Maggie died. I watched the life drain from her and I didn't feel a thing. You don't need to have the right words, or say anything comforting. I'm fine, I always will be, and nothing is going to change. The world will go on as it always has, no matter who dies. You'd better get used to that."

I get up and leave him there with his empty words and sad eyes.

———

"I can't believe you're still going to this thing," Fear hisses in my ear as I guide my truck up Sophia Richardson's driveway. Looks like everyone is here for the big birthday party. Her house is a couple miles from town, in a wooded area, a big two-story her parents bought before the divorce. As we pull up I see that someone's started a bonfire and the hot tub is uncovered. Kids are already getting drunk; someone is vomiting into a bush.

"Why wouldn't I?" I park my truck away from the other cars, between two trees, and kill the engine. Fear vanishes from his seat and appears beside me as I get out. He's gritting his teeth.

"I think we both know the answer to that," he says doggedly and tries to stare me down. I brush past him, the proximity to his essence causing the usual frightening images to race through me.

Ignoring this, I start toward the hot tub, which is where most of the kids are. I know Fear will follow me. "Do you want answers or not?" I challenge him, skirting around a loud couple making out in the grass.

He growls as he exhales. "You're a coward. I know what you're doing."

Music makes the ground shake, and a loud laugh rings out. It's dark, and Sophia has put up some medieval-looking torches. The flames flicker and cast strange shadows everywhere. I make sure not to look at Fear so nothing seems amiss. "What am I doing?" I question him, sounding genuinely curious.

A girl shoves past me, calling out, "Sean! Hey, Sean, over here!" and when I stumble, Fear steadies me. Once I'm upright he tries to make me face him, but I escape his grip and keep walking.

Fear stalks me now. "You never told Maggie Stone how you really felt, and it's the least of what you owed her," he snaps. "It's eating you up inside."

"And how did I really feel about her?" I ask, surveying the interactions around the hot tub like they really interest me. A few people have brought their swimsuits, and I watch a boy shove a girl into the water. She shrieks in mock outrage. There are many Emotions here tonight, and these kids are consumed by them.

If possible, Fear gets angrier. He disappears and bursts in front of me again. He seizes my shoulders in his zeal to make me see the truth. "We both know that you were affected by that girl's death," he insists. "Even though you never gave her anything back, she stayed. Even when all the other kids shied away and hated you, Maggie—a simple human child—loved you. And no matter what you say, I know you loved her back. I saw the way you looked at her in that hospital room."

"Sometimes you see things that aren't there, Fear. We both know that, too." I start to walk away again, but Fear grabs my arm and hauls me back to face him. His eyes burn. As if his touch isn't making my nothingness twitch, I raise my brows.

"I want you to admit that you care, Elizabeth," he growls. It's hard to hear him over the blaring music. "Say it. For once, tell the truth."

No one sees me standing in the shadows. We've made our way past the hot tub and toward the front door. I lift my chin, staring up at Fear. "I may have humored you in the past, but I'm done pretending. From now on, please accept that this is what I am."

He suddenly smiles, a bitter, sad quirk of the lips. "You know, sometimes you remind me of my kind in the way you act. The same deception, same games."

This conversation isn't sensible. Especially here. I look around me, pursing my lips. *Do not, under any circumstances, go to Sophia Richardson's birthday party.* The stranger—Rebecca—desperately wanted to hide something about tonight, so all I can do is wait and try to be in the right place at the right time. I head for the backyard.

What about the house? something reminds me.

I jerk around quickly, stopping Fear in his tracks. He scowls. I move to the right and he sidesteps, blocking me.

"Move," I order before thinking.

He doesn't react well to being told what to do. He grins at me, lazy and insolent. "Not until you tell me what you know," he retorts. "We did make a deal, after all. I come with you to this stupid little party and you tell me everything. Well, here I am."

I dart around him and continue walking toward the house. "You know, if you're so detached from it all," Fear says, following me again, "why are you looking for the truth? Why bother at all?"

"Well, well, well. Look who decided to crash the party."

Sophia, arms crossed, glares at me. I've wandered onto the lawn without realizing it, in full view of everyone. Sophia has a tiny army behind her—three girls all decked out in miniskirts and high heels.

"Happy birthday," I say to her, expressionless. Fear is cold at my back.

Sophia's eyes bulge out of her head now and Anger is suddenly standing beside her, looking bored. "You seem to bring me to this town quite often, human," he says to me. "You have a negative effect on this place."

As do you, I almost counter. I don't seem to have good control of my impulses tonight.

Sophia steps closer, her silly high heels sinking into the soil. The torchlight makes her face an ominous orange. "I didn't invite you here, freak," she hisses at me. "If you don't leave, I'm going to kick your ass."

"You can try." I don't back down.

Fear laughs. "Hit her. I dare you," he says to me.

Sophia actually shoves me. Caught off guard, I stumble back, and she laughs. She has a reputation to maintain in front of our peers. "I didn't invite you for a reason." She takes a step closer, menace in the movement. "Because you're not *normal*."

Everyone's paying attention to us now, and some kids start cheering. Encouraged, Sophia lifts her hands to shove me again, but I need to keep searching. Rebecca wouldn't mention this party for no reason, and I want to walk the entire property. I grab Sophia's wrists as she reaches for me, and before she can wrench herself free, I throw her to the ground with unexpected ease. Sophia screams as she rolls through the wet grass. There are scattered laughs through the crowd.

"If you're normal, then maybe it's a good thing I'm different," I tell Sophia in a mild tone. I step over her and sidestep her swiping nails.

"I'm going to kill you!" she swears, eyes blazing. She's cradling one of her arms. I turn my back.

The entire party has encircled this little tête-à-tête, and though most move aside for me to pass, one person stays where he is. He stares like he's never seen me before. I offer Joshua a wry smile, showing him that this is really who I am, not the perfect girl he's made me out to be. Why did he come?

To see you, that voice in my head whispers.

It doesn't matter.

"Elizabeth?" Joshua watches me walk by but doesn't reach out. Fear pats his shoulder, mockingly sympathetic. "Let her go, boy. She's a mess." Joshua doesn't hear or see him, of course, but he does frown, sensing something off about me and the air around us.

"*I'm* a mess?" I repeat blandly, going around to the back of the house. Fear just snickers.

The house is dark but clean. The place hasn't changed much from when I visited here as a child. Same wooden floors, same beige furniture. Sophia probably didn't want anyone to come inside because her sister is here. I travel through the kitchen, then the living room until I find some stairs leading up. My ears pick up the faint sound of *Wheel of Fortune* somewhere. I trip in the dark, and at the last second I throw my palm before me as a buffer to save my face from smashing the edge of a stair.

Wordlessly, Fear holds out his hand above me. A small

orb of light appears over his palm, illuminating the dark hall. Recovering, I keep going. I notice that while my weight makes the stairs creak, Fear is soundless. Using the light, I pause to study some pictures hanging up on the wall. Sophia hardly smiles in any of them, and in every single one she's by her sister, either supporting her or looking at her with indiscernible expressions.

I keep going. The stairs open up to a large hallway, and my eyes alight on a doorway at the far end, where sounds of the TV and a blue glow pours out. Without hesitation, I go toward it.

The room is small and pink. There's a rocking horse in the corner and a big, fluffy bed against one wall. These aren't the first things I see, however. What I spot first is Sophia's sister, sitting on a rug in the center of the floor, staring at the box that has been put in front of her. If my memory serves me correctly, she's four years younger than her capricious sister.

"What are you doing?" Fear stays in the hall when I enter the bedroom, so I leave him there and move toward Morgan Richardson.

She isn't startled by the sight of a stranger in the privacy in her house, this much I know. Does she remember me? As I approach, Morgan tilts her head back to look at me, and I in turn study her thick lashes, her round face and bleary eyes. She's in pajamas, and the material has frogs all over it. She's so tiny. The pants are too big for her. She must be in one of her withdrawn moods, since she doesn't say a word. In the past she wasn't able to communicate well, and it seems time hasn't changed that.

"Hello," I say, glancing around. Besides the furniture and toys, Morgan is alone. It looks like Morgan's babysitter has left and, judging from the fact I haven't seen her anywhere, doesn't intend to return tonight.

"Elizabeth, this is pointless," Fear says from the doorway.

Ignoring him, I squat down so I'm at Morgan's level. I smile at her and she stares back. But then, so quickly that I wonder if I imagined it, her eyes flit to Fear. A second later she fastens her gaze back on the TV. There's some cartoon on, something involving a talking sponge.

"Oh, fabulous," Fear mutters, stalking to the window. "Another human that can see me. That's just wonderful. You know, my ego can't take much more of this." He glares down at the lawn, the moon casting square patterns on his high cheekbones.

Processing Morgan's stiffness, I reach to brush a strand of hair back from her face. "You see things, don't you?" I murmur. She leans into my touch. "You know more than you should." The girl shudders. I acknowledge this with an incline of my head, understanding. "Sometimes the things you see aren't very nice, are they?"

Fear whips around, his glare burning through me. "I'm nice!" he protests.

When I still don't respond he steps closer, growling. "Elizabeth, we're wasting time. Hold up your end of the bargain."

"I will. Now hush." I keep my focus on the girl, but I can sense Fear fuming. Morgan meets my gaze directly, and for the briefest of moments, her eyes become clear and focused, as if she knows me and knows all my secrets. I straighten, alert.

"Do you want to tell me something?" I ask her.

"How long are we going to do this?" Fear seethes.

Morgan's strange brown-blue eyes go cloudy and clear over and over in an aching cycle. Her mouth moves, puckering. I lean in, putting my ear next to her lips. "Morgan?" I prompt.

She swallows, opens her mouth, closes it. Fear makes another sound of impatience behind me. "I have better things to do, Elizabeth."

The girl touches my cheek. My hand tightens on hers. "If you have anything to say, now would be an excellent time to do it," I tell her, forcing a note of tenderness into my tone. Longing arrives, that fickle Emotion. She kneels and embraces Morgan, smiling at me with luminescent eyes. This girl wants someone to be kind to her, just once, without the irritation and sense of duty that usually comes along with it.

Morgan's muscles spasm and her eyes go dull again. She looks in the direction of the window, soaking up the stars just as Fear had done moments ago. Seconds tick by. After a minute, it seems like she's not going to talk … but then she focuses on me yet again.

"Run," she says, clear as a bell.

Before I can move or react, Fear is hissing. He moves back into the hall, his coat snapping around his heels like a whip. I quickly follow, leaving Morgan there in that empty room with the box. "What is it?" I ask. The words echo.

When Fear starts for the stairs without answering, I stop and stand there in the dark. Realizing this, Fear snarls deep in his throat, but he stops, too, and faces me. There's a moment of silence. Frowning, he mutters, "I thought I sensed . . . "

He doesn't finish, but he continues to glare at a spot on the wall as if it's talking to him. "Are you going to fill me in?" I ask.

He lets out a frantic, frustrated breath, gesturing sharply to the room we just left. "Will you fill *me* in?"

Morgan holds no more interest for me. "Maybe," I tell Fear.

The word isn't even out of my mouth completely when he jerks and lifts his head, sniffing the air. His eyes go wide again, and he whirls around. He rushes down the stairs at an inhuman speed. Any moment now I know he'll disappear.

"This isn't a place for my kind," is all he says.

I try to stay close on his heels. "There are plenty of Emotions here," I note, raising my voice so he'll hear me. My grip is tight on the bannister. "Are you—"

"Just trust me on this," he snaps, reaching the ground floor. I quicken my pace as he reaches for the knob.

Just then a boy stumbles from the bathroom. He reeks of vomit. Before I have a chance to evade him he embraces me, slobbering on my cheek. I shove him away—Fear is already outside. I start running. Cool air splashes me in the face as I sprint out the front door.

Fear isn't anywhere to be seen. I've lost him. All the other Emotions are gone as well. The party is now just a writhing mass of kids, dancing, laughing, leering, drinking, shouting. Without any Emotions, they'll feel the same sensations for hours. And even if the Emotions don't return, they'll still feel something. Fear told me a few years ago that if there isn't the actual being around to instill an emotion, humans will draw from a memory of it as a last resort.

Sophia is standing with a group of her friends, obviously still incensed from our little dispute. Best to avoid her. I start in the opposite direction of the girls, toward the woods.

Why would all the Emotions abandon their summons?

Suddenly, the sound of sirens fills the air. Red and blue lights swirl around the house and lawn, reflecting off the water in the hot tub. Sheriff Owen's voice bursts out, tired and hard, "All right, kids, stay where you are. Ah, Dorseths! Don't you dare run!" Small-town party bust.

But Rebecca was so adamant about not coming to this party. I'm not finished. Distracted from the mayhem around me, I survey the whole scene with narrow eyes as I walk, trying to spot anything out of place.

"Get out of my way, you idiot!"

The unfamiliar voice comes from a distance, but it catches my attention. Male. Frantic. In the trees, I see bright headlights burst on. A girl falls at my feet in a drunken stupor. I hardly notice as I step over her. My gut insists that something important is about to happen in those woods.

"She's hurt," a new voice says, the words bouncing through the night. This voice I recognize. "We need to get her to a hospital."

Joshua. Again I begin to hurry, pushing aside branches. Morgan's urgent whisper invades my head: *Run, run.* As I sprint toward the sound of Joshua's voice, I spot an Emotion, no, an Element, cowering in some leaves. It's a tiny being with a slight glow. As I pass it, the creature actually jumps on my shoulder and pulls at my hair, her squeaky voice a piercing warning in my ear.

"He's here, he's here!" she shrieks. "Disappear, before he gets you, gets you!" She vanishes.

The argument ahead continues to drift toward me, though I still can't see the speakers through the trees and darkness.

"The cops are here, moron, and if you don't move I swear to God I'll run over both of you," the first voice says.

"Real smart, Tyler, because once you murder two people the cops definitely won't be after you *then*."

I finally come into a clearing where some cars are parked, spotting Joshua right away in the beam of the bright head-lights. He's on the ground, cradling Susie Yank in his arms. There's blood coming out of her ear. Tyler's behind the wheel of a pickup, revving his engine, glaring with red-rimmed eyes at the two kids in the way of his escape.

Neither of the boys is aware of me yet, coming at them from the tree line. There's the sound of footsteps behind me somewhere, but I barely comprehend this. All my focus is on the situation swiftly unraveling in the clearing. "Joshua?" I call out. "What happened?" A twig snaps under my foot as I get closer. Other people are rushing to their vehicles, not even noticing this show-down in their own desperate getaways.

Joshua keeps his eyes on Tyler. "Call 9-1-1," he says. "Tyler shoved Susie in his big rush and she fell and hit her head on a rock or something. I don't think I should move her."

"Move her," I say without hesitation. I see the frenzy in Tyler's eyes and in the way he grips the steering wheel. I'm still yards away, but even running, I see that I won't be fast enough. Tyler's truck rears forward, the engine roaring, about to bear down on Joshua and Susie.

"No."

There's no analyzing, there's no thought of consequences or benefits. All I can think is, *Not another one.* I surge, a blur in the clearing, scooping Joshua and Susie into my arms and wrenching them out of the way with a super-human strength and speed I shouldn't have.

Whooping in triumph, Tyler drives away, not even looking back.

Joshua breathes heavily beneath me, and I grasp that I'm lying on top of him in a protective position, having disregarded Susie completely. She's partially crushed beneath Joshua while the other half of her is flopped on the grass. There's no way I should have been able to save them. What is happening to me?

My senses are coming back together now. "Good thing I reached you in time," I say to Joshua, my voice even, casual. I stand up and brush my pants off. "Do you have a phone?" Silently he shakes his head, and he's staring at me. Shock is making his pupils dilate; big, small, big, small. I continue, as if we're discussing our English project. "I don't have one either, so we'll have to wait for the cops to come back here to get Susie help." I scan the kids in the clearing who are still dashing past us. None of them seem to have witnessed what happened, or if they have, they're too numbed by alcohol to realize anything. I walk away.

When I look back at Joshua, he's still gaping at me with that frozen expression. My nothingness reaffirms itself. I sense it prodding and poking, digging and building, strengthening the weaknesses. Again I proceed like nothing is out of the ordinary. "I thought I might be too late." I offer him a seemingly relieved smile.

Joshua has regained some of his senses, and he isn't buying it—I can tell by the way his jaw clenches. But there's no chance to confront me because we can both hear the deputies walking through the brush, shouting and swinging their flashlights. Joshua stands up and turns away. He lifts Susie and walks toward the cops, holding her against his chest. I stay where I am, looking after him.

He doesn't glance back, but his shoulders are stiff and determined, and I know this isn't over.

SEVENTEEN

All the lights in the house are on when I get home.

The farm is very, very quiet. Even the cows in the barn are subdued. I hop down from my truck, listening to the familiar sound of gravel under my tennis shoes. The screen door groans on its hinges, a noise I've listened to all my life, every time I enter this house.

The brightness of the kitchen hits me. It's not so friendly a place at one a.m. I stay in the entryway for just a moment, straining to hear anything, but it's silent. Both of them heard my truck pull in; they heard the screen door. They know I'm in here. They're waiting.

I step into their line of sight. Tim and Sarah look at me from where they stand behind the counter. Sarah is trying not to wring her hands nervously; she keeps pulling them apart and folding them again.

Tim, of course, is the first to speak. His forehead gleams. "Where have you been?" His voice is low and controlled, and the bruises Fear gave him have become simmering hues of blue and yellow. For the first time in a long time, he's not drunk. Sobriety seems even worse.

I take off my shoes so I don't dirty Sarah's clean floor, moving slowly, as if he's a predator and I'm prey. I look at that floor as I answer, "I went to Sophia Richardson's birthday party." I'd left after supper and made sure to do my chores, of course. Usually, after I shut myself up in my room, no one bothers me. But tonight, apparently . . .

"Your mother just told me the school called yesterday."

Ah. I'd forgotten about skipping classes when Maggie died.

"They said you were absent all morning," Tim adds tightly. When I don't respond, he clenches his beefy fists. "Well?" When I still don't respond, Tim steps away from the counter, closer to me.

Move, sense whispers.

Following some strange instinct, I hold my ground, lifting my chin in what could be perceived as defiance.

The faint scent of sweat and soil drifts to my nose. I look up at Tim. He seems taller than normal. He hasn't shaved in a while; scruff dots his chin and jaw. "You're going to tell me where you went," he orders. Again he waits for me to speak. Sarah's hands tremble as she reaches up to push her hair away from her face. She looks like she's focusing hard on thinking nothing, feeling nothing, being nothing. She's trying to be me.

And failing miserably.

"H-honey, don't you think—" she starts.

"Shut up." He's so cold, so empty. I should be seeing Anger, yet there are no Emotions present. Are they still avoiding whatever Fear sensed at Sophia's party?

At my continued silence, Tim leaves Sarah's side to tower over me. "Elizabeth." It's a warning. There's a vein jutting out of his forehead that always precedes pain. But for some reason, I keep ignoring those insisting urges to *run, fight!* and just stand there, silent. I don't answer his questions, and oddly enough, I don't plan to. That day in the hospital ... the time I'd spent at Maggie's side ... the words exchanged ... it seems pure, somehow. That day is ours. Mine and Maggie's. No one else should touch it.

Why do you care? that little voice whispers.

I don't see it coming. He slaps me. Hard. My head is tossed to the side, and my cheek feels as if tiny needles are being shoved into every pore of my skin. Tim gives me another chance to tell him what he wants to know. When I remain wordless for a third time, he tries to do it again, but I sidestep him. Tim bristles. Sarah doesn't seem to know what to do, how to feel. She can't watch, but she does.

"Answer me!" Tim thunders.

I smile up at him. "No."

Now Sarah looks truly frightened. Where is Fear? She opens her mouth to intervene, but before she can, Tim laughs. It's so unexpected, she stares at him. I just keep smiling. Tim laughs and laughs.

"You're a demon," Tim tells me, shaking his head. "You're no child of mine. I want you out of this house." His face is redder than I've ever seen it, and now veins stick out everywhere. He's not angry, exactly—Anger is nowhere to be seen—but this is who he is. Even without the Emotion. Tim lifts his hand again—

Even I don't anticipate Sarah stepping forward, resting her fingers on his shoulder gently. Tim's hand lowers, and he turns to look at her.

"You can't kick her out," she says timidly. He's listening to her; he's forgotten about me for the moment. Sarah swallows. "What would people say? We could get in trouble."

Tim thinks. A minute goes by, and slowly, all those veins and redness fade until he's normal again. The hand that was about to strike me inches up, twines with Sarah's. She flinches, but Tim doesn't see it. He's pursing his lips at me, squinting.

Finally, he points at me rather than trying to hit me again. There's earth under his fingernails. "You will do your chores every morning, you will go to school, and you will come right back here," he says through his teeth, nostrils flaring. He shifts his glare to the place just over my head as he talks. He can't even stand the sight of me. "You'll do the afternoon chores, you'll do your mother's work, you'll do your homework, and then you'll go to bed." Abruptly, Tim releases his hold on Sarah and storms out of the kitchen. Glancing at me with another anxious expression, she moves to follow.

I raise my voice to stop Tim. "Am I allowed to go to Maggie's funeral tomorrow?" Copying him, I ask it without looking at his face, instead studying that wall like it's the most interesting thing in the world. The right side of my face is on fire and the yellow flowers on the wallpaper consume me.

My father pauses. "It would look bad if we didn't go," he snaps as an answer.

As if that's all that matters.

———————

She lies there in the casket, her face small, white, still.

"Maggie spent her life always thinking about others," Pastor Mike says. He's the only pastor in Edson. He holds his Bible lightly, looking down at the body with a pasted-on expression of regret. This man didn't know Maggie. His words are hollow, automatic. He's probably thinking about what's going to be on TV tonight. "She would go out of her way to reach those who were in need."

Tim and Sarah stand behind me, as does a small portion of the town, including Joshua. He's been ignoring me so far. At my side are Maggie's parents, both drawn and gray.

The sun shines down as Pastor Mike continues his eulogy. We're all dressed in black. Not sensible, really, since it's sweltering out today—it seems even Fall isn't around to do her job. The stench of sweat permeates my senses. I look down into the fresh grave, examine the girl in there.

The freckles that always marked her and made her Maggie now stand out, a stark feature that looks strange on such a vacant face. She's wearing a neatly pressed dress. It's pink. She hated pink. And they've actually done her nails. Maggie liked them chewed down to the nub and only used black nail polish. This isn't Maggie. This isn't my best friend. This is a person I don't know. Where's the life, the illumination?

The sweetness, the contemplation, the wild abandon that made so many memories for us when we were young?

"Come on, Liz!" Maggie runs ahead of me to the ice cream truck, red pigtails bouncing all around her shoulders. I follow more slowly, feeling the heat of the day on my head. I can't get any treats because Tim got angry when I asked him for money.

Just as I'm crossing the street, I pause. There's an Emotion standing on the road, looking right at me. I recognize his white-blond hair.

"Why did you come back?" I ask him. Maggie is standing in line, getting her ice cream. She's forgotten about me for the moment.

The Emotion smiles down at my upturned face. "You interest me. Not much can do that anymore." There's a hint of sadness in his eyes.

I don't have a chance to answer; Maggie is running back up to me. Her cheeks are flushed and she breathes heavily. She holds two Dilly Bars in her hands.

"Here!" She thrusts the dripping thing at me, and I take it. "Happy birthday!"

I look at the bar and back at her. "It's not my birthday."

She grins, eyes sparkling. "It's not? Oops. Oh, well. Come on!" She takes my hand in hers, dragging me away from the road and the Emotion who's still staring at me, smiling.

The ice cream is melting in my hand, so I lick it quickly.

I stare down at the girl in that casket, feeling my nothingness dig a deeper hole inside of me. "She was often a counselor when her friends came to her in need," Pastor

Mike intones. Wrong, wrong. I was Maggie's only friend. I never went to her for counsel. I never went to her at all.

Fear's words come back to me: *You're a coward.*

Doesn't he know that if I really could, I would mourn my best friend? It's not a choice, no matter what anyone believes.

As if my thoughts have summoned him, suddenly Fear is here, walking through the crowd of black like he belongs. Maybe he does. Apparently the threat at Sophia's party is no longer a concern. I sense him coming up behind me. The crows on the gravestones hush.

"Look at her," Fear murmurs in my ear, his lips brushing my skin. I turn to face him, but he wraps his hands tightly around my arms, forcing me to stay where I am. "No. Look at her, Elizabeth."

He shouldn't be here. Not now. I focus on Maggie's face again, not really seeing it.

"Listen to me," Fear breathes, and the hair on the back of my neck prickles. "I want you to look at your best friend. She's dead, Elizabeth. She's gone, and she's not coming back. You were with her when all the life left her body; you saw every single one of her memories fade. Everything you two ever went through, every experience you ever had." Somehow he thinks of the exact day I'd been thinking of earlier and uses it against me. "Remember all the times she bought you ice cream because you had no money? Do you remember when Maggie dragged you to the homecoming game, and after everyone left you two sat in the middle of the field and looked at the stars? She told you everything. You told her nothing. She sensed that, but she didn't care. She always thought you would open up to her one day—"

"Stop."

I hadn't meant to speak out loud, but my voice slices through the still air. Pastor Mike does stop, staring at me expectantly. Someone coughs in the crowd. I can feel Tim stiffening. John—Maggie's dad—turns around to look at me, and as his gaze settles on my face, it softens. It's that expression that makes me realize something. Something bizarre; it doesn't make sense.

I'm crying.

Fear leans down, kissing my neck with his cool lips. He's accomplished what he came to do. "You will feel. I'm going to make sure of it," he promises. He leaves me there, sending a chilly breeze over the funeral. Some shiver.

"Did you have something to say?" Pastor Mike prompts, eyebrows raised. It's strange—his eyebrows are gray and his hair is black. Obviously dyed.

There are so many things I could say at this moment. So many words, meanings, memories, opportunities to make up for areas I've disappointed.

I just shake my head, backing away from the casket. I wipe away the strange tears with the back of my dark sleeve. "No, nothing to say. Sorry," I mumble.

The pastor eyes me, then seems to mentally shrug. "Everyone loved her and will truly miss her," he finishes, snapping the Bible shut with a *thump*.

———

I sit in the barn loft with a pad of paper and a pen. The bale of hay pokes at my bottom and legs, but I hardly notice. Mora is restless below; she snaps at another cow. I *tap, tap, tap* my way into nothing. No rhymes come to mind, not even free verse. Everything I think is numb and shallow ... there's just no inspiration to be found inside of me, and there lies the problem.

Something nesting in the ceiling beams flutters, and the faint tang of perspiration dots the air. Terror. A scream sounds through the loft a second later.

I lift my head from the palm of my hand, calling out, "Fear?"

He doesn't answer, but I know he's nearby. He's avoiding me and my questions about the night of Sophia's party, but at the same time he wants to be near. "You can't have it both ways," I say distractedly, pursing my lips in contemplation. Hiding. Pretending. Protecting oneself. I just have to start— that's the first step.

There are different kinds of hiding.

My handwriting is neat on the page. Fear remains uncharacteristically hushed, and I know he doesn't plan to come to me tonight. Which means not only is he avoiding me, but he knows something he desperately refuses to tell me. Something arrived at the party that night, something that sent all the Emotions and Elements running. What could it possibly be? It doesn't matter—the truth will probably come out one way or another, and if not, I'm no worse for wear.

I bring my knees up to my chest, becoming a ball. The paper rustles and I smooth it out, my fingers tracing the edges.

There are different kinds of hiding. I hide, I protect, I pretend. I will not go down in history for my poetry, but my promise to Joshua will be fulfilled; I will finish what I've started.

Will you? my little voice taunts.

I remember Sarah's pain as she asked me if I knew where her daughter was. Maggie letting her optimism crumble toward the end, lying there in that bed. Fear's impossible infatuation. Joshua's innocence.

I just realized that there are so many things I don't know about the kids I see every day. How many of them have secrets they keep from the rest of the world? How many of them wear masks everywhere they go? We're anything but typical.

Thinking about his words makes me think about Joshua himself. He, too, has been avoiding me. He doesn't look at me in class. He passes me in the hall without a greeting of any kind. He's guarded after what he saw at Sophia's party, after what I said to him on the steps. Just another person in Edson who knows what I am: something strange and unnatural. A freak.

I made a mistake, saving him and Susie that night. If I know anything about the world, things happen the way they're supposed to. I interfered in an event that should have taken place. Even the rebellious Emotions can follow the rules I've broken.

An event…

What if Rebecca warned me against going to the party because she was afraid something specific would take place? Something specific like me losing control. Was there a chance she knew I would reveal an ability I shouldn't have, an ability I never knew I had until that night? But what if I hadn't broken any rules? Maybe I'd been … meant to interfere. For reasons I don't know, maybe I was supposed to stop Joshua from being hurt…

I set my unfinished poem aside and stand.

Too many questions, not enough answers.

———

My truck rumbles into the school parking lot. As I reach for my bag in the passenger seat, I notice Sophia Richardson glaring at me. She's probably been making plans to get back at me for a few days now.

The first bell is already ringing inside. I haul the bag onto my back and start jogging to make it on time.

Just as I reach the front doors a shadow looms across me, and I turn my head to meet Joshua's intense gaze.

I've been expecting this.

"Not now," I say, stepping past him. "We have to get to class."

There's no trace of the shy, uncertain boy when he sticks his arm out to block my path. "You owe me this," he says sharply.

Two girls rush by, hardly noticing Joshua and me as they skirt around. It's as if neither of us is actually here.

I yield, stepping away from the doors. "How do I owe you anything?" I question.

"Because I believe in you," Joshua tells me simply. The bizarre statement causes my nothingness to twinge.

After a moment of consideration, I nod. "Okay. I'm listening."

This boy I've known most of my life takes my arm gently, leading me away from the doors so no teacher sees us. He pulls me around the side of the building, under the shade of some oak trees.

"We both know what happened the night of the party," he starts. He folds his arms across his chest in a resolute stance, and once again I notice the rubber band around his wrist.

"Why do you wear that?" I ask abruptly, motioning at it.

Joshua blinks. "What?"

"The rubber band," I clarify. "Why do you wear it?"

Suddenly self-conscious, he looks down at the band, toying with it. He allows me to change the subject. "It's kind of dumb," he admits. "But it's a therapy thing. Well, more of a habit, now. A couple months after my mom died, Sally gave it to me. You know Sally, right?"

When I nod, he goes on. "Anyway, I was ten and I wasn't talking to anyone. I was depressed, I guess; I started getting into fights with other kids. No one could get anything from me, not even the therapists my dad forced me to go to. So one day Sally comes up to me in the grocery store, squats down so she's looking me right in the eye, and gives me this rubber band. 'Every time you think about hurting yourself or someone else, snap this on your wrist,' she tells me. 'A rubber band has got to be better than a fist, right?'" He smiles faintly at the memory.

"Most therapists would try to stop the pain completely," I comment.

Joshua shrugs. "That was what was so great about it. She didn't try to change me or fix me. She just gave me another option. One that didn't land me in a hospital or more therapy sessions."

Joshua doesn't give me a chance to process this. "Now it's your turn." He raises his brows in challenge. He wants the truth—there's no need to say it out loud. The breeze picks up, and leaves stir above our heads. It's a content sound.

So I tell him. "I'm human. I know you're thinking alien or vampire or something like that, so you can relax. But I don't feel any emotions. I can run a little faster than a speeding car, and I also see things that no other human can see." There isn't much more, but I offer what I can: "I've been told I feel nothing because of some sort of power over me, and that I'm expected to break through it soon. I've already started to, actually." I go on to explain the other plane.

Joshua takes this in without the reaction I was anticipating; there's no wariness, disbelief, disgust. Even so, it's a little too much for him.

Once I'm finished I wait about a minute for him to think about it, then shoulder my bag again. "We really do have to go in," I remind him.

He looks around, as if seeing the school for the first time, and lets out a breath. His bangs lift off his forehead, and slowly settle back down, covering his eyes. An odd instinct consumes me to reach out and brush all that hair aside.

I start to walk toward the doors, and Joshua recovers quickly. He catches up with me. "We're not done talking about this, you know," he says. "Not by a long shot."

"What else can there be?"

"Hey." Joshua touches my elbow, stopping me yet again. His eyes—amber in the sunlight—are solemn. "Just because I know about you now doesn't mean I'm going to treat you like Sophia Richardson." He grins. "I mean, you're still you, right?"

I study his face. "And who is it, exactly, that you think I am?"

The boy frowns. "Well, first off, I don't buy the 'no Emotion' shit. You may not be obvious about it, but you're definitely human in that area."

Another person who's going to deny the truth. Even if I can't discourage Fear, I can set Joshua straight. "I meant what I said that day on the steps, Joshua," I say. "Maggie's death didn't affect me. You ignoring me didn't bother me. The fact that my own mother doesn't love me doesn't matter. When my father hits me, I feel nothing. My brother acting like everything is perfect and nothing is wrong doesn't infuriate me. I don't—"

"Knock it off," he cuts in with a downward slash of his hand. "I'm not the one in denial. You are." It's as if he's read my mind.

I think of all those little things that make him believe this. Memories that aren't just his. Seemingly human moments. Me offering him a smile in our kindergarten class. Me comforting Maggie on the playground after a boy had called her ugly. Me staring out the classroom window as one of our teachers droned on and on. Me studying the mural on my wall with an expression akin to frustration. Me looking down into Maggie's casket, those strange tears trailing down my cheeks. Our hands laced together on the table in the library.

I'm shaking my head. "Joshua, no matter what it seems like—"

He still won't let me finish. "It's a lot to take in, I'll admit," he says as if I haven't spoken. "But I've always known something was different. I didn't care. Do you understand that? *I don't care.* You're Elizabeth, and that is someone, no matter what you think or say."

"Joshua—"

He sighs. "And as far as me ignoring you, well, that wasn't just because of what you said on the steps or because of what I saw at the party. If you'd bothered paying attention to me at all, you'd know that the crops have me pretty worried, okay?"

Silence falls between us. A bee whizzes by. The only words that come to mind are *I'm sorry*, and I won't say it to him because it would be a lie. I've already lied to him, and now . . . it just doesn't seem like the correct thing to do.

"Do you want to come over tonight?"

It's out before I've thought it through, before I have a chance to stop it. Joshua seems just as taken aback as me. As if my hand has a mind of its own—no, I must be *losing* my mind—my fingers reach out, and gently, so gently, brush those persistent bangs out of the way for the first time. Joshua looks back at me, his gaze finally unhindered by all of that hair.

"It's always in the way," I offer by way of explanation. He just keeps staring at me, and I know he's wondering what this means.

Then he grins. A big, slow, smug grin that shows the extent of his renewed hope.

I spin on my heel and go into the school, my nothingness trembling inside of me. I can hear him following.

"So I'll see you tonight?" Joshua calls just as the door closes. I poke my head back out, trying not to think of all the repercussions this entire conversation could have on everything and anything.

"After my parents are asleep," I answer against my better judgment. "Late."

He nods, jogging up the steps. Just as he's getting closer I make to vanish again. He says quickly, "See you then, Elizabeth."

The way he says my name makes the trembling increase. As if we have a delicious secret no one else in the world knows.

It reminds me of Fear.

————

"Won't be back until morning!" Charles shouts on his way out the door.

Sarah waves at him, soap flicking to the tiles, but my brother is already in the driveway. We can hear his truck starting. Silence fills the house again. I'm in the laundry room adjacent to kitchen, standing in front of the washer. I know Sarah's listening to every move I make, unnerved by my being here. In an effort to put her at ease, I don't bother attempting conversation.

There are laundry buckets all around my feet. Bending

over, I find and pull a pair of Tim's jeans inside out, checking the pockets before dropping them into the wash. Next I find one of Charles's T-shirts and put that in as well. When I pick up a pair of Sarah's jeans, I check the pockets as usual, but pause as my hand collides with a folded-up piece of paper.

Maybe I should hesitate to look, invade Sarah's privacy, but I'm opening it before I think about it.

It's an airline ticket. One-way to New York City.

As I scan the words on the small piece of paper, I remember Sarah mentioning, long ago, that her mother lived there. It was Christmas morning; she'd had such a pained look in her eyes.

I glance at the date—three days from now—before shoving it back into the pants pocket.

EIGHTEEN

"Psst!"

Thunk.

"Hey, Elizabeth, are you up there?"

Thunk.

My eyes flutter open and I gaze up at the ceiling. I hadn't meant to fall asleep. I sit up, and my notebook falls to the floor. I lean over and stare at the poem staring up at me. The scribbled words taunt. *I hide, I protect, I pretend.*

Joshua calls my name again, his voice hushed and loud at the same time. He throws something at the window. He's going to break it soon if I don't get up.

When I get to the pane, his arm is arched back, getting ready to throw something small in his hand. He sees my silhouette too late. I watch a tiny crack bloom across the glass. If Tim notices it, I'll pay.

Joshua cringes. "Sorry!"

The window slides open with a slight hitch and I bend

forward. "What are you doing?" It's a cold night; the air numbs the tips of my ears and nose.

The boy shrugs, grinning. "You said late. I wasn't sure how late, so I took a wild guess. You're not getting away from me that easily."

A glance at my alarm clock shows me that it's 2:45 a.m. Joshua waits patiently. I hold up one finger to him, and he nods. I pull away, leaving the window open. I listen to the lonely sound of the wind as I pull a hoodie on over my tank top. I don't bother changing out of my sweatpants and slip out my door.

He's in the driveway, hands shoved in his pockets, still smiling. He looks so much like the little boy I used to know in this moment, with his silly-shy grin and a tuft of hair sticking up at the back of his head. My stomach does a bizarre little jump.

"I don't know why I invited you here," I tell him, my voice coming out icy. "Maybe this is a mistake."

He inclines his head, and I notice how his hair is out of his eyes—he's brushed it aside so that it sweeps across his forehead. The strands of red glow white under the moon. "Maybe," Joshua acknowledges. "But maybe that's what makes it so great. You're letting go."

For the first time in my life, I admit, "I don't know what I'm doing."

Fear's words come back to me: *For the first time in your life, you act without thinking.* It seems Joshua Hayes brings out a lot of firsts in me. But the thought of Fear brings on a whole new train of thought, and I begin to wonder if I'll see him again. After that conversation in the hallway—

Joshua holds his hand out. Clamping down on my roiling thoughts, I take it. His palm is rough and scarred from working on the farm all his life ... just like mine. He's warm and I'm hot. Our skins collapse against each other, and I imagine I can hear a sizzling in the air.

He senses my distraction and won't let it go any further. "Hey." He tugs on my hand, leading me away from the house. "Stop thinking for once. Come on."

"Where are we going?"

"You'll see."

He's leading me toward the road. We leave my house behind, and the fabric of my shoes rubs against my bare ankles—I forgot to put on socks. Joshua parked his car farther down the road. He probably didn't want the engine to wake up Tim and Sarah. He stops by the car, nodding to himself, and turns to survey the cluster of trees by the road. His hold on my hand tightens, and he starts to walk toward the woods. I resist.

"Joshua, what—"

"Just be patient," he sighs, tugging at me some more, and I allow him to lead me into the trees. But then I pull myself free from his grip. He lets me, acting as if it doesn't affect him. Darkness and shadows press in all around. I should tell Joshua about the possible dangers of this place—I think of the shadow in my dreams, Rebecca's obvious terror. But he's walking again, leaving me behind without waiting to see if I'll follow.

He knows I will. I hurry to catch up.

A delicate web above catches my eye, glistening between some leaves. A tiny black spider zips this way and that, its long legs weaving, weaving, always weaving.

"…and while I was walking to your house tonight, I found them," Joshua is telling me. "It would've been hard to miss; there was a bright glow." We duck under a low branch.

Glow? What does he mean? Rethinking this, I stop right there, shifting from foot to foot. Joshua notices right away and turns to face me. We're standing on a slanted ground, so for once I'm eye level with him. I notice the green flecks in his brown eyes. "We shouldn't be out here," I tell him.

Joshua laughs quietly and turns to start walking again. "What, are there werewolves?"

When I don't bother to answer he turns to look at me again, eyebrows raised. "*Are* there werewolves?"

My eye catches the faint gleam of a trap on the path, and I grab Joshua's elbow to swerve him around it. "What—" His head whips around and I point to the trap wordlessly. Joshua frowns down it. "Thanks," he mutters. "That's twice you've saved me now, you know." I hear the unspoken question in the statement but don't address it.

His elbow is warm in my grip, and I let go before he notices I'm still touching him. We walk for a few minutes more, and then he's lifting his hand to point, turning his shaggy head toward me. There's a faint light ahead, shining through the brush. Joshua is beaming with delight and a tiny bit of awe. He dares to take my hand a second time and pulls me forward against my better judgment.

A tiny clearing bursts open in front of us. It's alive and

soundless, illuminated by hundreds of fireflies. This is impossible, of course; the coming winter should have killed them, or at least made them go into hibernation. Either something is going wrong with the Elements or this is some strange happenstance. And I don't believe in happenstance.

They dart every which way, stunning, bright. Flashing, fading, becoming, disappearing. Dizzying and riveting all at once. "It's beautiful," is all I say.

Beside me, Joshua just continues to stare at them. "I wanted to show you," he whispers, as if speaking too loud will frighten them all away. Movement out of the corner of my eye catches my attention, and I don't respond to him. A small creature vanishes from an upturned bucket and appears on my shoulder. Joshua doesn't see her, which gives away the fact that she's not part of this world. I recognize her scent, a slight tang of pinecones—I've encountered this one before. Her countenance is not familiar, though. Her hair is long and black, dragging at her feet. Her chin and ears are delicately pointed, and her wide eyes are such a dark brown they're almost black.

"Who are you?" I ask her, my voice just barely above a whisper. I don't want Joshua to hear. I shift away from him to be safe. He doesn't seem to notice. He walks deeper into the clearing, looking lost in thought.

"Moss," the creature answers. "It's my specialty."

As soon as she speaks in her high, piping voice, I know where I've met her before. "Moss," I repeat. She giggles. I smile to appeal to her. "You were at Sophia's birthday party that night."

Her hands suddenly flutter; she's uncomfortable. I remember her words in my ear: *He's here, he's here! Disappear, before he gets you, gets you!*

"You were warning me about something," I add. I reach up and untangle the ends of her hair for her.

Her little hands flutter again, this time with pleasure. She nods hesitantly, her Cupid's mouth pink and pursed. "I shouldn't talk about it. It's not safe."

A firefly flits past my nose and Moss straightens, as if she wants to chase after it. "Please tell me?" I say, and her dark gaze goes back to my face. She flinches. Joshua is still enraptured by the lights, and he hasn't even noticed my quiet conversation. He's admiring the intricate dance.

The Element on my shoulder smiles at me, putting her hand on my cheek. She seems to like the texture of my skin. An instant later she squeaks and jerks her hand back, abruptly terrified, and she jumps off me, disappearing into the thick of the lights. The fireflies grow more frenzied, bright blurs of movement. I frown, sensing a disturbance. It isn't until I feel a cool breath on my cheek and feel him pressed against my shoulder that I identify the reason for their anxiety. Oh. I should have known.

I keep my eyes on Joshua. A boy that I've known all my life, a boy that has always watched over me from afar. He's smiling at me, motioning to join him. He doesn't see Fear, of course. I don't move.

"You almost look as if you feel something for him," Fear whispers, folding his arms around my waist from behind. His chest is hard against my back, his skin like marble. He rests his chin on the top of my head. "But I know that can't be right. After all, you don't care about anything, right?"

His hands are on me. The touch makes the wall of nothingness shudder, makes me think of those kisses and that brief minute in the hallway when I'd yearned to do it again. Despite this, I allow his touch. Maybe he'll tell me about the party. "That's correct."

He chuckles bitterly. "I never realized how stubborn you are. You hid it better when you were small." When I don't answer, Fear shifts so that Joshua is blocked from my view. I finally look up at him. "Well, at least I know that if you can't feel anything for me, you can't feel anything for him, either," he says in a low voice, his eyes burning into mine. After a moment he turns away to watch the fireflies too, his brow furrowed. He tries to hide his feelings from me, but I sense the turmoil inside him, a swirling mass of dark and light that constantly war with each other. In the midst of all of it is me.

Did … did part of me want him back, during that brief moment in the school hallway when the wall crumbled?

No. That couldn't be. "You've been avoiding me," I say in an effort to direct my thoughts in a more practical direction. "At the party—"

He sighs. "I won't answer your questions about that night, Elizabeth. There are some things a human shouldn't know. Even a human like you."

In the distance, an owl calls, a tenor that's gentle and luring. A symphony. Fear smiles now. "May I have this dance?" He doesn't try to hide his feelings as he gazes down at me.

His hands are freezing on my arms. Our frozen hearts are so similar. Too similar.

"Dance with me, Elizabeth?"

Joshua has come back. Once again he holds his hand out for me to take. His warm, rough, real hand. Courage chooses this moment to appear, and without saying a word to me or looking at Fear, he grasps the back of Joshua's neck.

I look at Fear, then Joshua, then at those lights floating in swirling masses. I clench my fists. *I hide, I protect, I pretend.*

I feel Joshua on my right, a balmy, solid presence, and Fear on my left, wintry and impossible. One human, what I should yearn for, and one from another world, part of the plane that has put me in this position. Just being near him makes my own world seem unreachable and surreal.

Surreal is dangerous.

I don't look at Fear. My fingers are so light as they wrap around Joshua's hand, and I try to say with my eyes what I can't with my mouth. *I choose you.*

———

Sophia has finally decided how to exact her revenge. I can tell by the way she keeps sneaking glances back at me, a catty smile curving her glossed lips. Her fingers caress the cast around her wrist, apparently from when I grabbed and sprained it. I keep my head down, debating on the best course of action to take: avoidance or endurance. Confrontation is probably not an option; I don't want another repeat of what I did to her the night of her party.

Joshua also looks back at me, but for another reason entirely. I'd guess he's uncertain about how I'll act today, in the aftermath of last night. Sleeping and dreams have strengthened my nothingness, yet there's still something deep down inside of me that stirs. Something deep down inside of me that can't stop thinking about Fear and the look in his eyes as I danced with Joshua. I'd done exactly what I'd set out to do: discourage him. Why, then, does the memory of his expression hound me?

" … read the chapters I've assigned you," Mrs. Farmer is instructing the class. The bell rings as she speaks, and everyone gets to their feet, gathering their books and leaving the classroom as quickly as possible.

Sophia darts out the doorway with the rest of the crowd, no doubt eager to find her friends and start the planning for my demise. Joshua lingers at his desk, waiting for me. I walk past him and approach Mrs. Farmer.

"Here." My palm slaps against the wood of the teacher's desk as I set down two pieces of paper stapled together. "My part of the project you assigned." At Mrs. Farmer's blank stare, I add, "The portfolio?"

"Oh!" Comprehension dawns in the teacher's face. Compassion appears beside her—she's a tall Emotion with a solemn light in her gray eyes. Mrs. Farmer reaches out to pat my hand but I move it out of the way. Hers flutters back to her lap awkwardly. "Joshua did well enough for the two of you," she says, glancing at him. "You didn't have to do this extra work. I understand the circumstances."

"That's nice of you, but I don't want special treatment,"

I counter. "Please look this over and give me the grade you think the work deserves."

She knows my meaning: I don't want to be graded on Maggie's death. Efficiency. That should be the focus. After a moment I turn my back on Mrs. Farmer and Compassion, leaving the room.

"When did you finish it?" Joshua asks me in the hall. His locker is in the opposite direction of mine but he walks with me anyway. We pass Susie Yank and she waves at me, timid. I don't miss how her glance lingers on Joshua, and her expression is almost worshipful. I return her wave but don't stop.

"I finished it this morning," I tell Joshua finally. "After we got back."

"Can I read it?"

I walk faster.

"Hey." He touches my arm, stopping me. It seems like he's always content to have our conversations in the middle of the hall. I pull my arm away, and he blushes. The sight of that twists something in my middle.

I rake my wild hair back; there was no time to brush it this morning between the poem and my chores. "I'm sorry." I stare up at him. "I'm not...good at this."

"Get out of the way!" One of Sophia's friends shoulders past. She glances at me with a strange expression before hurrying on.

Joshua ignores her. "Talk to me," he orders.

Now I give all my attention to the lockers to our right, studying the dents in the metal as if they hold some deep meaning for me. "I don't think that this is smart," I tell those dents. "You're going to get hurt. The people in my life have always been disappointed in me sooner or later."

"Huh." He takes my elbow to guide me out of the wave of kids rushing to their classes. I'm going to be late yet again. Joshua snaps his fingers in front of my face, forcing me to look at him. "I don't think you're really worried about me," he says bluntly. I blink.

"What do you—"

"You're scared."

That's not true; Fear is nowhere around. My hair is falling into my face. Ironic, since Joshua's is finally smoothed out of the way. "I don't have time for this," I say. I move past Joshua. He lets me go, his irritation obvious.

"If we don't take any risks, then we won't find the things worth living for," the boy calls after me.

"Go to class, Joshua," I toss over my shoulder. I think of the poem I'll never show him, never show anyone else but Mrs. Farmer.

There are different kinds of hiding.
I hide, I protect, I pretend.
I give no promises or look to tomorrow.
There is only this, only me.
A shadow and a whisper.
I hide, I protect, I pretend.
Everyone else.
No one else.
Impossibility and useless efforts.

Reasons?
I don't know.
I just know this.

During my lunch hour—among the aging stories and forgotten history of the library—I finally find the newspaper article I've been looking for. This time it doesn't disappear, but all my efforts toward finding it have been in vain; there's nothing more to know here than in what Sarah has already told me.

Girl Survives Car Accident
Yesterday, Elizabeth Caldwell, four years old, wandered out to the highway by herself. The driver of an oncoming car didn't see the little girl until it was too late. When questioned, he had little recollection of what had happened. An ambulance was immediately called, and paramedics say Elizabeth was conscious and lucid on the scene. She escaped with nothing but a few scrapes and bruises. Doctors say it's a miracle. She's already been discharged.

I'm beginning to wonder if there's a point to finding the answers about my past. Maybe the truth really isn't beneficial to my survival here in Edson, and this mystery is best left alone.

End of the day. Final bell. Girls shrieking and boys shouting down the halls. Teachers lecturing about assignments, calling for quiet. Lockers slamming shut, doors closing, lights dying. I wait in a corner with my book bag until everyone has left and the air is still, waiting for tomorrow. The school is ghostly after hours, and I chase my shadow when I make my way to the front doors. White light spills through the glass, beckoning to me.

I answer because there's no other logical solution.

I could avoid Sophia and her friends now, of course, but that'll only make her more determined to find me later. Even though her revenge will make me late getting home—Tim will definitely notice the delay—I think I'll let her do this tonight. And after her petty vengeance is out of the way, I can focus on my façade and she'll go back to her usual forms of torment.

Sunlight breaks through the clouds. I squint up at it as I step outside. I stand on the steps for a moment, studying the girls waiting for me in the parking lot. I'd guess that there are none that are actually upset with me—they're only here because they're afraid of Sophia. Most are probably glad that it's not them in my position.

"Hey, freak!" Sophia raises her voice so I can hear her across the lot. I hide my bag behind a bush so they won't terrorize my books. My keys jangle as I set it down.

If I had a sense of humor, the sight before me would be comical. Besides Stephanie Dill, a hulking girl Sophia keeps around for muscle, these girls are small. They're all wearing miniskirts and too much makeup.

"Come on, we don't have all day!"

My truck is a couple yards away from them. They wanted to make sure I didn't leave. Squaring my shoulders, I start toward the group, listening to my shoes scrape against the pavement. They all stare. So many Emotions…and so much emptiness where there should be actual beings. Which can only mean one thing: whatever sent them running is back. And nearby, maybe.

The flag whips against the pole, bringing me back to the situation at hand. As soon as I'm in earshot Sophia says in a low, furious voice, "You owe me an apology."

I realize my expression isn't correct for this situation; I try to look nervous and regretful. "I'm sorry," I respond, adding a wobble to my voice for good measure.

She clenches her jaw. "Too easy."

I stop just three feet away from her little group. "What do you want me to say?"

"She's so weird," I hear one of them mutter.

"Do you really think 'sorry' is enough for ruining my party?" Sophia snaps. "Do you think it's enough for humiliating me? Especially in front of…" She trails off, but we all know whose name is on the tip of her tongue. She's holding her cast with tight, enraged fingers.

Any answer I give will only rile her further.

Stephanie—the big girl—scowls impatiently. "Can we just get this over with?" she demands. "I want to get to the hardware store before it closes."

Sophia sighs. "Fine."

That one word is all it takes. All the girls tense, but it's only Stephanie who jumps at me. She clearly expects me to struggle or run, because the first thing she does is pin my arms to my sides. I just look at the ground. "Okay, I've got her," Stephanie says, triumphant, as if she's won a big contest. Her breath blows down on my face, and I can't hold back a gag. It reeks heavily of chewing tobacco and rot.

They're hesitant at first. The girls glance at each other, questioning this, questioning their leader. A blond opens her mouth, about to protest, then thinks better of it and shuts it again.

Sophia gives them a look of contempt usually reserved for me. "What are you waiting for?" she snaps, approaching. She grins fiercely and reaches up to grasp the collar of my T-shirt. The material is old and thin. It rips right in half.

Encouraged by Sophia's brazen behavior, two girls surge forward. The rest follow. One by one they take my pants, my shoes, my socks. And when I'm just standing there in my bra and underwear, Sophia sneers.

Fight back, instinct says. *End this,* logic insists. No, not logic. It's Fear's voice in my head, Fear urging me on. Will he come? Or have I finally driven him away forever?

Hoping to embarrass me, Sophia laughs, and the others laugh, too. Like a pack of hyenas. I just watch them throw back their heads and observe the way all the girls' teeth shine in the weak sunlight.

Stephanie's grip is firm. "Are we done?" she asks, cutting the cackling short. My bare feet curl on the ground; a small rock digs into my toe.

Sophia's smile dies as she looks at me, and now her eyes burn in a slow smolder of lost regret and hopelessness. She swiftly hides this behind a curtain of hatred. "One more thing," she hisses. Two quick steps, and her hand is flying. *Slap.*

"Don't ever piss me off again, or it'll be worse than this."

The threat is empty; Sophia's disconcerted by the coldness of my gaze, unhidden now, and my disarming smile.

"Just finish this," I say to her.

She doesn't voice the murderous thoughts emanating from her expression. Instead, she nods to Stephanie. The huge girl hauls me over to the flagpole, setting me up on the cement foundation. I hadn't known what to expect, but this definitely wasn't it; I start to rethink letting this happen. Stephanie's dull eyes watch me sharply for any sign of rebellion. Then one of the girls presents a chain—I hadn't even noticed it until now. It clinks as she moves.

They're hesitating again. Once more Stephanie is the one who takes action. I've taken too long to reconsider— before I can jump down from the foundation, she takes the chain in hand and wraps it around me quickly. Once, twice. She also loops them around my wrists. Finished, she then produces a lock. It shuts with a resounding *click*. The girls stare at me for a moment, waiting for any kind of reaction. Sophia is just smiling.

The loops of the chain dig into my bones and my bare stomach. Tight, tight, too tight. The telephone pole is a welcome coolness to my back.

When I give them no tears or pleading, Sophia's smugness melts into a mixture of disdain. "God, even now you can't act like a normal human being," she snaps, and her friends follow suit with the expressions of disgust. Mindless sheep. "Come on, let's get out of here." Sophia gestures to those sheep gathered behind her. They start to shuffle away.

They want a reaction? Fine. "Sophia." I attempt to put a

note of agony in my voice. "Please don't leave me here. I'll let you do anything else to me, I'll say anything you want, but you can't—"

"I can do whatever the hell I want. You had this coming. You should have thought about it before barging into my party uninvited and doing *this* to me." Sophia jabs a finger at her cast. Her words carry so much more meaning, though. She hates me for having her sister's affection without even trying, she despises the fact that Joshua sees me instead of her. I open my mouth to add something else—anything—but she's already walking away again. Her skirt flutters in the breeze, and the girls' high heels make sharp noises against the pavement. They take my clothes with them.

One by one, the girls get into their cars. The sound of waking engines erupts throughout the lot. Without honking or sneering or shouting, they leave me. In less than a minute they've all driven away. The last pair of taillights disappears around a bend.

When I can't hear their cars down the street anymore, I struggle against my bonds, and the rattle of the chains echoes in the silence. But I didn't think this through; I can't break free. The parking lot is cold and utterly empty. The breeze blowing past my ears is the only sound for miles. Even though it's futile, even though there's no point, I shout at the top of my lungs, "Help! Someone, help me!" Is there any way Fear will hear?

The parking lot is still empty, as it will be until morning. My truck is lonely in the corner. The sky is uncaring and I'm alone. Now what?

"Well, this is interesting."

NINETEEN

At first I think I imagined the voice. Just to make sure, though, I twist. The chains prevent me from angling my body too much, and the pole is blocking most of my view, but there *is* a person behind me. I see a head of black, tousled hair and some pressed slacks. How fortunate—I won't have to spend the night here. "Hello. Do you think you could help me?" I ask politely.

The man moves, stepping into my line of vision. I take in the tiny smile, the glint in the man's dark eyes. I've never seen him before. He's wearing a button-down white shirt with a black jacket slung over his shoulder, something that someone might wear to an office, and his free hand is behind his back, so casually. His shoes shine weakly in the looming dusk. Some women might call him handsome, with his groomed appearance and his contrasting tones. White skin, dark hair. But for some reason the sight of him makes my pulse quicken, a sour taste fill my mouth, my skin crawl.

"I don't have the key," I inform him, and an extraordinary quiver takes over my voice. Questions race through me, and the loudest... *Who is this man?*

Without answering, the man stares at me for a few heart-stopping moments, taking in my near-naked state. I begin to think he's not going to help, but then he walks around me to stand in the spot where Stephanie secured the chains. I catch a whiff of his scent. A combination of something fresh and something... not. As if one smell is supposed to hide the other.

He's still silent, probably examining the lock. "Lucky for you," he finally says, "I make it a habit to be prepared for situations just like this." His voice jars something inside of me—it's smooth and confident, like the strum of a violin—and an impulse to flee fills every corner of my being. *Do I know him?*

Mindless of my internal struggle, the man begins the work to free me. There's the sound of a pick digging around in the lock. I should thank him. For some reason, though, I can't. There's a lump in my throat, a rock, a cluster of...

Fear.

Where is he? Where is he? Why wouldn't he come?

Calm, a voice in my head advises. *Stay calm.*

My rescuer doesn't work in silence for long. "So how did you get yourself in this predicament?" he asks me. His finger slips on the lock pick, and his surprisingly sharp nail slices my arm. I wince.

"Some girls at school," is all I say. *Wrong*, my instincts keep whispering. Something about him is so familiar...

The man seems satisfied with this, and I hear a smile

in his voice when he replies, "Yes, I've been to a few high schools. Hard to believe children can be cruel so young. And it only gets worse."

When the lock opens with a loud *click* and the man unwraps the chains from around me, I manage to speak again. "So what brings you to the school at this time of day?" I rub my raw wrists. My stomach has indents where the links were pressed against me.

I look up and catch the man staring at me again. When I clear my throat, something in his gaze flickers, and that strange half-smile appears again. "I was passing by and heard you calling for help," he tells me.

I'm hardly paying attention because I'm so distracted by his expression. He doesn't even try to hide it. Rather than curiosity or boredom as I would have expected, this man who saved me is watching my every move with...hunger.

"May I borrow your jacket?" I ask, a bit too formally. Being alone with him is still causing my senses to quake. *Leave. Leave.* The power around me is cracking, I can feel it—fear still edges in, trying to consume. *Where is he?* Where are the other Emotions? Why don't they come? Am I breaking through the wall?

The man doesn't move to give his jacket to me. "You look familiar," he says instead, like he's reading my mind. "What's your name?" He cocks his head, and I'm suddenly picturing a wild predator about to pounce. I forget about covering myself and proceed with caution.

"I'm Elizabeth. And I really have to go. Parents waiting

and all that. But thank you for helping me." I'm not going to ask what I can do to repay him.

He doesn't respond, so I move to pass him. We do a little dance. I step to the left in an attempt to go to my truck, and he blocks me. It's clearly intentional, because when I start to the right, he follows again. His feet hardly make any sound on the ground. I purse my lips, trying to hide that faint feeling of agitation deep within me. Strangely enough, I want my nothingness back. I *need* it back...

Just barely, the floodgate in my wall opens.

Please come back, please.

You did this.

"What are you thinking about, Elizabeth?" The man has gotten closer without my realizing it. Reacting automatically, I dart around him.

"I'm sorry, but I really have to be going," I call over my shoulder. He doesn't try to stop me again. He just stands there with that strange smirk, head tilted. His hands are shoved in his pockets, and I get the distinct impression that the pick isn't the only thing hidden in those depths.

It isn't until I pull on the handle to the driver's door that I realize I don't have the keys—they're in my bag, which I stuck behind some bushes by the front doors of the school. I remember that I also might have a sweater in there. I can feel the man's unfaltering eyes on me the entire time as I quickly jog to my bag, dig around in it for both my keys and the sweater—it turns out to be a windbreaker—zip it on, throw the bag over my shoulder, and run back to my truck.

The man still doesn't say a word. The absolute silence

feels alien, and my fingers are still shaking as I grasp my keys and shove them into the door. The worn material of the seats rubs against my skin as I get in, but I scarcely notice. I'm concentrating on the steps, focusing only my hands.

Close the door. Lock it. Put your bag in passenger seat. Put the key in the ignition. Turn it.

Nothing. Silence.

I turn the key. Again. And again. *No, no, no, no...*

After a few more turns, I stop. It's futile.

The man has been waiting patiently. When he sees that I'm done, he lopes around to my window, tapping on it with the back of his knuckle, a delicate movement. My heart is pounding and my hands are sweating. There is something very, very wrong here. I roll the window down just a crack, choosing to stare at his perfectly white teeth rather than his cold eyes.

"Mind if I take a look?" the man asks. I shake my head.

He leaves my side and lifts the truck's hood. Moments later he calls to me, "It appears those children took out your battery." He shuts the hood. *Slam.*

I just sit there. My mind whizzes through all the possibilities. The school is locked, so I can't reach a phone. I could walk ... no, not without pants. Too many questions, and someone would see and probably get back to Tim. But getting home is probably more important than anything Tim will do to me ... maybe I should stay ... but when morning comes my classmates will see me, and rumors will spread like a wildfire.

I'm at a complete loss as to what to do. Seems to be happening to me often lately. Too often.

"You know, I could give you a lift home," the man says, his voice suddenly gentle. He knows I have no other options. No phone, no truck, no clothes. Fear hasn't appeared yet, which is odd in itself. I could wait a little longer—

Thunder rumbles the ground.

I start, glancing at the horizon. When did it turn gray? This strange fear flowing through my veins clouds my logic. It's nearing sunset already—how did that happen? Staying definitely wouldn't be safe...would it? Not with something out there that sent even immortal beings running for the hills. No, not safe. Especially not for a half-naked girl in a rusty truck, no matter what abilities she may have.

Clutching the steering wheel, as if the truck will spontaneously start and solve all my problems, I swallow. "You'll take me right home?"

If possible, the man's smile grows until it seems like it'll stretch right out of the confines of his face. Of course everything inside of me is shrieking, *Danger, stupid, stay where you are.* But I just need to get home. If he tries anything, I'll probably be able to overpower him.

"...straight home," the man at my window is promising. The thin piece of glass protecting me fogs with my breath, and I touch it with my finger, steeling myself.

The man has turned away. He's walking across the parking lot. When I remain in the cab of my truck, he glances back, lifting a brow. "Coming?" It sounds like a challenge.

Don't go! my instincts advise one last time. *Fear will come.* But I don't feel him anywhere near. I can't stay here. When once again I put the warning aside, the voice curls away like withering vines. Defeated.

Every sound is an explosion in my head. The lock clicking, the door opening, my feet slapping the pavement. I take my bag with me and drop my keys in the side pocket. Following this man is like letting a shadow lead me through the dark. No relevancy or light to guide me.

Since there isn't a single car in the lot now, I assume his vehicle is along the road behind the school, where the teachers park. We're both quiet.

Then he turns, walking backwards. This is strangely disconcerting, like an owl turning its head all the way around. "So, Elizabeth," he says in that violin voice, "how long have you lived in Edson?"

Around the side of the school we go, to the back as I'd suspected. There's one car and one truck along the curb of this road. Is there still a janitor here?

"All my life," I answer, my voice tight and careful. There's grass underfoot now, damp and freezing on my heated soles.

He nods as if this is so interesting. "I see." He stops under a large weeping willow, and the light and leaves cast intricate shadows on his face. I watch the patterns move over his skin in the breeze. I don't know which vehicle is his, so I'm forced to stop as well.

The man is doing that head-cocking thing again, and now there's an anomalous glint in his black eyes. "Tell me, Elizabeth"—my name is a hiss—"because I'm simply dying to know. Have you finished the mural in your room yet?"

A beat of pregnant hush between us. I'm frozen for a mindless instant.

And then I run.

He's after me before I've even turned around completely. I can hear his footsteps just behind me, a taunting drum surrounding, choking, laughing. There's something about the sound of his run, I dimly realize in my whirling frenzy. I fly back around the corner of the school, heading for the parking lot and the front doors.

"Oh, Elizabeth!" the man sing-songs. He doesn't even sound out of breath.

"Help!" I scream, willing someone, anyone, to hear me. Fear, just when I need him most, is far away. I rush through a line of bushes and some twigs scratch the vulnerable skin of my legs. There it is! The lot appears before me, open and empty. My truck in the corner, urging me onward.

The sound of the man somewhere behind vanishes, and then he's suddenly landing in front of me in the end of a giant leap. He exaggerates the swing in his arms, panting wildly, mocking. The veins in his eyes are huge. "What are you going to do?" he gasps. Then, just as swiftly as he evolved into this wild creature, he straightens, smoothing his hair and pulling at his shirt cuffs. "Shall we proceed?" he asks. "Or will you insist on trying that again?"

It's as I stand there, helpless—more desperate possibilities and disorienting panic whizzing through me—that I comprehend where I recognize his run from. The night of Sophia's party, when I was rushing through the woods, trying to get to Joshua ... there had been someone behind me. Following me. At the time I'd just assumed it was a kid trying to get to his car. But now I realize the truth. Is he what

Rebecca was so worried about on the night of the party? Oh. *Oh.* She'd been protecting me all along.

And that isn't all I remember. An image, like a blink or a flash, appears and vanishes. Burning eyes and a planted stance. That same tilted head. *He was in the hallway at school.* I remember now. He'd been staring at me with the same eyes he has now. Hungry eyes.

It's as I'm putting these pieces together that the man asks me, so casually, "Are you her?"

The words slam into me over and over again. *Are you her? Are you her?* A scrawled sentence on a lined piece of paper. There's a teasing lilt in the man's voice; he's mocking me. He wants me to know that the note was his.

"What do you want?" I ask, watching his every move warily.

"You know," he says as if I haven't spoken, "you're really a fascinating creature. You never responded to all the games we played. No one has done that before."

Creature. Not girl. He thinks I'm from the other plane. "You've made a mistake," I say, backing away. "I'm just a human. I'm normal."

He smiles again, advancing. "Oh, so wrong. You're far from human. We have a history, young lady. I've been looking for you for a long, long time. You had me fooled. You and that Emotion."

Even more comes together, suddenly, in my head. It's so obvious that I wonder why I didn't figure it out the instant I laid eyes on him.

There are some things humans shouldn't know. Even a human like you.

He's here, he's here! Run before he gets you, gets you!

This man—no, not man, something else entirely—is what has all the Emotions and Elements running. *He got me,* I think faintly. But he shouldn't be after me. I'm not one of them. "What do you want?" I ask again, backing away, down the hill.

As an answer, his bottomless eyes flare to red. "Where is she?" he purrs.

No. No, it isn't possible. But the truth is staring me right in the face. Nausea grips my stomach. *You killed me. Where is she? You did this. You ruined us.* I trip on my own heel and fall to the ground. My fingers burrow into the grass, into the soil, as if I'm on a ride that won't stop spinning. All the sleepless nights, the haunting dreams that felt so real … it was him. Never the boy, reaching out to me, begging me to know his story. No ghosts, as I'd secretly believed, no revelations of the past. Just the ugliness of this creature using and twisting my own mind against me.

"What are you?" I say, past the ragged air struggling in and out of my lungs. He approaches and leans over me, bringing that weird scent with him, and it's in that instant that I realize what that underlying smell is.

Old blood.

"Don't you know yet?" he breathes in my ear. When I don't—can't—answer, he whispers, his lips moving against my skin, "I'm Nightmare."

I stare up at him, frozen. He's silent now, waiting for me

to speak. He's a hole of quiet and malicious intent, and I have no idea what he's capable of. This is most dangerous of all.

The questions don't matter. I scramble to my feet and run again.

He lets me go. "I saw you save the boy when he was about to get hit by that truck!" Nightmare calls. He hasn't moved. "There's no way any normal human could have gotten to him so—"

The Element halts midsentence. Breathing violently, I glance over my shoulder and stumble. Fear stands between me and death. I can only see his back, his white hair curling on his neck. Nightmare doesn't say a word. He's looking at Fear with that pleased, ravenous expression.

"Go!" Fear shouts to me. Crouched, his body tensed, he doesn't take his eyes off Nightmare. "Don't look back, Elizabeth! Keep going!" he orders.

I obey without any more indecision, and the wind rushes past my ears. But at the sound of Fear crying out, I falter. I can't just leave him. I spin to help . . .

But I'm too late. Fear is crumpled on the ground, blood gushing between his fingers, from his middle. He struggles to stand up again, but the Element laughs and knees him in the face. Fear hits the ground. Nightmare stands over him, holding a long, wicked-looking knife. It's red all the way down to the hilt. Dripping.

Nightmare looks up, sees that I'm staring at his knife. He smiles. "Didn't he tell you to keep running?" he calls to me as if we're comrades, waving the scarlet blade back and forth. "We aren't indestructible to each other, you know."

I'm frozen again. Fear rolls his head back, his cheek scraping on the cement, and he sees that I've stopped. *"Go,"* he chokes, his eyes wilder than I've ever seen them.

Instinct takes over, and I find myself running once more. Behind me, I hear Nightmare make a sound of amusement deep in his throat before he's flying through the air again. He gives me a hard shove as he lands. I fall forward and throw my palms out to try to soften the blow. The skin on my hands shrieks at me as it tears, and then my face hits the hard ground. Black dots dance before my eyes, and I'm dizzy, so dizzy. Nightmare's shoes appear in my line of vision, and a moment later his voice sounds in my ear.

"It was ironic," he whispers. He brushes my hair back like a father would his child. "Those mewling humans chained you up and left you there, a fruit ripe for the plucking. Not to mention you brought a friend. Two birds with one stone. This is my lucky day. By the way," he adds, "the battery is behind the front left tire of your truck. I dare you to try and get it."

"Elizabeth!"

I would know that voice anywhere. It races through every part of me, filling all the corners with light, tearing apart the strong cobwebs inside my soul. Nightmare's shoes vanish. That fetid smell is gone. And then Joshua's actually there, holding me, rocking me, a cell phone pressed against his ear. "Fear?" I manage to ask, my voice so faint that Joshua doesn't hear it.

"Yeah, I need an ambulance. In front of Edson High.

Someone has hurt Elizabeth Caldwell pretty badly. Yeah. Okay."

I'm barely aware of any of it. All I know is that when I lift my head, indistinctly anxious that the Element will come back, he's gone. And so is Fear. I think I call his name again.

But Joshua's here. And he's whispering in my hair, telling me that everything is going to be all right, he's not going to leave me, I'm safe now, I'm safe.

———————

The moon is full in the sky when the girl emerges from the house. She closes the door as softly as she can, glancing around to make sure no one's watching. When she's certain that there's nothing but the howling wind and the disapproving stars, she runs. The woods aren't far, and as soon as she plunges into their cover a tall figure steps out from behind a tree.

"Rebecca."

She gasps, whirling, and presses a hand to her chest. When she sees who it is her eyes narrow. "Don't do that," she snaps.

Fear grins back, unrepentant. Rebecca smiles back reluctantly. Coy now, she puts her hands behind her back and sways. She's wearing nothing but a tank top and boxer shorts. Fear's gaze flicks up and down, and she has trouble releasing the air in her lungs when his pupils dilate.

"Like what you see?" she tries to tease, but the breathless quality to her voice ruins the effect. Fear reaches for her wordlessly, but she quickly bounces away, laughing. The Emotion stalks her across the clearing, his long coat flaring. Just as she

darts to the left to escape, he snatches her hands. Her struggle is half-hearted, and she lets him tug her to him despite the way his touch makes her heart pound and her palms sweat.

Embracing her, Fear's lips skim Rebecca's collarbone, hot and cold all at once. She gasps, throwing her head back. Her eyes latch onto the night, but she hardly notices the velvet expanse of galaxy. Somehow they're on the ground. Fear is kissing her everywhere now, her arm, the spot beside her belly button, her thigh, her calf, the bottom of her foot, back up to her cheek, her breast, and finally, finally her mouth. He's so tender, but she's impatient. She's hungry for him. She wraps her legs around his waist.

He gasps her name as she pulls him closer, forcing the kiss into something more powerful. She loves his taste—strawberries and horror. She loves his eyes-nose-lips-cheeks. Their passion consumes them, and they drown in each other as they tumble in more sweat and ragged gasps. The grass is wet on their skin; dew permeates the dark.

"Don't go tonight," the girl whispers, her eyes sparkling with abandon and adoration. Her long dark hair drapes down her back and Fear smooths it away, kissing her shoulder. His mouth is soft.

"I love you," he says simply. The girl cups his cheek with her palm, smiling. She doesn't need to say the words—her uneven breathing says it all. He grins at her in return, a slow, sensual, loving smile. They clasp each other close once again, sinking back into the grass.

———

"I just want to run a few more tests. It's always better to be safe than—"

"No, it's not necessary. She'll be fine. You said yourself, you've never seen anyone recover so quickly."

"Yes, but her blood cells are nothing I've—"

"I said no, Dr. Pruett. Now please give me some time alone with her."

When my eyelids flutter open and I take in the smooth white ceiling above me, I'm instantly aware that the power has realigned itself and stands strong once again. My nothingness is back in place, blocking any Emotion that should try to come my way. It takes me a moment to recall all that's happened. I can't conjure any excitement at the fact there's one more piece added to the puzzle: Rebecca, the beautiful, angry, sad, mysterious girl that haunts me . . . Fear knew her. Fear loved her.

Oddly enough, my chest aches at the thought. Is Fear alive? Where is he? Only Nightmare knows.

My mind skitters away from thinking of him.

There's a poster of a kitten taped to the ceiling. *GET WELL SOON!* it reads. Focusing on it, I wonder about the relevance of the feline.

"Are you awake?"

Sarah stands by my bed, staring down at me. She looks tired. There are bags under her eyes and there's a slump to her shoulders that I—not Tim—have put there. She shoves her wispy hair out of the way and sighs. "Joshua is out in the waiting room. He's been there all night."

"Where are Tim and Charles?"

She plucks a Kleenex from the box next to my head, dabbing her eyes with it. They're watery from exhaustion. "When they found out you're going to be fine, they both left. Tim is at home, in the fields. Charles is at work, I think. He says if you're better by the time you check out, you should come to the track and watch him race." A rueful smile just barely crosses her lips.

"You should sit," I tell her. She does, probably just because her feet are aching and she doesn't want to go home. The chair squeaks at her weight.

The hospital room I'm in reminds me of Maggie's. Same beige paint, same curtains, same tiled floor, same cheap TV nailed to the wall. The thought of Maggie causes the newly fixed wall of nothingness to twinge.

I fold my hands on my stomach and face Sarah. I decide to be straight with her.

"You're leaving tomorrow night."

She gives a little jerk, her gaze darting to the doorway as if Tim will be standing there, glaring murderously at the two of us. "The doctor decided to keep you overnight for observation," she informs me, unwilling to discuss it. "You only have some scrapes and bruises. You were weak for a while there, but they say you're healing extraordinarily fast." She purses her lips, concentrating on the floor. "Just like last time." She says it so quietly I'm not sure she means for me to hear.

A pipe in the wall drips. A bird lands on the sill outside the window. We both look at the little creature. It's a kind I've never seen before, all green and blue and black.

"They usually don't make it this far north," Sarah murmurs, her lined face suddenly alight with awe. "Especially this time of year."

"What kind is it?" I shift to get a better angle of her.

She doesn't take her eyes off the bird. It's still there, washing itself, and I imagine images of the sky and of worms and eggs zipping through its little mind. "I'm pretty sure that's a Green Jay," Sarah tells me after another pause. "They live in Texas and some of the other southern states. They like the warm weather all year round."

"How do you know so much?" The bird on the sill is staring back at us now with its beady black eyes, its little neck bent to the side. The pose makes me think of Nightmare again, and my stomach clenches.

Sarah swallows. The nervous action is audible. "It used to be a hobby of mine," she replies softly.

It's something I never knew about her. How bizarre that you can know someone your entire life, see their most hidden pains and hopes, and not know the tiniest detail about them. If I had done things differently, if she had been a slightly different person, if *I* had been a different person, maybe everything could have been better.

Careful, Elizabeth, it almost sounds like you're regretting something, I can practically hear Fear say to me. But he's not here. I don't know if he will ever be back. An image of the desperation in his eyes, the blood spurting from that hole, shoves its way into my head. Shuddering, a bitter taste in my mouth, I focus on the bird. It's fluffing its wings now, spreading them out, showing the bright colors off. Vain little thing. But it's truly admirable, its stamina and determination. Few others would leave behind everything they knew to venture into the unknown. What was so different about this bird that it would abandon the warm breezes of Texas and fly hundreds of miles across the country, just to arrive here, at my window? What was the purpose? Just because it could?

"I'm going home." Sarah's announcement doesn't surprise me, of course, but it does come out of nowhere, like she pulled it out of the air, magic.

I think about this. She isn't venturing into the unknown, exactly, but she is taking flight. It seems unjust that no one will care, after everything she's gone through. No one will tell her story. Not her, not Tim. A few in Edson may notice her absence and gossip about it for a while, but eventually, she'll be forgotten. Maybe she wants it that way.

But I won't forget.

She seems to expect me to say something. Words that will make her feel brave, that will make everything all right. I told her once that the past can't be changed, but the future can. She married Tim, she lost the love of a daughter, she spent years in isolation and misery. But her story isn't finished, and for once she's picked up a pen.

"Go," I say to her, smiling. It feels strange on my face, but the sight of it doesn't frighten or embitter her. Sarah nods, slowly, hands tightly clasped. As I watch, her fingers unlatch, one by one, until they're lying loosely in her lap.

Voices drift by the doorway, two nurses talking. Sarah glances toward them, then back at me. She nods to herself once more and stands. There's a stain on her jeans that looks like gravy. "Owen's men haven't been able to find the person that attacked you. They're still looking, I guess. They want to ask you some questions once you've recovered. I didn't let the doctor run more blood tests on you," she adds, like an afterthought. "I thought you might not want him to."

I lie there. Parts of me are still tender, but somehow I know that I should hurt much, much more. *You've healed*, something in my head whispers. I don't wonder at the implications of this. Not now, at least. "Thank you," I say to Sarah.

She nods a third time. There's not much else to say. Giving her the opportunity to slip away—I know she hates goodbyes—I look at the Green Jay again. It's gotten bored with us and is observing some clouds with sharp attention.

The chair squeaks again, and Sarah leans over, setting her elbows on my bed. Together, we watch the Green Jay lift its wings and take flight, heading deeper into the unknown, to unbury all the secrets of a land it's never seen.

He stands in the doorway, uncertain, quiet. There's so much I should tell him, because somehow I sense my time is almost up. The clock is still ticking inside my head, a warning. I'm almost at the end of the road, an end I've been running to ever since I decided to seek out the truth. Was it ever a conscious decision? Did I ever have a choice in the matter, or does fate really control everything? There's no telling what this end will look like, but I have a feeling that nothing—especially whatever this is between Joshua and me—will be the same.

You will need that boy in the end.

"You look better," Joshua finally says, breaking the long stillness. He tugs at the hem of his T-shirt, an anxious movement. He looks a lot like Sarah; the shadows under his eyes, the drawn features. His hair is greasy and hanging in front of his eyes again.

"You can come in, you know." I glance at the chair Sarah vacated a few minutes ago, but Joshua doesn't move. He just stares at me as if he's memorizing my features. He looks torn.

"I'm okay," I say, and it's the truth. My voice is normal, my minimal wounds are healing. Will Fear heal? *Stop it*, I tell myself flatly. But it takes a huge amount of effort to stop thinking about him.

Joshua draws in a ragged breath, his fists clenching at his sides. "It was the weirdest thing," he tells me. "I was at home with my dad, and suddenly I got this feeling that you needed me. I didn't even think about it; I just left. And for some reason, I went right to the school. There was your truck, just sitting there. I heard you scream." He closes his eyes, and I study the veins in his eyelids, such tiny things.

Someone is speaking over the intercom and we both listen to the words for a moment. "Annie Harkin, please report to the third floor nurse's station . . ."

Joshua rubs his eyes with the heels of his hands, sighing some more.

I straighten my blankets. "Joshua—"

"You are *really* trying my patience."

Joshua doesn't open his eyes or even move, but I glance away at the sound of the familiar voice. A hooded figure is standing in the open doorway, huddled, fists clenched.

Rebecca.

TWENTY

She stomps into the room like she owns it. She points at Joshua with a hand that's covered by her too-long sleeve. "You, out."

Joshua blinks. Frowns. He glances from her to me uncertainly. "Do you...?" he starts.

Our intruder sighs impatiently. "You suddenly feel an urge to go home and do whatever it is you do there. *Go.*" Power leaks into the words.

Joshua's body jerks, and he resists for a moment—he's strong, but not strong enough. "I'll see you soon, okay?" he says to me, already walking out. "I need to go home."

I just watch him leave. Then I turn my gaze back to this creature who's barged into my world yet again. She waits, utterly still, probably prepared for more questions about the past or the influence on me. After all, she's my only link to any of it. But even I don't expect the words that come out of my mouth, as unstoppable as a meteor hurtling to the earth: "Is Fear alive? Have you heard anything about him?"

I picture it again, his expression, his cheek scraping over the ground, the blood between his fingers. For some reason my heart picks up speed; we both hear it from the monitor beside my bed. *Beep, beep-beep, beep-beep-beep.*

She tilts her head a little. The hood falls against the side of her jaw. When it becomes apparent that she isn't going to answer, it occurs to me that she probably has no idea what I'm talking about. "You've been gone for a while," I say after a moment of stiff quiet.

At this she moves to stand by the bed. Her jerky movements speak volumes. Irritation and maybe a little relief at seeing me alive. "I shouldn't have come back," she snaps. "No one else is stupid enough to be in this horrid little place while that monster is around."

"Ah, yes." My eyes narrow. "Him. Are you trying to get me killed? Because I'm assuming he's the reason you told me not to go Sophia's party that night. You knew he would be here."

Rebecca breathes through her nose, a visible sign she's striving for control. All I can see of her is the bottom of her chin. "The key words there are *told you not to*. You deliberately went against my warning. He's been looking for you, and I knew he'd be drawn to that party like a moth to a flame."

"Why was he after me?" I ask bluntly.

Now she sighs, walking to the window to peer out. "You're so stubborn. If you would just..." She stops, begins again. "One of the side effects of the illusion on you is that I can't tell you a thing about why I placed it in the first p-place. If I'm around when you discover something from the past, I have no choice b-but to remove the evidence." She grips the windowsill with white fingers. "My own essence makes sure I do, and that I don't speak of it, or it causes me searing pain. Which is part of the reason I've been so vague with you."

An illusion? That's when I put another piece of the puzzle together. *She's the one who made the newspaper disappear.* How long has she been watching me?

Putting aside thousands of questions—about this, about Nightmare, Landon's murder, their mother and the stone house, my past, the power—I ask the question that's been stalking me since all this began. "Do you know why Courage told me I would need Joshua?"

"Because I told him I thought the boy could break through!" she explodes. She's agitated; she speaks with her arms, waving them around her head and pacing the floor. "It would've been the quickest way. It seemed like you were feeling something for him. All the signs were there! You were smiling, letting him close. I saw the way you looked at him when he brought you to see those ridiculous bugs." Then, abruptly, she stops, rubbing her temples. She forces her tone to be even. "I haven't seen you look at anyone like that since…" She trails off, shaking her head.

Since when? Where do I fit into all this? For a moment I experience the faintest, faintest stirrings of frustration. So many questions she won't answer. Even though it's useless, I can't help but ask, "Who am I?"

She blatantly ignores the question, of course, preferring to finger the edge of my blanket and focus on the material. Her nose wrinkles with disgust. "Hate hospitals," she mutters to herself.

"This … illusion, as you call it, was put on me a long time ago, and you only recently sought me out. Why did you hide for so long?" I ask next. "Why all the games?"

Restless again, Rebecca stalks over to the wall to examine a painting hanging there. Her hood slips a little, and she catches it with fast fingers, putting it back over her face. "I already told you," she says. "I can't do anything but watch. In the beginning, I did stay. After a while I realized how pointless that was, so I left. But when I caught wind that *he* was hanging around Edson, I couldn't just do nothing, so I came back. I had to warn you. Little good it did. My only hope of the illusion breaking was the kid. That way, you would have your powers to defend yourself against that monster."

Powers? What am I? But of course I won't get an answer if I ask. "You can't remove it?" I ask her instead, following her with my eyes as she moves around the room.

She shakes her head. I study the small scrap of her face that I can see; she has a full bottom lip. "No. It fades with time, and if it's to be removed sooner than it's meant to be, only you can do it—by feeling heightened emotion, like love or terror or grief. It's happening, though; I bet you've noticed. Emotions are breaking through. Your own power really is too strong to be restrained for long."

"It's been restrained for more than thirteen years," I tell her, resisting the urge to ask about my abilities.

"Because you are unbelievably adept at lying to yourself. Truly, I'm amazed."

Maintaining a firm hold on all of this information is a bit difficult. I'm silent, taking it all in.

Rebecca isn't going to give me much time. "But"—she whips back around—"you need to break my illusion *now*. I could take you away from here. Then again, there's really no point. Now that he's found you, he'll hunt you down no matter where you go. Until you remember, you'll be helpless."

"And how do you suggest I feel 'heightened emotion'?" I ask her coolly.

Air hisses through her teeth as she exhales. "That's the point, stupid. You could remember right now if you wanted to. All of this is a choice on your part. If you really want to know the truth, it's there at your fingertips. Take it so that we can all get on with our lives."

I purse my lips, nodding slowly. "So you expect me to sit and wait for Nightmare—"

"Don't say his name!" She whirls as if the Element will be standing in the doorway, staring at us. When she sees we're still alone, she relaxes slightly, her alarm turning to fury. "Stupid," she spits at me yet again. "You're endangering us both. You don't have to be asleep for him to reach you."

"What does he want?" I repeat, more sharply this time. "Why is he after me?"

"Power," is all Rebecca says. Then she relents and adds, "Blood from the other plane is like a drug to him. A rush. He no longer feels the need to answer his summons. Our kind knows that he's gone insane, but so far he's managed to avoid getting killed." She continues to pick at the blanket some more.

"Are there others like him?" I ask.

"Members of the other plane have no desire to start a civil war," she answers in a dismissive tone. I turn my face to the window. Outside, it's getting darker. The sun is almost gone as it sinks into the ocean of sky. There's a small lamp on in the corner of my room, casting deceptive serenity over the room.

Fear should be here, harassing me. The thought comes from nowhere, and a lump forms in my throat. Thinking of him continues to causes that odd, painful sensation on my chest. I recall that vivid dream, the way he'd run his fingers down Rebecca's spine. Something curls in my stomach. Something like ... envy.

" ... even listening?" Rebecca snaps, springing. She flicks me on the temple with her nimble fingers. Hard. I swat at her like she's a fly, but she's already yards away.

"How much you have to learn," she mocks. "And unless you learn fast, little girl, that monster will find you, and he'll take your power for his own."

The words hit me suddenly. Nightmare isn't gone. Of course not. He's out there somewhere, waiting for a second chance. And unless something changes soon—I regain all my memories and I break the illusion, or I leave Edson behind forever—he'll seize the next opportunity and I'll be dead. What happened to Fear will be merciful in comparison to what the Element will do to me.

My stomach lurches at the thought, and again the memory of Fear's anguished expression assails me. I sit up, debating whether or not to leave the bed and the room and go. Follow Sarah's footsteps in venturing beyond this tiny town, leaving behind the conflict and the malicious, petty intents. What was once keeping me here doesn't seem to exist anymore, or maybe it just doesn't matter.

Rebecca sighs yet again, suddenly losing her fire. Her shoulders slump. I appraise her thoughtfully. How strong do you have to be, to go on after an experience as horrific as hers? The bloody death of a brother, running for years and years. I try to picture what she looks like under that hood, an expression other than the one that she wears in my dreams over and over again. "Why—" I start.

She shakes her head, scowling. "No more questions! Think! Haven't you noticed that p-people are d-drawn to you?" She bends to hold her stomach but continues determinedly, "Why is that? Haven't you ever stopped to wonder? Just break the damn illusion! And stay alive until you do. I might not be able to get the boy to you in time if this happens again."

Wait. Rebecca is the one who saved me? She's the one who warned Joshua? I open my mouth to respond, but then the rest of her words sink in. *Drawn to you.* Morgan. Maggie. Fear. Joshua. There was no reason for any of them to pursue me. She's right. But I can't begin to puzzle out why. I lift my gaze again to implore, "Can't you—"

She cuts me off with a downward slash of her hand and walks away. Her footsteps are soundless. At the door she pauses, inclining her head thoughtfully. "One more thing." She turns and flattens her palms against either side of the doorway. Her tone is hard. "Fear isn't dead. He's nearby, in fact, since he was too injured to move very far. While that monster was distracted with you, I pulled him into the woods. I'm doing my best to make sure that he lives. I'll return once you've remembered everything." She gives me her back again.

I raise my voice to stop her. "Fear thought you were dead. All this time he was mourning you. Why didn't you tell him? Did you think you were… protecting him?"

She pauses but doesn't turn this time. Finally she says, so softly, "I wasn't the one he was looking for." I frown. But before I can utter another word, she's gone.

Maybe not quite gone. A second later, her voice sounds from farther down the hall: "If you get killed, I swear I'll bring you back from the dead just to kill you again myself!"

———————

The house is a mourning skeleton of a place. Without Sarah, it's lost its soul, its purpose. I imagine it misses the tender hands that tended to every corner of its insides, misses Sarah's gentle footsteps and her soothing voice. Even the shadows feel abandoned and empty.

It's been three days since she left. Three long, tension-filled days. Sheriff Owen tracks me down to ask me his questions, to which I give vague, useless answers. Tim drinks himself into oblivion for hours on end now, leaving the fields and the livestock untended. Charles avoids the house like a plague. And since Tim isn't exactly around to notice, Joshua has been by every day, once in the morning to pick me up, once in the afternoon to drop me off. He's not taking any chances now, and won't take no for an answer. To anything.

Now. Now. Now. It's all I am. All I can focus on. To think of anything else would only bring me around in circles. The questions are too many, the solutions too few. Should I leave? Is Nightmare nearby? When will he pounce? Is Fear still alive? And then there's Tim to think about—he's a ticking time bomb, set to burst at any second. Will I survive the explosion this time, especially since Fear won't be rescuing me again?

I'm lying in bed, staring up at the ceiling, the smell of dry paint filling my nostrils. When a loud creak sounds through the walls, I instantly sit up. My first thought is that Nightmare has finally come back for me. But after a moment, I recognize my brother's tread: slow, light. Somehow I know what he's doing. Change is in the air. For a second I ponder if I should confront him or not. Then I slide out of bed and pad to the door.

"What are you doing?"

Charles twitches, dropping his bags right there in the hall. They hit the floor with two resounding *thuds*. He looks at me over his shoulder as if he's been caught doing something wrong. For a moment it seems like he's actually considering pretending that he's not leaving, that nothing is different.

Moving in a way that won't startle him, I approach my brother in the dark, bend down, grab the handle of one of his bags, and press it into his sweaty hand. I smile up at him, this boy who will never grow up.

He swallows. I watch his Adam's apple bob up and down. We both know there's no pretending this time. And finally he does mutter, "I have to go." As if the words have a bad taste, he clears his throat. I don't have the reaction he's probably expecting: hurt or maybe anger. My calm appears to bother him even more, and, unable to keep eye contact, Charles looks down at his feet. Now he looks like a child about to be scolded.

I give him what he wants. "It's okay. I would do the same if I could."

Charles laughs a little, shaking his head. "No, you wouldn't. You've never wanted to be anywhere. You never seemed to care about any of it."

I pick up his other bag and hand it to him. "That's not true. I think deep down, I always wanted to paint Venice." The lie is sudden, effortless. I don't know why I give it to him.

He raises his head. "Yeah?"

"Yeah." He looks even younger here, in the dim. I remember Charles as a child, always leaving me behind to play with his friends, always running off when Tim was in one of his moods. "You're going to live the life you want," I tell him. "And you shouldn't feel guilty about that."

The grandfather clock at the end of the hall dongs. We stand there, and the song plays. Charles sighs. "I'm staying at my buddy Garrett's house for a while. If you … if you need me for anything, just give me a call, all right?"

We both know I won't. But it's nice of him to make the offer anyway. "See you," I say, reaching out to give him a one-armed hug since he's carrying the bags. He doesn't try to hug me back, but I do feel his chin rest on the top of my head, just for a moment.

I watch him go down the stairs. Before he reaches the bottom step I turn away to go back to my cold, lonely bed.

"Liz?"

I poke my head out the door one more time. Charles has stopped. He's looking up at me. When I don't respond, he bites his bottom lip. "You asked me a while ago if I remember what you were like as a baby." He meets my gaze suddenly, determination in the lines of his face. "The truth is, I don't really remember that girl. She was so different from who you are now. But I do remember one thing. I've never forgotten, really. It was right after you had your accident. I asked you once, 'How are you feeling, Liz?' It was … scary. You looked right at me and said, 'Liz is dead.'"

I force a smile. "Thank you for telling—"

"I'm not done." His hold on both bags tightens. "I asked you why you would say that. You didn't answer me right away. In fact, it wasn't until after supper. I was outside hitting some balls. You came up behind me and you said, 'I took her place.' I was just a kid, but even then I saw how real it was. You've never been my sister, but I still treated you like one, because I always thought you needed someone to show you some kindness."

I blink. Once. Twice. "What—"

"I'm not as ignorant as I act. None of us are. We all saw the change in you. No accident could do that. I don't care what the counselors or the doctors said. I've always believed that there are strange things in the world, even though we can't see them. You're just one of the mysteries, Elizabeth. I accepted that."

The words hit me like bullets to the chest. *You've never been my sister*. Some part of me did always believe that even though I'm different, apart, I'm blood to these people. This— the need to belong to a family I should have already belonged to—might have been the real thing that urged me to find the answers. Their pain drove me to try to become the girl they once knew.

But I can't think about this now. Later. Because it's time for another goodbye.

I study Charles. Maybe I've been too quick to judge him. It just goes to show that what's on the surface is never all there is. "Charles." I smile down at him. "Go. You were a good brother—the best you could be—and I'll never forget you."

It's as if a weight has lifted off of him; his shoulders slump and he sighs again. "See you in another lifetime, Liz," he murmurs, grinning. That flop of hair shines beneath the entryway light. He nods at me and turns his back for the last time, leaving this life behind to seek out a new one. Just as Sarah did. A life that won't hiss with secrets from every corner and where pretending is unnecessary.

The door shuts with just a gentle *click* and Charles Caldwell is gone. Somehow, I know I won't see him again.

I go back to bed, settling into the sheets as if I'd never left. The filmy curtains around my window flutter, and I focus on them as sleep claims me. The dream waits in the recesses of my mind, waits patiently to take me down into the depths.

———————

He stands with his back to me, in that pose I'm beginning to identify as his: arms behind his back, hands clasped. We're on a clear platform of some kind, surrounded by nothing but white, open air. The wind tugs at my hair. It hangs loose, long—I never wear it like this. I look down and see that once again I'm wearing the yellow sundress. It seems out of place now that all the illusions are gone. He isn't using Landon this time, isn't hiding behind meadows or stone houses.

"What are you waiting for?" I ask his back dully. "Go ahead. Finish it."

He doesn't turn. After a moment he says, "I find that I like my opponents to be invested in the game." His tone is light, casual, as if he's commenting on the weather. His clothing presses against his body; he's facing the wind. I glance around and wonder for a brief moment where we are. Then I remember that it doesn't matter. None of it is real. He's in my head.

When he doesn't get a response, Nightmare finally faces me, and it's difficult to look him in the eyes. They're round black jewels. Snake eyes. "It's time for a short intermission," he informs me. His hair reminds me of Fear's in the way it rests against his skin like silk.

His words register. "Is this a game or a play?" I ask, taunting him for some reason. Foolish. I can't take it back, though.

His gaze narrows. "Perhaps you'd rather continue now, then."

Again I don't answer, but my heart stumbles. He sighs, waving a hand. "Go, little one. You'll see me soon. I do hope you regain some of that charming emotion I saw so briefly."

I open my mouth to speak, maybe ask the questions I'm unable to ask Rebecca, but an invisible hand pushes me right in the center of my chest. My arms flail, but it's too late. I fall into the white oblivion. Down, down, the air rushing from my lungs.

I land in my bed.

———————

As soon as the sun rises in the sky I know the house has turned into the fiery, cackling depths of hell. I just didn't expect it to happen so soon. Tim has woken with a vengeance, still drunk from the night before; I can hear him muttering through the walls. He needs someone to blame for Sarah leaving him.

Too bad I'm the only one left.

I consider running for just a moment. But I can't seem to bring myself to move. Thoughts of Fear, memories, dreams fill my head and I lie there, listening to the heavy thump of Tim's feet against the floor. He's still muttering to himself. I think of Landon. So much death in this story. How did he end? Was Rebecca with him during his last breath? I think of Fear, of Fear and Rebecca clasped in a passionate embrace. She had been the girl he'd spoken of in the loft, the one he'd loved. The one who I'd once thought was dead. And now they're together, after all this time. Is she explaining why she stayed away so long? Is he telling her how much he missed her?

"Elizabeth!" Tim slurs, banging on my door. He can't seem to figure out how to work the doorknob. It keeps slipping in his grip.

Please, please come back.

How painful it must have been, to hold someone she cared about so much in her arms and watch his blood run into the ground. How strange. Other than Maggie's misplaced dedication to me, I've never witnessed any kind of real love.

"Open this door, you little bitch!"

Which is worse, Tim or Nightmare? They seem the same in my mind. What's the point? Even if I leave here, I'll walk into a trap just like this one the moment I fall asleep. There's nothing to fight for, now; not survival, not love of my own. And this is no longer my home—I have to face that; nothing will ever be the way it once was. But I find myself clinging to it just the same. Pesky emotions. Even when weak, they're a hindrance to the logic I'm accustomed to.

After Nightmare's attack, after speaking to Rebecca in the hospital, I've been remembering more and more. Their past—Rebecca's and Landon's and their mother's—comes fast at me now. I don't know if it's an unconscious decision on my part or if it's just time, but the illusion is growing thin and my nothingness is a weak, feeble thing deep inside of me.

"Elizabeth!"

That's not who I am. Now I'll face the truth. As the threat of pain and darkness drools on my door, I close my eyes and say the words that I've been avoiding for so long.

"I'm not Elizabeth."

Nothing happens, not that I expected anything to. There's no explosion of realization or power or memories. No Emotions come to touch me, the untouchable girl. All I know is who I'm not, and not who I am. I open my eyes again, staring at the mural. It's still unfinished, but I'm almost done. There's just one more wall to do. I concentrate on that stone house, Landon's still face, Rebecca's pain, the death and the agony, the feelings I can't reach.

"I'm not human," I say next.

Still no earth-shattering epiphany. The pieces that are me remain scattered, incomplete, and there are no patterns to follow.

Tim has been pounding at the door, and now it gives way. With a *crack*, his fist bursts through, and he's cut his knuckle. He roars, shouldering the door now. More of the wood drops to the floor in jagged chunks. Tim keeps at this until there's a hole big enough for him to fit through. He ducks inside, eyes wild and red-rimmed. They scan the room frantically until they come to rest on me.

"You," he breathes. "You did this."

I did. Without my encouragement, Sarah never would have started thinking, and she never would have left. But still I don't move, even when Tim advances in a snarling rage. He seems so out of place in my small room—he's never been in here before, actually.

"What makes you tick, Tim?" I ask, looking up at him, causing him to pause for an instant. Death at this man's hands will surely be better than the slaughtering at Nightmare's.

This human who is not my father growls, reaching down to haul me to my feet. I'm limp in his hands, my thoughts a gnarled haze. We stare at each other for what feels like eons until Tim grunts once, then throws me at the wall as hard as he can. My back slams into the depiction of Landon. The plaster cracks. Ignoring the blaze of pain ripping up my spine, I reach up to touch one of the tears on Rebecca's cheek.

Tim advances, stumbling. He reeks, the sting of his scent filling my senses. Anger is absent—this is born purely from Tim and that amber liquid he loves so much. Just as he reaches down to pull me up yet again, I tell him, "What happened to me isn't your fault, you know."

It's the wrong thing to say. A dark reminder. I know it, of course. Tim's an animal now, wounded and furious. He throws me down and jams his knee into my stomach, clenching his fists around my throat. I cry out in pain, half-laughing, and dry-heave a second later; I haven't eaten for a while. I forgot.

"You're a demon," Tim mumbles thickly. He tightens his hold. As he leans his weight on me, his knee buries itself in my stomach until I can feel my organs crumpling. I don't fight him. My instincts are a dull, throbbing mess. All I keep thinking is, *I'm not Elizabeth. I'm not human.* Who am I, then? Where do I belong? Again I envision Fear and Rebecca. He's lying in a bed, slowly healing, and she's sitting at his side, smiling into his eyes. The image hurts; just more pain to add to the onslaught.

Dots dance in front of me, green and blue and red, and they're so close that I reach up with one slender finger, trying to touch one. Tim's talking again, but his words don't register. Exactly six seconds tick by and I give up on the dots, eyes drifting shut.

"Wake up," someone—Landon?—orders. "Open your eyes. Now."

I smile sleepily. His voice is familiar, comforting. "No point. No point."

"Tap, tap," Landon says. Now I frown. It doesn't seem like something he would say. I don't know how I know this; I just do. "Tap, tap," Landon says again, and now I do open my eyes, looking past Tim's red, bulbous face to the window. A little figure stands on the sill, her pretty face pressed to the glass. It's sprinkling outside, and her hair sparkles with lingering droplets. As if she doesn't even notice the rain, the creature clenches her tiny fist and knocks on the window. *Tap, tap*. She looks worried. Why is she worried?

Darkness is clouding in again. I lose awareness of anything besides Tim's grip on my air supply, the consuming dizziness, something humming in my ear. No, wait, there's a fly in the room. It buzzes past my nose.

And then, like a star illuminating the black night, a new voice explodes through the shrinking space. "Get out. Get out now and never come back, or I swear to God I'll call the cops and have you put away for the rest of your miserable life."

Without warning, the crushing weight is gone. Coughing and gasping simultaneously, I gulp in gallons of air, my lungs greedy. Suddenly time is utterly still, and it's over. I lie there, my back to Landon, gazing around my room until my vision clears up completely. I'm alone except for my bed, the dresser, the rickety desk, a mirror, and the mural. I try to figure out what was real and what was illusion when Tim was choking me. For a wild second, I thought I'd actually heard Landon...And had Moss really been standing at my window? One quick glance shows the empty sill, the lonely glass. No. I'd been half-delirious.

Which brings me to wonder where Tim went. The house is so still—he must really be gone. How...? I lift my nose and sniff the stale air, wondering if an otherworldly being saved me...maybe Fear...there's nothing but the scent of alcohol. Tim.

He might come back.

I try to stand and find I can't. Pain grips me and draws me completely beneath its murky waters. I struggle against it, but then darkness cackles and whooshes in with its inescapable embrace. This time there are no dreams, just a face. Pale hair, crinkled azure eyes, conceited grin. Fear...

Quiet.

A gentle touch.

I must have fallen asleep. When I wake, I blink rapidly. The blurred world comes into focus, as does the face of my champion. And of all the people who could have rescued me this time, it's the boy who's not my brother. He's squatting in front of me, his eyes clouded with concern. His mouth moves as he speaks, and I crane my neck to see past him.

I struggle to my feet, Charles supporting me and all the while still talking in my ear. Tim wouldn't actually leave just because he was told to, would he? I whisper with a pang of hope, "Fear?" No answer. No tang of terror. Just then the clock chimes in the hall. *I'm late for school.* A simple thought, reflex.

"Elizabeth, answer me, damn it!" My not-brother's face looms close, demanding and concerned.

"Charles?" I squint, as if he's an apparition that'll disappear any second. When I realize that he's real, he's not going to fade, I ask with slight disbelief, "What are you doing here?" I see that Courage is gazing at me, his hand on Charles's shoulder.

"Only for you would I risk coming back here," Courage tells me solemnly.

My not-brother is still holding my arm, and when he sees that I'm finally lucid, he lets out a breath of relief and lets go.

"Are you all right?" he says rather than answering. "When I first came in, it seemed like you were in pretty bad shape. I had to take care of Tim, so I left you for just a second, and when I came back, you were passed out. But now it doesn't look that bad."

He and Courage watch as I study my arms, legs. Nothing. No bruises, no cuts. No pain. My throat is fine. I must have healed as I slept. I look at Charles again, at his achingly familiar mop of hair, ruddy skin, fidgeting hands. Of all the people I would have expected to save me, he was the unlikeliest possibility. "What are you doing here?" I repeat. I already know, of course, but for some reason I need to hear the words out loud.

Charles just shrugs. "I had a bad feeling. I came back to make sure you're doing okay, and I heard ... should I take you to the hospital?"

"I'm fine. I think I'll even go to school today." I rest my hand on his arm, right next to Courage's dark-skinned fingers. The Emotion's heat enfolds me, and my quailing insides calm a little. "Charles," I say. Just the one word, just his name. He has to hear the question in it. We're standing in the middle of my room, surrounded by the mural, by the pieces of the past, the truth that I'm not his sister. We both know it—but still,

Charles came back. I didn't expect this. Very few times in my life have I been wrong about a person.

Experiencing Courage's influence for the first time, Charles makes a choice. He reaches for me and jerks me to him for a quick, awkward hug. I hug him back. When he pulls away, my brother clears his throat. He does it again. Finally he blurts, "I'm going to be here from now on, all right?" He means to sound gruff, but his tone is laced with relief and a faint tinge of pride. Right before Courage disappears, I catch sight of a tiny smile curving the Emotion's normally serious lips.

I smile, too. "I believe you."

Charles spoke the truth; Tim is nowhere around. His truck is gone. Seeing this, I hurry to get dressed, grab my bag, and get into my own truck. There's something oddly comforting in the routine, and I drive to school like it's any other day. As if Sarah is at home in the kitchen, Tim is out in the fields, and Charles is sleeping in before his shift at Fowler's Grocery. Everything is different now, of course.

The parking lot is full by the time I pull in, and my normal spot is taken. I don't want to park at the outer edges where anyone, or a certain someone, can attack me, so I park in one of the open spots beside Sophia's red convertible toward the front. Bought with her father's money, of course. I've heard Sophia's friends say that he buys her off to make up for never visiting. Sophia always demands that the spaces on either side of the car to be empty so no one scratches the flawless paint job. How thrilled she'll be to see my tank by her precious car.

I'm through the front doors, just a few feet away from my locker and moments away from class, when I'm spotted through the office window.

"Elizabeth?" Sally Morrison shoves the door open and stands there in her perfect clothes, with all her good intentions, staring at me. I slowly turn. Her eyes are so sad as she keeps looking at me, waiting for me to say something. She really does want to help. I clutch my bag tightly.

The counselor sighs after another moment. "Do you want to come into my office?" she asks, motioning for me to walk before her. I do, remaining silent.

Together, we enter the room we're both so familiar with. Sally shuts the door quietly and takes her normal seat, smoothing her skirt. Again, the woman gives me an opportunity to talk first, but I don't take it.

"Is there something you want to tell me?" Sally sits back, sighing. She doesn't expect the truth. She's waiting for another lie, like I've given her every other time I've been in here. Her crossed legs and her shiny shoes hold all my attention as I think.

Sally waits. She doesn't speak or even glance at the clock. Finally, finally, after we've been silent for ten minutes in this tiny room of hope and pain and lies, I give Sally Morrison my first truth. I don't know why. Maybe it's because I have nothing left but this.

"Remember that day in your office? The bruises?" I ask. She just continues to wait. So I finally tell her, "A cow didn't kick me in the face."

TWENTY-ONE

The only unchanged variable in my new life is Joshua. He calls every night, walks me to my classes. As time goes on, though, he stops insisting on giving me rides. He begins to believe that I'm safe again. Tim is still mysteriously missing, and I haven't seen or heard from Nightmare. But I know it's a lie, this delusion of peace.

He's coming.

Fear still hasn't made an appearance. When I think of him, I experience a twinge in my gut. Worry, trying to claw free of the illusion.

On Wednesday morning, a week after Sally Morrison called me into her office, I pull into the school parking lot. The sky is gray, the wind dismal. Winter, a striking Element with white eyelashes and blue lips, is on her way. I remove the key from the ignition and drop it in my jacket pocket. Through the windshield, I watch the kids walking by, chatting. All of them are secure in who they are and where they stand. If it weren't for the illusion that still holds on, I think I'd be jealous.

Joshua is waiting on the front steps of the school. I see him before he sees me, and I hop out of my truck, watching him. His bright eyes scan the crowd climbing up the steps, and when he can't find me, his gaze expands out to the lot to pick out everyone in the clusters by their cars. He's so kind, so good, and I know that the best thing to do—the right thing to do—would be to free him. Even if the illusion does fully break, even if I do come out of this alive ... he's only a beautiful idea.

Just like Fear. Who must be enjoying Rebecca's ministrations. Since I haven't heard from either of them, they must have reached the happily ever after they've been denied all these years.

Thinking this, my stomach tight, I shoulder my bag and start toward Joshua.

"So it's Elizabeth now, correct?" a voice breathes in my ear. A beat later it adds, "It's time."

My spine stiffens and I stop in my tracks. Tyler Bentley gives me an annoyed glance as he passes. He doesn't see the urgent message in my eyes. I open my mouth—

"I wouldn't do that, *Elizabeth*. Ah, don't turn around, please. What are you going to do, call the sheriff? Tell one of your teachers? None of them can see me, and you'd look like a hysterical schoolgirl. And then you'd have the boy's blood on your hands. Wouldn't want that now, would you? Start walking."

He means Joshua. He's threatening Joshua. I obey, my

gait halting as I begin the trek across the parking lot. "You're not going to touch him," I say through my teeth.

Nightmare laughs quietly. He's following me, moving with the group around us as if he belongs. He's still leaning over my shoulder when he warns, "Then I suggest you stay quiet." Before I can say anything more, my hair is stirred by a sudden breeze and Nightmare is gone.

But I can feel him nearby. Even when Joshua spots me, smiling soothingly as his warm palm cups mine, I can sense the chill of Nightmare's presence.

Between classes, I pass him in the hallway and his strong scent—blood, darkness, hunger—assails my senses. Our eyes meet, blue against that infinite black, and then I look away, acting as if I can just wish him into oblivion. He turns as he passes to keep those eyes on me. He's playing a game of cat-and-mouse, toying with me before he makes his final move.

Yet Nightmare still doesn't attack. Even when I notice him behind some shelves in the library, watching me and Joshua study, even when he passes the doorway to one of my classes and winks at me.

It's one of the slowest days I've ever experienced. At the end of it, Joshua kisses me on the cheek. "I have to go home real quick," he tells me. "But I'll swing by your place later, okay? Make sure you're never alone."

His concern causes more spasms in my wall, more digging in the hole.

Sophia, for once, ignores me when I pass her group. She's been acting this way ever since the town found out about Tim—instead of mockery and pranks, she now pretends I don't exist. It's the best she can do, I suppose. Sally doesn't talk about any of it, of course, but my brother does. Some of Sophia's friends see me and look away. Most with guilt.

At the end of the day, I get into my truck with no trouble from Nightmare. Get on the road. On my way home. Back to Charles. Safety is only a few miles away.

And then he appears in the back of my truck, his eyes gleaming back at me in the rearview mirror. I slam the gas pedal all the way down, intending to knock him off balance and leave him behind in a cloud of billowing gravel.

Pop. One of the tires explodes beneath me.

Now I smash on the brakes, open the door, and fly out of the driver's seat, heading for a field to my left just through a line of trees. I don't bother checking to see what's ruined the tire. Nightmare expected it to happen; he's already disappeared. I'm a blur through the trees. There's no way he can possibly catch me. Where is he? I turn...

...and he wraps his hand around my throat.

"Sleep," he purrs. His grip tightens, just barely. A fierce desire to curl up and succumb to darkness creeps over me. I fight it but my eyelids are so heavy, as if my eyelashes are made of iron. Somehow, I manage to lurch away from the Element and stumble in the opposite direction, back toward my truck. I hear Nightmare sigh impatiently. "Fine, have it your way." When I glance back, a gun materializes in his hand. *Not real, not real,* I tell myself in a daze, staggering.

A sharp pain billows through my shoulder and down my back. I gasp, faltering, and as I do so he shoots again, another bullet slamming into my lower back. Colors swim before me and unbearable waves of heat spread through my body. I stumble to my knees, rendered helpless. For a shivering instant time stands still. Then I drop, landing face-first into the dirt.

I watch his shoes approach, all shiny. I'm powerless.

"You do like to make things harder for yourself," Nightmare says, squatting beside me. "It's quite amusing." He reaches down to grasp my chin, turning my head to the side so he can see my face. I can't speak; it's so hard to keep my senses straight with all this pain burning through me. My vision begins to cloud until the face leering down at me is nothing but a blur—all that stands out are those voracious eyes. The whiteness of his shirt.

"... please ... " I manage to say, moaning.

"You'll be fine. We both know you'll heal."

My head starts to pound and I can't suppress another moan. A rock is digging into my stomach, but I hardly notice it compared to the agony of the gunshot wounds.

Lying. It's all I have left. "... not one of them ... " I say, tears slipping out the corners of my eyes.

Nightmare rests the butt of the gun in the dirt, leaning on it. He balances gracefully on the balls of his feet, as if he wants as little dirt touching him as possible. "I beg to differ, my girl," he replies. "As I said, I've been looking for you, and even though you're wearing a different face, I know. Not to mention the fact you have those abilities. How foolish do you think I am?"

The pain is consuming. I make a strangled noise. The Element shakes his head, sighing. "Our kind really can be so arrogant. As you're finding out, we're not everlasting. I've drained more of you than I can count. And we just keep coming back!" He smirks. "It's a game that never ends. Kill Guilt once, and a new one pops up to take her place."

At my silence, the monster cocks his head yet again, examining every inch of me. He doesn't seem to be worried about anyone driving by and seeing my abandoned truck. After a minute, he sighs. "Well, let's get this over with." He reaches down again and digs his finger into my hair. He begins to drag me through the long grass, and I barely feel the pressure on my scalp before the rest of the pain tightens its hold on me, and my world goes dark.

Something soft against my cheek. Something cold. I stir but don't open my eyes. Instinct drives me deeper into the shadows. But then the soft, cold thing on my face leaves and quickly returns in a decidedly less pleasant manner. *Slap*. Frowning, I come awake. My vision is swallowed whole by a pale oval. I swallow to wet my throat. "Where am I?" It comes out as a croak.

"Don't worry. You're safe."

I blink rapidly, and the oval solidifies and becomes a face I would recognize anywhere. "Fear?" He's lying next to me, head propped up on his hand, looking down at me with a gentle light in his eyes. His fingers brush a strand of hair away from my face.

"What—" I start. My memory chooses that moment

to come back in a roaring current and I let out a gasp. My hands clutch at Fear's shirtfront of their own volition. I sit up, head swimming. "We have to get out of here." I look around, and Fear's nearness must be affecting me, because my heart is pounding against my rib cage so strongly that it just might break it. "Nightmare—"

Fear shushes me, smoothing my hair back from my face. "Don't worry about him," he says. "He won't touch you." Dimly, I realize that I'm drenched in sweat.

We're on a bed in a huge, shadowed room. The sheets are twisted around my waist, pearly white. The walls are elegant, painted in a muted shade of lavender. There's one large window to my right, and curtains have been drawn over the glass. It's warm in here, a feeling of safe isolation crowding close. My pulse slows.

The Emotion shifts so that his hip rests against mine, and I lift my chin to look up at him. I didn't think I'd see him again. Where is Rebecca? I study his expression, wondering what this means. Before I can open my mouth and let out a torrent of questions, he tells me, still in that calming tone, "Nightmare just needs to know where your father is."

The words bring the dread back in a rush. Forgetting Rebecca and the rest of the questions clogging my throat, I shift uneasily, struggling to breathe. "M-my father? Tim? Is Nightmare here? Where are we?"

Fear lowers his mouth to mine. It's so startling that every coherent thought flees my mind. Fear doesn't wait for me to recover. His palm brushes over the bare skin of my stomach and his lips are sweeter than anything I've ever tasted. He shifts so that his body is turned toward mine. My back falls against the mattress and I drown in the fire of Fear. His hand becomes a fist in my hair. Different sensations gust through me, and for the first time in my life, I feel that place *down there* tingle. My grip tightens on his shirt and I pull him closer, as if every part of him isn't already fused to me. This is what I wanted that day in the hallway, this is what the illusion stops me from—

Fear pulls away so abruptly that our lips make a smacking sound. "Just tell me where your father is, and I'll go relay it to Nightmare so you won't have to," he says with a drowsy look in his eyes. "Then I'll come right back."

I open my eyes. "W-what?" The haze of lust begins to ebb. My brow furrows and I look up at Fear. His expression is impatient, demanding. After a moment I tell him, my voice a rasp, "I have no idea where Tim is."

He shakes his head, caressing my spine. This time the touch doesn't distract me. "Not Tim. You know I don't mean Tim. Please, Elizabeth, just tell me. Then this will all be over and you and I can be together."

I stare. "No, Fear, I don't know who you mean. Charles kicked Tim out, and he left. Who are you talking about?"

He stares at me three full seconds. I count them. *One. Two. Three.* Then, without warning, the beautiful Emotion screams. Before my eyes, a cut slashes across the mouth that just kissed me with such passion. He rolls out of the bed and hits the floor with a dull *thud*. I scramble to reach his side and Fear rolls, holding his stomach. "He'll kill me if you don't tell him!" he says through his teeth. Then he jerks and lets out another cry of pain. Blood spurts from a fresh wound in his gut, caused by an invisible weapon held by an unseen hand. I try to cover the gushing hole with my shaking fingers, shaking my head dumbly.

"I-I don't—"

"Tell him!"

Tears stream down my cheeks. *"I don't know!"*

Everything freezes. And then Fear is gone. One second he was on the floor, bleeding and dying, and the next Nightmare is standing in his place, looking down at me with an unfathomable glint in his eye.

I recoil, landing on my bottom painfully. Nightmare sighs. "Let's try this another way, shall we?" he asks blandly, straightening his shirt cuffs.

My lip lifts in a snarl and I struggle to my feet so I can launch myself at him, claw his eyes out. But before I can, I lose myself in swirling, cackling shadows once again.

———————

"It's simple. All I want to know is where your father is. Please, *Elizabeth*. For your own sake, tell me."

Another shock jerks through my body, and I cry out.

The light bulb above us flickers some more. It hangs on a wire, which is nailed to a wooden ceiling. No rays of light burst through the cracks, leading me to believe it's night. I can't see much, because my vision is still blurred and it's dark in here, but from what I can tell he's brought me to some sort of shack in the woods. I can hear the trees rustling outside, smell the richness of the earth, barely feel the breeze slipping past. There are no animals, no Elements, no Emotions of any kind. None of them dare tangle with this creature.

Which means no one will be coming to rescue me. I'm on my own.

And this is the ultimate truth. Because here, I've realized, is where I'm going to die.

Nightmare circles the table I'm lying on, sighing. "You'll have to forgive the décor. My powers of persuasion seem to be lost on you." When I still say nothing, he bends so his face is level with mine. His voice is kind as he adds, "You have to give up at some point, my dear. I've already won. You're just prolonging your own pain."

Snot runs down my mouth, and I try to spit it out. It only clogs my throat, and I gag for a few moments. Nightmare's expression twists into one of disgust. His pupils are slits, like a cat's. "Give me your father's location and I'll let you go," he says gently, brushing some of my hair out of my face with his sharp fingernails. He draws little pinpricks of blood. I can't even move away from his touch.

Nightmare toys with my earlobe, then, without warning, he digs his nails into the side of my head. I scream. He leans down and growls through his teeth, "Tell me where he is right now, or I swear I'll put a knife into your stomach so many times that it'll look like Swiss cheese."

His fingers dig even deeper into my skull, and I whimper. My fingers twitch a little—the closest to moving I can get.

When still I don't speak—I've already told him dozens of times I have no idea who he's talking about, because he can't possibly mean Tim—Nightmare straightens, pulling his fingers out. Tears slide down my cheeks, soundless rivers. He circles me some more, his footsteps thunder in the tiny space.

"I don't mean to be so vulgar. Come, now," he coaxes. He's playing nice again. "The fool can't mean that much to you. Honestly, I watched your family all those years ago, waiting for him, and I never saw him once. Doesn't seem like he cared, otherwise he would visit, wouldn't he? Wouldn't he show up now to save you? Is he really worth dying for?" When I still don't reply, he sighs. "Such a slippery fellow. Every time I waited at a birth, he didn't make an appearance. The others know about me now, and this is getting harder."

I barely hear this last part. *He knows something about me*, I think. *He knows who I was before the illusion.* But I don't have any answers for him, and I can't utter a single question. So when I just shake my head, tears running out of the corners of my eyes, Nightmare smiles a little. His teeth glow in the darkness and his anger fills the tiny space. Slowly, his hand reaches for the light switch on the wall next to the door. I open my mouth—try to shout something, *no, please, no*, anything, but I can't—and his finger lightly flips it, as if it's the smallest thing in the world.

Electricity sizzles through my body again, and I rock the table from side to side, coming dangerously close to tipping it as I convulse. Now spit, combined with the snot, runs down the side of my neck, pooling on the surface by my cheek. My fingers grip the edge of the table in desperation and a weird sound manages to escape from my mouth, a half-shriek, half-sob. Nightmare instantly flicks the switch back off when he hears it, and his eyes are alert.

"What?" He strides back to my side, cupping my cheek in a tender way. "What did you say, little one?"

I wait a beat. Then, summoning up what energy I have left, I hack the slimy glob from the back of my throat into his leering face. It hits his eye with a satisfying squirt.

The Element jerks back, freezes for an instant. Slowly, he wipes the mess away with the back of his hand, revealing dangerous, scorching eyes. Lumps of coal with depths of perilous fire. "You really shouldn't have done that," he informs me. He goes to another table at the side of the room, where he has an assortment of knives and tools stacked against the wall.

As he runs his fingers over every one of them, taunting me, Nightmare gives me accounts of all the Emotions and Elements he's hunted, tortured, killed. The manner is very similar to how Fear had once told me his own tales, but there wasn't such malevolence in his eyes.

I can barely see Nightmare now. His elbow moves. When he turns around to face me, I can finally see what he's holding in his hands. One of the shorter knives. He approaches, surprising me when he just plays with the blade, doing a trick by balancing it on the tip of his finger. Instead of more pain or more talk, the Element gets an old-looking chair from the corner of the shack, pulling it across the dirt to the table. He sits on the edge of it, almost primly, and crosses his legs.

"You know, you're the only one that got away," Nightmare says. The light bulb above illuminates the harsh angles and planes of his face. "I'd given up on you. Then, a month ago, I happened to eavesdrop on a couple of Emotions. They were talking about a girl who could withstand their touch and not feel a thing. Curious, I began to investigate. When I got here, I soon stumbled upon you and your dreams. That's when I put two and two together. Your new face didn't throw me—that's easy for one of us to do if we have enough power. But I'll admit, I began to doubt after watching you for a while. My nightly games didn't ruffle you a bit. You were quite dull, even for a human. But just as I was about to leave I saw you save the boy from being run down at that party, and I knew."

Nightmare jerks, and suddenly the tip of the knife is buried in my hand. I try not to scream, try not to give him the satisfaction, but it's impossible. My screech fills every corner of the shack, a deafening sound. Nightmare kisses my temple. His lips are dry.

"You know, besides Landon, you're the longest to ever last in my clutches," he whispers.

Time slows until it stops completely. The world around us disappears. What did he just say?

Landon.

My insides heat up and up until my blood is lava inside of me. There's a loud rushing in my ears, like a wave or a billow of wind before the tornado hits.

Nightmare moves out of my line of vision and I see a flash of his hand as he goes back to his torture instruments. That hand touched Landon. That hand hurt Landon. That hand *killed* Landon. How didn't I see it before? Nightmare is the shadow in the trees, the villain in the siblings' story. My breathing grows shallower, and my chests rises and falls so quickly I feel like a blur. An image of Rebecca's brother fills my mind, a picture of him sitting at that kitchen table, shoving a huge bite of cereal in his mouth.

I want to make Nightmare feel the same pain he caused Landon. I want to watch him die. I want him to regret what he did to that sweet boy who loved his books and his family with limitless, quiet devotion.

Would you like to hear a story?

From the dreams and the flashes, I remember the way he turned the page of a book. Such reverence, such concentration. For the first time, the memory causes pain. Because of this creature, that boy is gone. Ripped away from this world forever. Destined to haunt my dreams.

"I'm going to kill you," I whisper. The words burn up my throat and blood is pooling on the table; the gunshots haven't healed and my hand is screaming. My strength—what pathetic little there is left—is almost gone. I won't last much longer now. No more time to seek out the deeper answers.

Nightmare turns to face me again, a different knife in his hand. This one has a crooked end. "What was that?" he asks, quirking a brow. I fall silent again. He pats my arm. "I do hate to be left out of a joke. Share!"

Even though I still refuse to answer, Nightmare senses he's struck a nerve. "What did I say?" he muses out loud. "Oh, does talking about Landon bother you? Don't worry, dear. He didn't suffer... much. After I was done with his blood—that's where all the power is, you know—I burned him alive. And I hope he keeps on burning in the worst kind of hell there is. Where I'll be sending you shortly here if you don't tell me where I can find your father."

With an image of Landon standing beside me, holding my hand, I look right into Nightmare's empty eyes and rasp, "See you there."

TWENTY-TWO

The Element just throws back his head and laughs, teeth glinting in the feeble light. He bends down, presses his cold lips against my ear once again. "Shall I tell you how he died?" he whispers. "Should I tell you every tiny detail? Oh, he was so much fun, that child."

I honestly don't know how I'm going to kill him. There will be no spontaneous surge of power, no burst of strength. I'm alone and weak and dying. I'll be joining Landon and Maggie soon. Too soon. I close my eyes and remember the way Fear's fingers felt on my cheek.

"You're not listening, little bird. How can I hold your attention? Hmmm. Ah, did you know that as I pulled out his nails one by one, Landon screamed? No, wait, how thoughtless of me. You wouldn't know because you weren't there. He was completely alone when I killed him."

"I...hate you." For the first time, I feel it, that Emotion. It's weak, without the actual being around to force his essence on me. It's a subtle slither through my veins, a memory wrapping itself around me until I'm caught in its mesh. A bitter taste on my tongue.

Nightmare doesn't hear me—my voice is barely a whisper and he's walking to the table again, apparently unsatisfied with just knives. The light bulb above flickers again, and it would be just too fortunate for the power to go out, so I don't even entertain the hope.

The Element comes back, settling down onto the chair again. The legs scrape in the dirt. He rests his chin in his hand, elbow on the table, examining me in a detached way like I'm a fascinating painting.

"You're leaving me no choice," he says, sighing. "Though I don't enjoy getting messy." His other hand appears, an odd clamp positioned between his two fingers as if it's a cigarette. Then he picks up a knife, and I have no idea what he's planning to do. He moves his face closer and the single ray of light bearing down touches his skin. It casts disconcerting shadows over his features. "One last chance. Your father?"

My father? I don't know who that could possibly be, much less where he is. I look away, because Nightmare isn't the last thing I want to see in this lifetime. I close my eyes and think of Fear, of Joshua, of Charles, of Sarah, of Maggie, of Landon and Rebecca. *You all got me to care.*

Just as Nightmare is adjusting his hold on the clamp in one hand and the knife in the other, something hits the wall. Something heavy; we both hear the *thud*. It's just outside the door.

He pauses, pulling his tools away. "I should drain you

now," he mutters, distracted by whatever's outside. Belying his hard tone, his face is caked in frown lines. *Go to the door, see what it is,* I urge him silently. Nightmare's hand lowers as he considers the best course of action, and suddenly the knife is just inches away from my twitching fingers.

I need to act quickly. Nightmare takes one step toward the door. I find one last scrap of stamina within me and jerk over and reach for the blade. I have no choice but to snatch it by the sharp edges, and I gasp as pain licks through my hand. I try to sit up and my body screams at me. The world blurs in a wild blend of colors and heat. My torso is tilted from the movement, and now the upper half of me hangs off the table. I can't get back up, but I clench that knife as tightly as I can, trembling.

"How—" Cursing, Nightmare leaps at me, about to take the knife back from my limp fingers, but then a figure appears briefly on his shoulder, shrieking.

"Get up, get up!" the thing squeaks.

Talking to me, I think distantly, moaning. Something tugs at my hair and I struggle to move again, but then Nightmare is there, digging his nails into my skull to lift my head. He grins in my face.

"What are you going to do with it?" he taunts me. "Go ahead. I'm curious." He releases my hair to wrap his fists around my hand, the one holding the knife, and dares me with his smirk. I struggle to keep my head up. Neither of us moves. I look into the depths of his gaze and see all the darkness he's done and caused. I loathe him and wonder how one individual can go so wrong.

Before I can decide what to do, the tiny being is back, darting between the two of us with another high-pitched shriek. "Get him, get him!" that same tiny voice orders, and suddenly through the haze I recognize it. Moss. Little Moss.

Nightmare is still as a stone, watching the Element appear and reappear at random spots around the shack. He's wearing that odd smile. Just as Moss runs along my other side again, begging me to "stab him, stab him," Nightmare flies over me and the table, arm shooting out, and then Moss is in his grip. "Drop it," he orders me, meaning the knife.

I do, with just a moment of hesitation. But even when it falls to the floor with a woeful *clink*, Nightmare doesn't let go of Moss. With an intense expression, he closes his fist and begins to squeeze, squeeze, squeeze. She's probably not worth draining.

A million images and memories pound into me like the bullets in my back, drawing blood and tides of Emotion despite the illusion that's still miraculously intact. Rebecca was wrong—even danger such as this, facing death itself and choking on a sensation of feeling, hasn't broken it. I sense the power hanging on by a thread. Most of the wall has crumbled.

I remember Landon and the way he squinted at words on a page. *She'll be back. She always comes back.*

Rebecca and her passionate abandon as her skirt twisted around her thighs. *Please come back!*

Their mother and her constant, wrinkled worry. *No more dancing.*

I see Maggie and her sweet smile. *Since you can't go to the ocean, I thought I would bring it to you.*

It wasn't supposed to end like this.

I witness Sarah and her pain, scrubbing vigorously at the kitchen sink. *When someone is pretending to be something, or hiding who they are or what they believe, they're really more ... protecting themselves.*

I'd like to think that it's never too late to change the way things are.

I invoke Joshua's image. Frustrating, stubborn, kind, enduring, irrevocable Joshua. So many words, so many looks, just a few unrequited touches. *How many of them have secrets they don't want the world to know? How many of them wear masks everywhere they go? We're anything but typical.*

What more can there be?

And then there's Fear. His impossibility, his adoration, his infuriating ways. His kisses, his persistence, his sacrifice. *At least I know that if you can't feel anything for me, you can't feel anything for him, either.*

Why are you the only one who can't let go?

I should have—

"Elizabeth!"

The name jars me, and I crane my neck to find my little friend. Moss is gasping, her tiny fists pounding on Nightmare's finger. She grapples and keeps making weak, frantic sounds. Her big eyes fasten on my face. *Help me,* she mouths. Already she's fading. Her inner light sputters as her life drains.

I can't do anything but watch. The edge of the table digs into my stomach as I observe Moss's time slipping away. Her gaze meets mine one last time, and she reaches out with her hand, flailing for me. At just the right moment, Nightmare shifts closer—he's laughing, riveted on Moss's face—and her fingers land to rest on my ear.

There's a surge of power, and suddenly I can move. Gasping, I shoot up to a sitting position, and Nightmare's head whips around. He hisses in shock. Before he can react, I reach out and shove him with everything I have.

The monster flies back and crashes against the table of weapons and toys with a loud shattering sound. I sway for a moment before I fall. My head bounces painfully on the edge of the chair, but half of me remains on the table.

"Elizabeth..." Moss gasps, warning me. I can't see her, but I can hear her wheezing and swallowing heaps of air somewhere.

Nightmare is already stirring, muttering under his breath. He braces himself against the wall, swiveling around to find me with his eyes. They speak murder.

Just a little more strength. That's all I need to end this.

Nightmare stumbles to his feet again, blood running down the side of his face from a cut on his temple. The sight of it gives me a fresh surge of resolution; he's not indestructible. I can kill him—I can survive this. He glares at me through the crimson stream and wipes it away with the back of his hand. "You're going to die slowly," he promises in a hiss, stalking back toward the table.

"Moss," I rasp, my eyes rolling painfully as I search the room for her. "Moss!" I need her to give me power again. But I can't find her. Nightmare laughs at me, drawing even nearer. He kicks the chair out of the way.

"You didn't burn Landon," I say in a wild attempt to

gain more time. I don't know why this is what I choose to say, but it feels so important.

Nightmare pauses and does his head-cocking thing again. "And why would you say that?" He sounds genuinely interested. He's stopped smiling, and I don't think he's even aware of it.

I swallow. Pause. Purse my lips. Then, in a voice that shakes like a frightened child's, I tell him, "Because someone found his body."

The paintings, the dreams, the memories. All of it led to this. I may not remember a life before being Elizabeth, I may not recall the illusion or who I was, but I do remember one moment like it's my own—when Rebecca cradled her brother in her arms, screaming over his lifeless body. Never again would she hear his laugh. Never again would he say her name. Never again would they dance in the woods.

Nightmare is speaking, but his voice is a senseless hum, the shack and my own pain a blur.

Because now, finally, I'm remembering.

Rebecca wakes up in her tiny room, and the first thing she notices is the silence. She has no idea how she knows, but something is wrong. There's a taste on her tongue—something bitter and sweet, like salt and strawberries.

Fear.

She whips the blankets aside, her feet touching the chilled floor. She casts about for some pants and settles on a wrinkled pair of jeans tossed carelessly over a chair. Yanking them on, Rebecca hurries out the door. The house is so small that she knows in an instant she's alone. The kitchen is dark, the bedroom doors all open and mournful. Where are Mom and Landon?

She whirls and runs to the front door, bare feet slapping against the tiles. Just as the girl is reaching for the knob, though, Fear bursts into the space between her and the outside. She screams, leaping back.

"Rebecca, you can't go out there." Looking panicked, Fear grabs her wrists and stops her when she recovers and grabs for the knob again.

"I have to," she says frantically, trying to shove him out of the way. He flattens his back to the door. Uttering a half-terrified, half-infuriated cry, Rebecca wrenches herself free of his hold.

"Wait—" Fear attempts to seize her shoulders, but she moves more quickly this time. "Rebecca, your brother—"

"Leave me alone!" she screeches up at him. "You've answered your summons! We're done!"

Hurt flashes across his beautiful face, but she doesn't care. There's a window in her room that she can fit through, so Rebecca turns her back to him and hurries away, her mind filled with her mother and Landon. Fear appears at her side again. "You can't help Landon!" he insists shakily. "But your mother is alive, so please, let me take you away from here." She gives him a look of loathing as his words roll off of her like dew on a leaf. Undeterred, Fear grabs her arm and shoves her against a wall. "You don't understand, Rebecca. I can't answer Landon's summons because—"

Taking him off guard, the girl brings a knee up and slams it in the tenderest of places. Bending, Fear wheezes. As soon as his cool hands are gone she rushes away once again. This time he lets her go.

Scrambling through the window, Rebecca falls to the ground and glances around wildly. It's a cloudy morning, and there's no sign of Mom in the garden or Landon in the yard with one of his books. The ocean roars, oblivious to her world cracking. Something urges her toward the woods. She doesn't question the instinct. Rebecca sprints through the trees, full speed. Her terror is so strong that it's a choking sensation. For the first time in her life she can't breathe.

"Landon! Mom!" She starts screaming their names, over and over. Her shirt snags on something and she hears it tear, doesn't pay it any mind. She senses Emotions and Elements running from this place as quickly as they can. Why? Why? She's too frantic to pause and find out.

The girl trips over something. Something solid and warm. She sprawls on the ground, getting a mouthful of dirt. She hacks, shuddering. After a moment, she struggles back up to her feet, glancing back to see what tripped her.

The world stops spinning.

The trees darken.

Her veins pound.

Landon lies on his back, his beautiful eyes staring up at the sky. Glassy. His blood sinks into the soil around him. His body, his achingly familiar body... it's ruined. She stares down at him, and abruptly she feels a laugh bubbling up inside of her. Vicious Fear and his games. How could anyone make an illusion this cruel? She kneels down beside this fake boy, poking him. *"This isn't funny, Fear!"* she calls out, clutching her middle as hysterics overtake her. There's a loud ringing in her ears.

A buzzing overhead. A fly lands on Landon's blood-flecked arm.

For some reason, it's the sight of the fly that breaks her.

No, no, no, no. Screaming, Rebecca crawls closer to him, pulling his head onto her lap. She rocks Landon back and forth, sobbing. Because she can't deny it now. He's dead. She starts to whimper. Back and forth, back and forth. "No. Come back, please, please," she begs, a broken whisper. His blood soaks her jeans. "Landon..."

He doesn't answer.

Her soul shatters, and her heart stops beating. She clutches his face until her knuckles turn white. "Wake up, Landon. Wake up now!" She starts to pound his chest furiously. It's the first time she's ever struck him. Realizing this, Rebecca stops. She holds his cold body close again, shaking her head.

Her power leaks out, affecting the land, and the skies open up and start to sob with her. Her hair plasters to her head and her clothes grow heavy with water. They sit there together in the mud, the girl and her brother. Trembling, she starts to tell him a story. She bends over him to shield him from the wetness, and her hair trails through the mud.

"They all lived happily ever after..." Rebecca says in his ear, kissing his cheek. His eyes are closed now—she must have shut them at some point. Rain falls harder now, soaking her to the skin, washing all the blood away.

Thunder shakes the ground, but she hardly notices.

"We need to go."

The voice makes her jump, and Rebecca looks up dully. "Oh. It's you," she mumbles incoherently, then puts all her attention back into rocking Landon.

The woman kneels beside Rebecca, tugs at her arm. Her gray eyes are sharp and wary. "It's not safe here," she adds in a low voice. "We need to—"

"Leave me alone!" The scream echoes, becoming lyrics to the song of the storm. Rebecca shakes. A moment later, however, she's returned to the mindless grief. "You can't leave me all alone. Please, please, please, come back . . . "

The woman apparently decides to forgo asking and seizes Rebecca's arm. The girl hisses, swiping at her as if she's a wild animal. Jerking back, the woman lashes out. The blow hits Rebecca in the head, and she slumps. Swearing under her breath, the woman gathers Rebecca up in her arms. She's not much bigger than the girl; she stumbles back a step. The rain continues to come down in torrents. The woman sloshes through the mud toward the cover of the trees. She leaves Landon there, bleeding, rotting, dead. It's too late for him. Her eyes prickle but she doesn't look back.

Rebecca stirs. "W-where's Mom?" she asks bleakly, head lolling in the crook of her rescuer's elbow.

"She's gone. I think . . . I think your father took her. I could feel his essence in the air. You were probably too distracted to tell the difference between yours and his. By the time I realized what was happening and went to warn you all, the house was empty. I heard you screaming in the woods."

The words don't seem to register with Rebecca. "Where's Mom?" she asks again. Her companion lets it go unanswered this time, breathing hard. When she trips over a root she curses, setting Rebecca down.

"You're going to run," she orders her. "If you don't, I'll hit you again. Harder."

"Oh, Rebecca! Rebecca James!" The playful, unfamiliar voice comes from behind.

The woman's eyes widen in panic and she yanks at Rebecca's arm so hard that it might pop out of the socket. Rebecca just stares ahead, empty.

"Where's Mom?" she murmurs yet again.

"Rebecca! I have some questions for you, if you'll spare a second!" that male voice calls.

The woman shudders in terror. She glances down at Rebecca with a manic light in her eyes, as if she's thinking about slapping her. Reason isn't working, so she stoops again, slips the girl's arm around her neck, and straightens, trying to drag her soundlessly through the trees. Nightmare is close by; the power rolls off of his skin.

The woman's fear is so strong that Fear actually comes, appearing right in her path. Drawing up short at the sight of him, the woman smothers her gasp just in time, chest heaving. Fear assesses the situation in an instant. "Take her somewhere safe. I'll distract him," he says quietly, touching the woman's back. His gaze is focused on the way she came. She doesn't protest. She nods sharply and continues to pull Rebecca along. She knows the girl's car is parked back at the house, a mile away, so she heads in that direction. Sweat makes her shirt stick to her torso.

They reach the tree line twenty minutes later. Without going out of the way to get clothes or food from the house, the woman bundles Rebecca into the ancient Cadillac and goes. She doesn't look back, but when she senses Nightmare near, her pulse picks up speed again. He doesn't appear. The only destination she has in mind is far, far away. They bump onto the highway and climb up to seventy miles an hour.

They spend hours on the road. Five. Eleven. Nineteen. Twenty-six. They stop only for gas and bathroom breaks. Blearily the woman finds a half-full bottle of Gatorade and a bag of Doritos in the glove compartment. The car becomes hot and cramped, but neither really notices. Rebecca might as well be a corpse. She doesn't move, speak, eat, or drink. She stares out the window at the passing scenery, not really seeing any of it. Rather than letting her worry consume her, the woman concentrates on the run. Getting as far away from the Element as fast as possible, so that he can no longer sense them.

It's somewhere in Wisconsin, at twilight, that she finally steps on the brake, frowning. "What's going on?" she mutters.

There's a red pickup truck in the middle of the road, one door wide open, the headlights still illuminating the night. The driver isn't behind the wheel; he's kneeling next to something on the blacktop, his movements jerky and frantic. CPR. Rebecca and the woman watch, both realizing at some point that the figure lying there prone is a person. A little girl. Her yellow hair splays around her head, a bittersweet halo.

After a few seconds the woman tears her gaze away from the tragedy, shifting gears to pull around them. "We need to keep moving," she mutters. "He's still—"

"No, don't." It's the first time Rebecca has spoken since they fled from her home. The woman pauses with her hand poised

over the gearshift. The look in Rebecca's eyes halts the question in her throat. Rebecca slowly turns from the chaos of the accident, staring at her companion with an expression of desperation. "I have an idea," she whispers, so quietly that the woman has to strain to hear.

The woman frowns. The truck driver is sobbing into his cell phone, hysteria thick in the air. "What do you—" She starts, then breaks off with an impatient hiss. "Rebecca, we don't have time for this! If he gets too close, he'll be able to sense you. Please, can't you just—"

"I have an idea," Rebecca repeats, like some broken toy.

The woman grits her teeth. "Fine. What's your idea, Rebecca?"

An odd smile curves the girl's lips and she continues to stare at the crying driver, the too-silent child. Both of them can feel Death coming. Closer, closer. Nervous, the woman turns away. Rebecca watches. She doesn't say a word as Death takes the little girl's soul, but part of her wants to call the Element back, beg for his touch. Something keeps her silent. And then all that's left is a shell, a half-delirious driver, and the endless possibilities.

Wordlessly, Rebecca reaches out and touches the woman's wrist.

The woman looks at the body on the road and back at Rebecca. Understanding dawns; she realizes what her charge is suggesting. Her expression twists into a combination of instant revulsion and reluctant speculation. Rebecca just looks at her with a sort of flat pleading. Even with the unique blood running through her veins, she has smudges under her eyes that *have never been there before. She looks white and too thin. The woman is tired, too. Tired from the running, tired of holding her form in one place for so long when it's in her nature to go from place to place, summons to summons. If something doesn't change, there won't be an end to any of it.*

Three minutes tick by. Rebecca counts the seconds. In the distance, they can hear the wail of a siren. No more time to decide.

The woman heaves a sigh, her shoulders slumping. She faces Rebecca. "Okay," she says softly.

Rebecca's relief is so palpable it's almost overwhelming. "Okay?" she echoes.

"Okay." The woman looks at the driver, steeling herself. He's the first loose end to tie up. Then there's the body to hide. She rolls up her sleeves and gets out of the car. She approaches the man, kneels in front of him, and says something softly. She rests her hands on his shoulders. His eyes glaze over and he nods. He stands. As he lumbers back to his vehicle, the woman turns her attention to the little body still lying in the middle of the road.

Rebecca waits where she is, holding her knees in an effort to make herself small. It's the only way to keep calm when there's a moment to think. She watches the clock on the dashboard to distract herself. Six minutes... seven... ten...

"Rebecca." The woman returns. She stands by the passenger window, gripping the car door with white knuckles. The power has already taken a toll on her; her countenance is gray and lined. Rebecca nods, unbuckling the seat belt, and follows the woman off the road, into the ditch.

Rebecca waits until they're facing each other to say, "I want you to make a block so none of the Emotions can touch me."

The woman hesitates. A crow swoops overhead. "First, I'm not sure I'm capable of doing that, and second, won't it make the humans suspicious? It'll complicate—"

"Just try it, okay?"

Pursing her lips, her companion nods. "You will forget every-thing," she agrees. She holds out her hand, preparing for the big-gest illusion of all. "Too bad you won't be there on the other side to restore me," she adds. There's a note of uncertainty in her voice. Not the case with Rebecca. She stands there, waiting, thrum-ming for the moment when she'll open her eyes and not remem-ber a thing, not feel a thing. This constant shooting pain in her chest will be gone, the memory of blood on her hands, gone. Landon... Landon... No. Rebecca won't think about it. Her insides twist and her fists clench at her sides. "Do it," she breathes, eyes burning with a manic need.

But the woman can't leave it at that. "I'll give you ten years. The Element will be off your trail by then."

"Fifteen," Rebecca counters, need coiling like a snake within her.

The ambulance is almost there. Time for arguing is over. "Fine," the woman replies shortly. Then, "I'm not going to say goodbye." She closes her eyes. The man is sitting in his truck now, still blinking in dazed confusion, and the body is gone, hidden forever. Too late to go back now, and Nightmare will still be look-ing. This really is the best solution, the woman tells herself. She takes a breath, then twitches as her power flows toward Rebecca James.

The girl screams as it latches onto her. It hurts, it hurts, it hurts! She drops to her knees. It's like a fire licking over every inch of her skin. She tries to dig her fingers into the tar and her nails tear away, bleed. A vein bulges from the woman's forehead as she concentrates, and there's pity in her eyes. But the woman keeps her hand over the writhing girl. Feature by feature, piece by piece, the things that make Rebecca are wiped away. Brown curls turn to straight blond tresses. Long slender fingers shorten to a chubby child's. Elegant legs become knobby knees. The woman focuses on the block, now that the illusion is complete. Nothingness. She says it over and over again in her head. Nothing. Rebecca feels nothing.

And then it's done.

Spent, the woman sags against a tree. She struggles for breath. The ambulance is coming over the hill now, lights flashing. Before they can spot her and her car, she leaves the girl in the ditch, hating herself, hating Rebecca for asking her to do it. But she comforts herself by saying that it was the smartest thing to do. A necessity.

She's driving away when it happens. When it begins. She doesn't see it. But she feels it, feels the knowledge sealing itself inside her, not to be spoken of for fifteen years.

Elizabeth Caldwell opens her eyes.

"Elizabeth," peeps in my ear. "Wake up, wake up! Please, please!"

My eyes flutter open. The illusion trembles, so close to being broken.

Moss has given me strength again. I can feel it whizzing through my muscles, brightness illuminating me from the inside. I see movement out of the corner of my eye, remember the Element, where I am. Nightmare dives at me, the knife I'd dropped catching the light in his hand. Reacting swiftly, I roll off the table, and the blade clatters behind me.

I scramble toward the door on all fours, panting, scraping my knees and the palms of my hands. Nightmare shoves the table out of his path—it lands against another wall and shatters a hole through it—and dives for me again. I don't move fast enough, and his hand encircles my ankle. I scream and he laughs, yanking me back toward him. I jerk my leg, startling him, but the knife buries itself deep in my calf. I scream again, and the sound pierces the air so sharply that Moss covers her ears. Nightmare groans at the sound, wincing as he leans away. That's when I see it. The smaller knife from earlier, the one he'd used to stab my hand, abandoned in the corner. Just inches away from my fingers.

It's quick. It's so quick that it seems surreal. I grab and raise the small knife, then shove it into the Element's left eye without thinking.

I'll never forget his cry. Half-man, half-beast, so frightening that my heart twists inside of me. He recoils, his back slamming into the wall closest to us. Dirt showers down on our heads. The blow doesn't kill him instantly, as I'd hoped it would, so while he's weakened and distracted, I yank the other knife out of my leg. Ignoring the shooting pain, I reach forward again, my hands slick with blood, and slit Nightmare's throat.

He stares at me for an eternity. He touches the cut, and when he pulls his hand away he looks at the vibrant, scarlet blood on his fingers as if he can't believe it. Then he falls. Doesn't get back up again.

Once I'm certain he's dead, I join him in darkness. For once there are no dreams. Just the peace of surrendering to oblivion.

TWENTY-THREE

I wake up on the ground. Above, the trees hover, shielding me from the bright glow of the moon like a protective mother. Nighttime. There's only a portion of the sky visible, but somehow the fact that the stars have come out is comforting. A cool breeze stirs my sweat-drenched hair.

Remaining on my back, I look around. I'm in some kind of clearing, in woods I don't recognize. It takes me a moment, but when I do remember everything that's just happened, I wish I hadn't. Landon, knives, Moss, Rebecca, the illusion, the woman who saved me, Nightmare—it all comes back. But the shack is nowhere to be seen. The Element is gone, dead, and I'm alone.

The same instant I realize this, I also comprehend that the pain is gone. All my cuts, bruises, the bullet holes in my back, the stab wounds in my calf and hand—they're healed.

Is this because of the woman I'd been calling Rebecca? Because of Moss? Or just ... me?

Now that I've thought of her, she actually appears, crouching beside me. For the first time, she isn't hidden in layers of clothing. I recognize her face from the memory, and her hair as well—long and straight, the color of leaves after Summer has left. She's dressed simply, in jeans and a long-sleeved green shirt. On her feet she's wearing stylish, heeled boots. There are lines on her face that indicates she's not as young as I'd originally assumed, though her eyes are bright and sharp.

I lean up on my elbows, my lips trembling as I relive the whole ordeal. The woman brushes my hair off my shoulder, a tender, unusual gesture for her. We sit there like that, quiet. I should know her. Our pasts are intertwined. She saved my life. But even having possession of the truth doesn't make me feel connected to any of it.

"Looks like he found me after all," I finally murmur. Because of Nightmare, I've been alone for thirteen years, empty and surrounded by a web of lies.

She hops to her feet. "I'm sorry you went through all this," she says abruptly. And I know she means it. She never intended for any of this to happen. For a few more minutes, we stay there in comfortable silence, sharing the overwhelming knowledge that it's over. It's all over. There are more questions I'd like to ask her, of course, so many more. For now, though, I let us simply exist.

Then the woman ruins the moment by saying, "But I can't *believe* that none of it broke the fucking illusion. You still look like Elizabeth, and I still can't talk about anything."

Sighing, I think of the day Landon died. The pain of remembering isn't quite as strong now as it was in the shack; the illusion is attempting to realign, to hold on. I find myself falling back to my old ways, thinking of the facts. And they're simple: *I* am Rebecca. Landon was *my* brother… my twin. Fear loved *me. I* lived in that house by the ocean. *I* am something more than mortal. And to run from Nightmare—to deal with my twin's death—I asked this woman to do the impossible: make me human.

The thought of my family urges me to ask one question. "So you can't tell me where Rebecca's—" I stop, correct myself. "Where my mother is? She wasn't killed; I know that much." Moss appears on my shoulder, humming, and I touch her cheek. She giggles.

The woman—I still don't know what Emotion or Element she is—just shakes her head.

I purse my lips, wishing I didn't have to accept this. And I still don't even know what I am. *Later,* something says inside my head. *Later.* I settle back on my elbows, deliberately emptying my mind. "So what now?" I murmur.

Still standing, my companion looks up at the sky, and I follow her gaze. The stars stare back down at us—cold, timeless rocks. They make me think of Fear, and a pang of longing consumes me.

After a moment, she just shrugs. "Now, you live."

"Wake up. We're almost there."

The woman's profile swims into view. It's still night, so the moon's shadows hide her features, but I recognize the slope of her lip, the lines of her chin and jaw. I blink up at her, my cheek resting on a cracked leather seat. Is this one of the dreams?

When the woman hisses impatiently and reaches over to smack my cheek, I know it's no illusion. The hours before drift back: we're in her car, on our way back to Edson. We'd been over eighty miles away, she told me.

I sit up in the passenger seat and my body protests. "Almost where?" I ask. A road sign flashes by, bright green: *10th Avenue*. "This isn't where I live ... what's wrong?" I've suddenly noticed how fast she's going; the speedometer is inching past seventy. As if we have somewhere we need to be. As if there's not much time. But isn't the danger, everything we've been running from, gone? The answer occurs to me before she has a chance to answer. *Fear*.

"Where is he?" I ask next. There's no panic or worry, just a need to get to him. The windows are rolled down, and the air is curiously warm now, the stillness disrupted by gunshots rather than the moans of the lonely wind. Hunting season. I wonder if Winter knows the threat is gone, that the way is safe for her.

This leads me to thoughts of Nightmare, and I go rigid, clenching my jaw so hard it hurts.

The woman still doesn't answer. She stares out at the expanse of black sky. Remembering that she'd once said Fear was too injured to take far, I'd guess that we're heading toward the outskirts of town. For once, I don't pepper her with endless questions.

I've never been on these back roads, and the headlights

sweep past foreign trees and unknown houses. It isn't until we pass an old windmill that I know where we are. The Halversons' place. It's a farm that's been abandoned for years. Presumably a huge family used to live there and they all died from some sort of plague. Kids come out here on Halloween and dare each other to go inside for five minutes. It's a rickety house with gray paint, a drooping wraparound porch, and falling shutters.

The woman shifts into park and kills the engine. Still silent, she swings out of the car. I follow. The grass is long and uncut all the way up to the front door, and the hinges moan as she pulls it open. Inside, the air is musty and thick with dust. This was probably the only place she could bring Fear without being noticed. Tense, I follow her through a grimy kitchen and an empty, moonlit living room. There's a single table in the dining room, and as soon as we round the corner I draw up short.

There … there lies the Emotion who's taunted and tormented and loved me almost my entire life. Both my lives. The white moonlight slants down on him, making him glow, his flawlessness more pronounced. Even now, he's beautiful. But his eyes, usually so sharp and vibrant, are closed. His chest is barely rising and falling, and his skin glistens with sweat. I've never seen Fear sweat before. My own breathing grows uneven.

"He's dying," I observe quietly, and it's as if his wound is mine, because my stomach feels like a knife has been thrust into it. He tried to save me. This happened to him because of his unhealthy obsession with me. *Stop saying that,* my mental voice snaps. *It wasn't obsession.* And now I have to admit that the voice is right—it was something so much more. And I should have done more to discourage him. I knew what happened to those around me. Even without the knowledge I have now, I knew.

I drown in a battle of detachment. And it's while I'm standing there staring down at him that it occurs to me: this is Fear's consequence for interfering the day Tim attacked me in the barn.

"You're going to help him," the woman says matter-of-factly, interrupting my thoughts.

I look at her, trembling. "What can I possibly—"

She tries to snatch my hand and I jerk back, a reflex. She rolls her eyes, letting out an annoyed breath. "I just need you to touch him," she growls. "Put your damn palm on his forehead and keep it there until I tell you otherwise. Think you can do that?"

I do it without an instant more of protest. He's freezing to the touch, even colder than usual. We wait, and it's hard to keep still. Ten seconds. Twenty. Nothing happens. I don't know what I expected, but something inside of me sinks. Fear is slipping away. *No. No.* This can't happen. He isn't mine anymore, and I've pushed him away for so long, and he loves someone that doesn't exist, but all of that is so insignificant now. My grip tightens so much that if he were conscious, it would hurt. I close my eyes and strive to cope with the knot inside me.

"Damn it," the woman says through her teeth. "I thought the illusion had faded enough that…" She stops mid-sentence, and I immediately see why. Before our very eyes, the wound in Fear's stomach is folding, drying, closing, until the skin is smooth and unblemished. My throat clogs with more questions, but instead of voicing them, I kneel so I'm right by Fear's head. With trembling fingers, I smooth his hair back, and it occurs to me that this is the first time I've actually touched it in this life. It's just as silky as I imagined it would be.

The woman watches for a moment. Then she rests her own hand on my shoulder. "He'll be fine," she tells me. "I'll take you back, if you want. Or I could make up a bed for you here."

"No," I respond instantly. "I don't want to stay here." There's really nothing to go back to, but I find myself leaving Fear's side and following the woman back to the car. The door hinges shriek as we leave, and clouds of white swirl through the air with each exhale. The woman doesn't ask any questions as we get back into the car—which she probably stole, now that I think about it, since she has no need for one when I'm not around.

The night whizzes past once again, less urgent this time. Pressing my forehead to the glass, I close my eyes and try not to think about Fear. But it's impossible not to. I know why I don't want to be there when he wakes up; I can't get those images of him and Rebecca out of my head. Knowing that he once loved me—someone that I destroyed—I can't face him. I keep picturing those moments of passion, the way Rebecca and Fear touched. Gone. Fear's been wandering the earth in pain just as long as I have. He found Elizabeth and loved again. And again, I ripped that love away from him. His pain, his struggles, his torment. All my fault. I can't pinpoint the sensation that makes my chest hurt…or maybe I'm not willing to explore it. Not right now.

Once again the woman and I are silent in the car. The white lines on the road shoot by. It isn't until we're back in Tim's driveway, back at the house that isn't really mine, that she speaks. The engine idles as she shifts gears again, and the leather seat creaks when she twists to face me.

"I want to tell you something." She hesitates, and stillness fills the space between us. "About the illusion," she asserts.

I angle toward her, too. "Okay."

The woman taps her knee with her finger. "When it breaks…it's going to hurt. A lot. Not just physically."

"Well." I take this in. "Thank you for letting—"

"That's not what I want to tell you," she snaps. "I should have told you this the day you asked me to do the illusion…I just want you to know that you're strong. Okay? You didn't need the illusion to overcome w-what you'd g-gone through." She clenches the steering wheel at this, and I know she's struggling to speak past the power that not only affects me but both of us. She breathes deeply, then continues. "I only did it because we needed to get Nightmare off your trail. And it did, for years. So I don't regret doing it. But you didn't need the illusion to survive…to survive what you did. Do you understand me?" The power stops her from giving me details, and there's still a portion of the illusion standing, so I don't understand, not completely. But I nod. The woman nods, as well. "Good," she says. "Good night."

That's my cue to go. Her polite way of telling me to get out. She's never been polite before, so I quickly comply. The house is dark, but Charles's car is in the driveway, so I know he's home.

Preparing myself for the scene ahead, I watch the woman drive away into the night, back to Fear. And I have a feeling that when I see her again, things are going to be very, very different.

Even though it felt like a decade, I was only in the woods for two days. My not-brother yelled at me when I got home, and it wasn't horrible for his first lecture. When he was done, his face was as red as Tim's. But the menace was missing. Instead of looking furious, he just looked ... weary. He'd returned to this house for me, altered his life for me, and this is how I repaid him. But the guilt I should have felt was absent, as the illusion taunted me with its resoluteness.

Three more days have gone by. I can't bring myself to go back to school. My thoughts are consumed by my real family and the few glimpses of my old life that I've been given. No, that I've fought for. Why? Why fight for something I tried so hard to forget? That was what I was doing, throughout all of this. Fighting. Looking for the truth. Seeking to find a place where I belonged. In this way, I'm so human. I've observed it many times, thought it on countless occasions: give a person what they want, and it turns out it's not what they wanted after all.

As the hours pass, I lie in the bed I've slept in for thirteen years. It feels strange now. Like I'm burying myself in someone else's sheets. They smell like me, Sarah picked them out for me, but the ghost of what should have been fills this room like a choking perfume. The mural looms closer and closer and Landon's prone form swallows my attention whole, no matter how much I try to concentrate on something else.

Charles doesn't hover. No matter how much he's changed, he was never good at that kind of thing. He loses himself in the car he's invested so much hope in, and continues his shifts at Fowler's. I've seen him poring over bills, though, Worry pressing close. I really didn't give Charles enough credit over the years—he's just as extraordinary as Maggie.

Maggie.

I try not to think about her. The memory of her pallid face causes an uncomfortable sensation in the pit of my stomach. Every time my guard slips and she slides past, one word pounds at the inside of my skull: *Should.* I should have tried breaking the illusion sooner. I should have been able to lay my hands on her and heal her, as I had with Fear. I should have been more for her. If I hadn't been so weak, so desperate to cling to logic and escape the past, her death could have been prevented.

It's a mantra: *Don't think about her.*

Finally, though, one thing drags me from that bed, from that room, from the pieces that are me and someone else. And that thing is Joshua Hayes. Charles must have told him I'm back, because he calls the house relentlessly. Whenever Charles tiptoes through the doorway—as if disturbing me will set off some sort of grenade—I pretend to be asleep. But Joshua is there, lodged in my head. Past all the questions and torment about Landon, our mother, what I am, why Fear hasn't come to see me now that he's better, Joshua is there. Waiting. *I saw you.* The words replay over and over with all the tenacity of a blaring radio. I pay my dues, and I owe him. He was nothing but kind to me. The only problem is that he wants. Wants Elizabeth, who's fragmented and fading. Wants a future, which I can no longer imagine. Wants more, which I just can't give. Because so much else stands in the way, and it isn't just the illusion.

So, as I shower and dress for battle, the decision is easy: I'm going to lie. I feel nothing, for him or for anyone. Once he believes me, sees that I'm a monster, he'll let me go. Quite easily, I imagine.

My face void of all expression, I head outside. My truck is parked by the barn. Charles must have had it towed back from wherever Nightmare abandoned it.

As it always does, the thought of the Element sends a jarring shiver down my spine. But Fear doesn't come—I can't help but notice. No, I won't let myself wonder. I'm becoming an expert at avoidance, and there's no reason to abandon the skill now.

I climb into the truck, find the keys on the dashboard, and go.

I haven't been to the Hayes' farm since Joshua's mom died. Everything looks like it's falling into disrepair. The roof on the house is sagging, and whatever color paint it had is long gone. The fence alongside me is missing sections and the driveway is full of potholes. And the crops … the beans aren't right. I can tell, even when looking at the field from yards away. They should have been harvested by now. The plants are yellow, half-withered, low to the ground. Joshua wasn't exaggerating when he voiced concern; this place is slipping away.

Even when the sound of my truck rumbles through the air, no one emerges from the house or the fields. Killing the engine, I get out and wander.

I'm not surprised to find Joshua in his barn. Like me, he seems to takes solace in the quiet there. He's shoveling manure out of a stall and into a wheelbarrow, the muscles in his arms standing out as he works quickly, intent only on this. I watch from the doorway. I wait. It doesn't take him long to notice me.

He stares like I'm a mirage. Disbelief stands beside him—the sight of the Emotion confirms that Nightmare is dead, and I feel the faintest sense of relief. Disbelief nods in greeting; he's a tall, skinny being with pinched lips and a skeptical light in his eyes.

"Elizabeth?" Joshua says in a whisper. When I just stand there, shifting from foot to foot, his expression breaks into a smile, his relief so evident it causes a twinge in my chest. So many Emotions. I think of how peaceful it is for those without the ability to see it all.

Then, as quickly as he was happy to see me, Joshua becomes furious. "Where the hell have you been?" he shouts, dropping his shovel. Two quick steps, and then he reaches out and shakes me. "Why haven't you called me back? You were gone for, like, two days! Charles went out of his mind! And then when we found your truck abandoned on the side of the road, we thought you ran away or had even been kidnapped. The sheriff—"

"I'm sorry," I say tonelessly. "I'm fine. I only came back to tell you goodbye."

Joshua's arms drop to his sides like I'm diseased. "What?" he says hoarsely.

I just shrug, as if I don't care. Wrong move. Joshua clenches his jaw and grabs me again. "Oh hell no," he snaps. "You're not going to be this stupid. I won't let you. You're seventeen, and you have nowhere to go. If you won't think of me, think of your brother. Charles cares about you—"

He's not understanding me. This goodbye isn't because I'm leaving; it's because I'm already gone. I have to cut this bond, now. "I'm one of them," I say, sharp now. Joshua jerks back. I don't give him time to react. "I'm not human," I say. "I'm not like you. You're weak, and this would never work, not that I even want it to."

Joshua flinches as if I've slapped him and his expression is hurt, still angry. I try not to cringe. His jaw works some more, and he just stares at me for what seems like hours.

Suddenly Joshua's gaze narrows and he raises his brows in challenge. "Really?" he snaps back. "So you're just a heartless bitch, right? That's the story you're sticking to? Okay then. Let me hold you while you remember everything we've been through, and then look me in the eye and tell me that again."

I'm shaking my head before he's even finished. "It doesn't matter, Joshua. I told you—"

"Look, I don't care about what you are, okay? *I don't care.* It's *who* you are that I fell in love with." He stops, red spreading up his neck and face. He didn't mean to say it, but it's too late; the words are already out, floating in the air between us. He thinks he speaks the truth, but I know better.

"I'm no one, Joshua. You can't love me any more than you can love a statue."

"Bullshit."

I shake my head again. "I've tried. For years, I tried to pretend. I've hunted for the truth. I've endured more than one person should in a lifetime. But it's all hopeless. I am nothing; I feel nothing." *You're still pretending,* that voice in my head says, snide. An image of Fear assaults me, his crinkled eyes, the way that coat constantly flapped against his boots. The tender way he ran his fingers down my spine in the woods that night, so long ago…

"No. There's always a solution," Joshua says doggedly, filled with unshakable determination. "You should know that more than anyone. A month ago, I didn't know that anything nonhuman, or from another world—any of it— existed. But it does. This incredible power, these creatures that aren't bound by human rules or boundaries—"

"It's not as grand as you seem to think."

"—and no one knows about it. Just because we're so shallow-minded that we can't accept the idea there's something more."

It's easy to guess where his thoughts are heading. "Even

if you'd known about the other plane years before now, you couldn't have saved your mother," I say gently. "One of the few rules my kind has is not to interfere in the lives of mortals, other than to perform our purpose."

"You interfered," he counters.

He knows I'm rejecting him. He sees right through the lies. There's nothing I can do to ease his pain. "I disobeyed," I say, taking a step back. "I was...sad and stupid. I still am. I shouldn't be here. But I pay my dues; you saved my life, so I thought you might want an explanation for—"

"An explanation isn't what I want."

"I can't give you what you want." I'm blunt now. Even if it means hurting him further, I have to get it all out of his head. Me, his feelings, any shred of hope. "If it comforts you, I would feel sorry if I could."

"Shut up, Elizabeth," he says, breathing heavily. He takes two quick steps and he's suddenly there, too close and too demanding. He grasps my shoulders, so impassioned that he doesn't realize his fingers are biting into me. The hurt boy is gone, leaving a heated man in his place. I study this new creature, his blazing green eyes, that ridiculous long hair.

"Joshua—"

"You feel," he tells me through his teeth. "I know you do. You cried at Maggie's funeral. You were afraid when that man attacked you in the parking lot that night. You painted that mural...for what? Because everyone else expected you to? No. Because you *wanted* to."

I'm shaking my head, but he'll have none of it. Making

a sound of frustration deep in his throat, Joshua pulls me against him. Before I can react, he's pressing his lips to mine for the first time. He's a little clumsy, uncertain. But then his warm hands slide from my shoulders to my waist, cupping the small of my back, and he relaxes. I close my eyes, instinctively kissing him back.

Even irate, Joshua is infinitely tender, holding me so close I find it hard to breathe. Thinking to shove him away, I flatten my palms to his chest. Unrelenting, he pushes me against the wall and presses closer. My mouth opens to his, and our kiss deepens. He tastes a little like the sweet corn he must have had for supper. His arms are stronger than I'd realized, refusing me escape, challenging. Wishing everything was this simple, I keep kissing him, but somehow, someway, someone else slips into my thoughts. Someone with an infuriating smirk and silky white hair...

When Joshua pulls back, I'm unprepared. A small gasp slips out, and at the sound Joshua grins, a slow, warm grin. "Elizabeth," he says. "Don't you get it? I'm not playing games. I don't expect anything. I love you."

The simple words spark something inside me. I've heard them before, but it's different this time. I freeze in his arms, carefully analyzing the strange sensation deep inside me.

"You..." I take a breath, struggling to regain my analytical way of thinking. Joshua won't let me; he kisses me again, catching me by surprise.

"Yes, I love you," he says. His breathing is more ragged than mine. The Emotion herself shimmers into existence, touching his cheek before leaving us alone again.

I swallow. I can't say the words back. Because I yearn to say them to someone else. The realization isn't a blow—it's been waiting, just beneath the surface. And it means more pain for Joshua, more guilt for myself. No one can have their happy endings.

"You don't even know my real name," is all I mumble to Joshua in response.

He presses his forehead against mine, inhaling my scent, seeming to savor it. "Then tell me."

I hesitate for just an instant before whispering, "Rebecca. Rebecca James."

"Rebecca. It's a beautiful name."

"Thank you." I allow his touch, ignoring the instinct to pull away. This is the last time he'll ever hold me like this, and I stay to give him memories of his own.

Joshua and I stand there for a few minutes—minutes that feel like peaceful years—just two people in a barn, alone, together, separate and apart, yet one. A human and…something nonhuman. Love and nothing. Love and everything.

A noise nearby. I lift my head. I should pull away. I should leave. But I don't.

The boy in my arms notes the alert movement. He rubs a thumb across my lower lip, smiling. Then, softly, softly, Joshua says the words: "Just you and me, Rebecca."

There's an instant of silence, and I can feel the illusion trembling. Then there's the sound of thunder all around me, something breaking into a million pieces.

Whoosh.

The wall collapses.

Pain. Pain. *Pain.*

I remember. I remember it *all*, this time. And with the remembering comes the rush, the waterfall, the shrieking earthquake of feeling. Joshua disappears as the world crumbles. Emotions surround me, murmuring in wonder, touching me everywhere. I fight them, making sounds that don't even sound human. Their faces crowd in, bright and dark, hideous and beautiful. As their skin makes contact, my eyes roll back in my head, the room around me fading into fuzzy shadows. I want to laugh, I want to cry, I want to scream, I want to pound my fists, I want to tear my hair out, I want to throw up my arms and dance and dance until I'm too dizzy to dance anymore and fall to the ground.

And in the midst of it all, the memory of one face presses in, filling every corner of my being. *Just you and me, Rebecca.*

Elizabeth is gone. I am completely Rebecca James once again. And I know what I am. Daughter, sister, lover…Element. I'm a hybrid. A half-blood. *Haven't you noticed that people are drawn to you?* I know why now. And I know why Nightmare wanted to find my father. Because my father's blood is the most precious, the greatest addiction, the highest power, the ultimate nectar. Blood that runs through my veins, making me only half human.

Life.

And I couldn't even use it to save my twin. "No!" I scream, tears streaming down my face. "I don't want to remember! Take it away, please, take it away!"

"Too late for that," a voice says, close by. "Back off, all

of you. I know it's exciting, but she shouldn't have to deal with it all at once."

"Rebecca, Rebecca," the Emotions are saying over and over again, still touching me. My twin and I used to join their parties all the time, intoxicate them with a single touch. Life—that's what I am. Why, then, do I crave death? I feel hands in my hair, on my shoulders, on my back, on my legs, my feet, my cheeks, my stomach. Their touch, their essences gush through me, bursting out of my pores, oozing through every part of my body.

"Get away from me!" I scream, wild-eyed, thrusting my arms out. Power rushes through every part of my body, making me tremble all over. The gust is so strong that the Emotions all around are thrown back. Many of them vanish. Others gaze at me in awe, standing a safe distance from me. I'm barely aware of any of it. I crumple into a ball, weeping.

I remember him. Everything. I remember his smile, his pensive tones, the way his eyes twinkled, every moment of every day we spent together.

His words, his companionship, his love—gone. All of it, gone.

My brother. My twin. I sink into a black hole of despair.

"Landon."

TWENTY-FOUR

I stand in the middle of Elizabeth's room.

I gaze at the walls, the mural I'll never finish. Green everywhere, trees and light and mystery. My eyes fall on me and Landon. I take in the silent anguish, my arms embracing death. It's the thousandth time I've seen the image—through flashes of memory, through dreams—but now it means more. So much more. That was the moment I denied the blood running through my veins. What was the point of being Life if I couldn't use it to bring my brother back?

Something wet falls to the wooden floor, the sound like a crash all around me. I look down, see the drop of water. I touch my cheek. I'm crying.

That's when I realize I'm no longer alone. Someone stands behind me, someone with gentle fingers as they rest on my shoulder. I turn and meet Sorrow's bottomless eyes. He doesn't say a word, and as always, he's crying, too. There's nothing to say. We grieve together for a few moments before the Emotion fades into nothing, leaving his essence as a token. As the salty taste in my mouth.

It's being in this room. It's thinking of him. It's Sorrow's brief presence. But suddenly I can hear his voice—something I've done everything to avoid—in my head, warm and alive.

Just you and me, Rebecca. We'll be travelers. We'll see everything and no one will tell us what to do.

A sob hitches in my throat. Wanting to block it all out, I bend over, picking up a bucket of green paint by my feet. I hurl it at the wall. It splatters everywhere, ruining the mural and bleeding across the floor. It's not enough. I pick up another bucket, throwing it at the next wall. The bucket cracks at the force of the impact. But the paint simply drips down the wall—not enough, not enough. I collapse against the wet paint, screaming, rubbing it with my hands, spreading it over me, the trees, and the shadow that is Landon.

"This is the last place I expected you to go."

The woman stands behind me. In another lifetime, my mother considered her a good friend. She's proved to be more than worthy. She helped me run, she created the illusion, she tried to protect me when Nightmare found me a second time. This woman, with her cryptic warnings and ever-present pain. I should have known who she was, even when I was Elizabeth. It's so obvious, so simple.

"Leave me alone, Denial," I whisper.

She glowers. Trembling, I just lie there against the wall, paint dripping down the side of my face and staining my hands. The sensations coursing through my veins are overwhelming.

Denial watches me. "It'll take some time to adjust to," she says, waving her hand at me dismissively. "Now, back to the matter at hand."

I barely hear her. After the illusion broke, I fled Joshua and the barn and all the Emotions. This was the first place I could think of to go. So far, Charles has yet to make an appearance.

Denial only endures my silence for a minute before she grows impatient. She smashes the stillness. "Your time for mourning is done. I told you, Rebecca. You're strong enough to—"

"I haven't even *started* to mourn!" I hiss, pushing myself up, clenching my fists. Even now, I'm still trying to hold on to Denial's essence, to the nothingness that's desperately gone now. I want to balk at all of this, refuse to accept it. I want the oblivion back!

I take a step away from Denial and collide into a warm chest—Anger. "Nice to see you again," he murmurs, and I can see that he actually means it. Smiling with a trace of smugness, he reaches out and takes hold of my shoulder. The fury is devastating, and the ever-present pain makes tears spring to my eyes. Finished with me, the Emotion vanishes. I turn this new wrath onto Denial. I feel my eyes burning, but she isn't afraid; she just glares back.

"And whose fault is that?" she challenges. "I did what you asked. I did the illusion. I hid you here. It's time for you to grow up and face reality again."

I whirl away. "You agreed to my terms, Denial. You

shouldn't have tampered with any of this. You should have *let me be.*"

"Don't you dare turn this around on me. I saved your life—Nightmare would have eaten you for breakfast if I hadn't come back to warn you."

My fist slams against the wall of its own accord, and the plaster crumbles. I shake my head, my wild hair sticking to my skin. Now I'm a sniveling hole of regret. "You shouldn't have let me do this. You shouldn't have—"

"You remember that day, Rebecca. You were desolate. No, that's not strong enough. You acted like you were dead, too. You asked me to take away the pain. You asked me to change who you were. Not to mention that he was still looking for you. This is the result we *both* came up with."

I just keep shaking my head. Ignoring me, Denial approaches the nightstand beside Elizabeth's bed. She studies a picture there of her and her brother. "It was so simple. I'm surprised it took you this long to figure it out. The only tricky part was coming back every so often to alter the illusion so you appeared older. Couldn't have you looking like a little girl forever. And you clung to the lie so hard that you never even sensed me."

I straighten, glaring at Denial through my tears. I can taste a blob of paint on my lip, and green hair hangs in my eyes. "What do you want from me? Your part in this is finished. The illusion is broken. I remember. You can go."

Denial doesn't soften. "I care about you, despite what a pain in my ass you've been the last thirteen years. I'll leave when I'm sure you're not going to slit your wrists. And I won't let you sit around and wallow. You either continue your existence here or start anew somewhere else. Your choice."

"That's no choice," I retort, but the words are weak.

She sighs, but I'm not done. There's something that's been haunting me, and I can't let it go. "Just tell me one more thing," I whisper, briefly closing my eyes as if my eyelids alone can keep away all the shadows and the mistakes. "If... if I'd broken the illusion sooner, if I'd gotten my powers back... could I have saved Maggie?"

Pity blooms in Denial's gaze, and I hate that. But she doesn't mince words. "Probably. There isn't much you can't bring back with a touch. But, Rebecca... I'd guess that you just being there prolonged her life. You gave her more time, even with the illusion intact."

It isn't enough. I hate that word. *Probably.* I turn my back on her, wishing so hard that none of this had ever happened, that I could destroy all the *probably*s, that I could go back in time and save Landon, tell Fear that I loved him too, stop my mom from leaving that day. But maybe she didn't leave... maybe my father forced her away, and by the time she escaped him, got back, we were already—

The reflection in the mirror next to the door catches my eye, and I freeze.

If I needed anything else to prove that I'm really not Elizabeth anymore, the face staring back at me would be it. The girl gaping in the glass is someone I haven't seen in a long, long time. She's so different from Elizabeth Caldwell. Her cheekbones are high, her brown eyes slightly slanted. Her skin is paler, her hair so dark it could be called black.

It tumbles over her back in exotic, uncontrollable curls. Her nose is slightly upturned, and her lips are full, pouty. Her collarbone is so delicate it looks like it could be snapped with one blow of a fist. When I raise my hand, the girl in the mirror raises her hand, too. Her fingernails are round, oval-shaped, and there, there is the one thing that reveals that she was once upon a time a girl who worked in a barn, hauled rocks from a field, withstood the abuse of a man who reeked of alcohol: there is dirt under those nails.

And one random thought that shouldn't even occur to me in the wake of remembering my twin's death: *what will Fear think?*

Shuddering, experiencing so many things I feel like my skin is going to expand, I turn back to Denial. She's studying the mural with something akin to sadness in her eyes. She almost seems ... drained. Her gaze lands on what was once Landon before I ruined him, and now real sorrow does bloom in her expression. How could I have forgotten? She loved him, too. Many times I would catch the end of a lingering glance between Denial and my twin. Whether something ever came of those looks I'll never know, but I do know there won't be anything more.

I swallow. I look back at the destroyed mural, this room that no longer belongs to me. Never belonged to me, really. There's nothing here for me anymore. All I'm leaving is emptiness, and memories that should never have been mine.

I turn my back to it all. "I know what I want to do."

———

There's a note for Charles on his bed. Three sentences, one farewell: *I'm going back to where it started. Thank you for saving me. You were the one who made me believe in humanity.*

There's a suitcase in the passenger seat of Elizabeth's truck, stuffed with her clothes—which don't quite fit me now, since she was taller than I am—and I have a new destination. There's a map in my lap, and the route to Gig Harbor, Washington, is highlighted. Where I'll find the stone house I grew up in, where Mom cooked breakfast every morning, where Landon and I were homeschooled, where we grew into our Elements.

It's raining again. There's been a steady downpour ever since the illusion broke. Trees speed by. It's easier to focus on them than on the reflection staring back at me from the glass. After thirteen years I've grown used to the blond hair and blue eyes. These dark curls and brown irises are disconcerting, to say the least. No one would recognize me now—not Maggie, not even Joshua.

Joshua. I swallow, trying to shove down the feeling that swells up. He served his purpose. *You will need that boy in the end.* Joshua needed to love me, so that one Emotion could break through my defenses. In the end it wasn't death or terror that shattered them. It was someone else's love. How poetic.

It takes me a day and a half to get there. Since I'd never left Gig Harbor before Nightmare came, I don't recognize the signs or the landmarks. But I follow the directions I got from Google Maps, and as soon as I take a right onto the last dirt road, I know. That's the driveway, up ahead. I'm here. This is the place. There's a mailbox in the ditch, no name on the side of it since Mom was always paranoid about someone finding us.

She turned out to be right.

The clouds have broken up just a little, enough that a few rays of sun touch the ground in sporadic splotches. I'm stiff, holding my breath as if I'm about to drive off the cliff into the ocean. Nothing yet... just the woods on either side and the overgrown road. No one has been back here in a long, long time. It feels like it's all been waiting for someone.

Waiting for me. I roll down the window and let the humid air in. Smelling like salt and wind, it toys with my curls as I listen to the sound of the gravel under the car. The crunch of rocks and dirt makes me think of Elizabeth's life in Edson. All that's missing is a slamming screen door...

The house comes into view.

It's lonely. It's old. No one has bothered to chop away the tangle of vines climbing up its side. The shingles are rotting and falling off. One of the windows is broken, and the front door is wide open. It's different and it's the same.

My head feels light, too light, and I remember that I'm holding my breath. I let it out in an audible *whoosh*. So many memories, so much pain. I can almost hear Landon's voice, reading aloud, or Mom's gentle tenor as she firmly instructs us to sit at the table and work on our math for an hour.

I expected to feel... happy, maybe. Or at least whole. But all I feel is empty. After everything, after all the years and the pain and the pretending, I expected more.

It doesn't matter, though. What matters is that I'm finally home.

Everything is still here. Landon's textbooks, Mom's cook-books. I found one of my old sundresses in a drawer—the one I was wearing in all the dreams. I remember Mom hugging me once when I had it on. Her scent has long since faded from the material, but I haven't taken it off since discovering it, despite the cold. I like to pretend I can still smell a hint of her lavender shampoo.

I drift through the long grasses and trees of the woods that Landon and I loved. Since our father never took an interest in us—we were two among dozens he's probably fathered, since Life can't be contained—we used this place to feel closer to him. His presence is palpable here. He didn't play a domestic role for us, but the trees emanate his very essence. Not that I care anymore, now that I see the truth for what it is. He slept with my mom and abandoned her. Moved on. Left us. He has to know we exist. His blood runs through our veins. But even when Landon was dying, when I was dying, the only one Life apparently cared enough to save was our mother.

There was one person who did save me, though, every single time without fail. And *I* abandoned *him*. I know that's why he's staying away. He thinks I don't want him. When I became Elizabeth and left Fear in another lifetime, it was the ultimate betrayal. And how ironic that he fell in love with her. Does he hold any feelings for Rebecca, anymore? Or has my deceit obliterated any remnants of that love? Thinking of him adds to the pain, and I'm already confronting too much, so I avoid any more thoughts or memories.

Once, all I wanted to do was sing, dance, celebrate always and mourn never, but now I am consumed by what I have lost. Is Mom looking for me? Will she ever come back here? I try to imagine her somewhere else, leading an existence without me or Landon. She had no illusion to help her endure. Does she think I'm dead, too?

Sometimes I wonder if I could find comfort if I were to return to the niche with Charles. Memories are so easily erased, patterns simple to find again. But then I imagine Tim's red, swollen face, feel the rage of his fists and hear the slur of his words. I remember Sarah's trapped pain, the guilt that constantly consumed her. I think of Maggie, my only friend. I contemplate Joshua and what could have been. I relive Charles turning his gaze away when he noticed a new bruise on my cheek. And I know I don't want to go back. Not really.

I lean against the trunk of a tree, huddling into myself in the twilight. I close my eyes, torturing myself with more memories.

"Someday we'll leave," Landon tells me, eyes so bright, so alive. He holds a book of maps in his hand. "Just you and me, Rebecca. We'll leave the country, even." His gaze focuses on something in the distance. "I've read about things I can't even begin to imagine without seeing for myself. I mean, there are pictures, but…" He sighs. "They're not enough."

"Things like what?" I ask, lying on my back and squinting up at the sun. I pluck a blade of grass loose from the green beneath me.

Landon finally lies down beside me. We both smell like earth and excitement and daydreams.

"I want to see Mount Rushmore," he tells me, his voice soft. "Can you see us there? Looking up at huge mountains that have faces carved into them? And cities! New York! It's full of towers so tall they touch the sky."

Days go by. One morning I sit on a mossy bank by the river, staring down into the currents. The water by my feet is clear and trickles gently over the smooth rocks. There's a splash nearby, and when I glance over, all there is to show for it is an oily sheen, floating on the surface. The river quickly carries it away. Trout?

"He'd take you back, you know."

Jumping, I turn to see Fear leaning against a tree, arms crossed in that arrogant manner of his. He's staring at me with an unfathomable expression on his frozen, lovely face.

I haven't seen Fear since I healed him, since we both thought I was a human girl called Elizabeth, since I was wearing her mask. At the sight of his achingly familiar face, the breath catches in my throat.

"Fear." I stand, brushing off my bottom, swallowing audibly. My dark hair—still foreign to me—tumbles into my eyes, and I'm grateful for the curtain to hide behind. I don't know what to say. I'm vulnerable. He can see me now; he knows the truth. Does he hate me for what I did? For hiding all this time? I resist the urge to throw myself at him, experience his hands on me for real after so many years of restraint and lies. I know that he wants another now. Someone who was never real to begin with.

Fear doesn't seem to sense my inner turmoil. "Are you going to go back?" His tone is so distant it hurts.

I blink. "Go back where?"

He sighs impatiently. "To the humans. Back to the boy."

Joshua. He means Joshua. I turn my back to Fear, trying to muster the courage to tell him he's wrong. I can't. I've faced so many things, but this... this I'm not ready to confront. I can't handle his rejection. I'm good at running from the truth. As I bend toward the skeleton of a dead flower—fresh color streaking through the petals at my touch—I try to change the subject, asking, "Have you done something to Tim? No one's seen him since Charles ran him off, and I don't think he'd stay away just because Charles threatened to call the sheriff."

But Fear isn't going to let me run. He strides toward me, bringing a cool breeze and all his horror with him. "I warned him never to touch you again," is all he says. Then, "Answer me. Are you going to go back?"

I cringe, and butterflies erupt in my stomach as his essence wraps itself around me. My pulse starts to race.

Fear breathes down my neck. Helpless, I am assailed by images of us together. His lips pressed to my neck. Legs intertwined. Grass sticking to our backs. I whirl around to glare at him. "Get away from me."

"Oh, you're mad now. You must really miss him."

"I don't miss him." *I'm mad at you for staying away. I'm mad at you for falling in love with someone else. I'm mad at myself.*

But he doesn't hear my thoughts. "Now you're the one pretending, Elizabeth."

"Don't call me that," I snap, glaring at him. Is he deliberately being cruel, throwing it in my face that I can never be the one he loves again? "Elizabeth was the little girl whose life I stole. I'm just the fool who tried to be a human, and I damaged everyone I came into contact with. I'm not Elizabeth. Even if it hurts so much sometimes I want to kill myself, I'm going to remember myself this time."

Fear lifts a finger in the air, teasing. "Ah, but you are Elizabeth. You've brought a little of her back with you. Don't you remember who you were, Rebecca, before Landon died?" Before I can retort or hate him for mentioning my twin's name, Fear silences me by putting his finger over my lips. A jolt runs through me at the touch, and I struggle against the terror suddenly edging in.

"Listen to me," Fear whispers now. His breathing is uneven. "You're a little of both now. Rebecca in all your beauty and grace, and that little bit of snobbery"—he doesn't let me utter a protest—"and Elizabeth in your gentleness. The way you endured my feelings for you because of your compassion. Really, I feel like an idiot for not seeing it. Maybe some part of me knew."

And in his search for me, he found a new obsession. I swallow, all my sharp words and outrage fading again. *Endured* his feelings? As Elizabeth, maybe. Now I *crave* them. I remember those nights we spent together, the way his fingers felt brushing over my skin. "Fear—"

"It's fine," he cuts in, dismisses what he thinks is an apology. When I lift my gaze, Fear sighs. Removing his hand from my cheek, he brushes his silky hair out of his face and looks away. "It's always been my lot to want what I can't have," he says. "This is no exception. I'll survive, Rebecca." His grin is tinged with sadness and defiance, something he tries to hide from me but miserably fails.

Heart in my throat, I move as if to touch him, but Fear shakes his head, moving back so he's out of my reach. Doesn't he know that if I could bring Elizabeth back for him again, I would?

I chew my lower lip, wishing again that I had the strength to tell him how I really feel, that I don't want him to leave me again, that it's him I think about, not Joshua. It never was, even that night I chose him over Fear. Where is that damn Courage when you actually want him to appear? "Fear—"

"Don't." Again he doesn't let me finish. "You've given me enough. Just a glance in my direction was a rush." He winks, shoving his hands in his coat pockets. He's moving even farther away and I don't attempt to stop him. What more is there to say? As if to agree with me, Fear shrugs, and his form begins to lighten, go transparent, as he leaves me yet again. Even though I hate myself for it, I don't stop him.

"You don't have to say anything," Fear murmurs. "Just go to him. Love him. Be happy again. After all you've been through, you deserve it. I was right, by the way," he adds unexpectedly.

I swallow. "Right about what?" I ask faintly.

He fades completely from sight. "You do look beautiful in a dress," his voice whispers in my ear. Then … silence. I let him go.

TWENTY-FIVE

Sometimes I think I hear my twin's tread on the ground, coming closer. It always turns out to be nothing. A deer, a breeze, my imagination. That voice in the back of my head has been nudging me lately. The numbness is gone, along with everything else, and the voice of feeling hisses at me, demands that I acknowledge it's not the absence of my family holding me back from life now. From the very thing I can't make disappear with an illusion. Forever a part of me, no matter how much I resent it.

One afternoon, as I pick my way across a creek, Courage is suddenly beside me. When I don't stop he walks with me. I glance at his profile sidelong, curious as to what he could possibly want. But I refuse to ask, so we trek in silence together. The bare trees watch us.

Courage doesn't let the stillness remain for long. "So is this your plan? To wander around here and mope for the rest of your life?" He walks so perfectly, so controlled, arms behind his back, shoulders straight. His boots hit the ground with tidy *clips*. I can't help comparing him, over and over, to his brother. Fear has a bright façade and dark insides; he's horror and a windy recklessness that carries millions over the plains with no hope of ever stopping. And Courage…he's dark on the outside but carries a light within; he's calm and encouraging and his very breath is a soothing dash of water on a hot, hot day.

"You're easily distracted," Courage notes. He stops, and I choose to stop alongside him. A slant of sunlight falls across my face, but I don't move out of the way. Instead I revel in the warmth, shivering when I remember the darkness of Nightmare's shack.

Suddenly, when Courage speaks, he is hardness and determination. He cuts right to the point, wills me to accept his words. "The other plane loves you. They always have. It wasn't your brother that was the strong one. You were able to bring us all together as no others could, because of the sound of your laughter and your smiles. Your very step on the forest floor had the trees stretching tall to impress. It was you, Rebecca, and not Landon that survived Nightmare. And why do you think that is?"

I consider walking away, but Courage has me intrigued. Instead of answering his question, though, I tilt my head and study him in a removed way, as if I'm hardly bothered by his confrontation. "Why do you care so much?"

Finally his stony expression cracks. He sighs, impatience leaking into the sound. A small breeze stirs a strand of my hair. "Because not only does my brother care for you, silly creature, but I hold some affection for you as well," he snaps. "Have you forgotten the dances? The stories you told me on the days I thought my brother would smother me with his zealous campaign of terror?"

Of course I haven't forgotten. I do remember all those nights in these woods. Courage always stood by in the shadows, watching the festivities. If he continued on in that manner for most of the party, I would eventually drag him into the noise and the lights and force him to dance with me. And the stories … they were Landon's, but I repeated them to Courage when I found him rubbing his temples, deep in contemplation. Fear is strong, and sometimes courage is not so easy to instill in a human inclined to succumb to the panic.

I turn my back to Courage, smiling. "It's nice, seeing you ruffled. It's been too long since I've kept you on your toes."

"Yes, much too long," he agrees, wry now. "No games, please, Rebecca."

Frustration bubbles up within me. "What do you all expect me to do? Go back? Live with the humans? No. No one can make me." I hate how that last part comes out so petulant, as if I'm a child. Scowling, I feign interest in a withering tree. It crackles and grows taller, greener, at the brush of my fingers, a strange appearance in the middle of this sleeping forest.

Courage touches me for the first time, grasping my arm. A surge of feeling rushes through my body, and I'm seized with a desire to conquer the world. There's nothing but horizon before me—I can run and leave this place of ghosts and do whatever I want—

"Stop it." Stubborn, I keep my gaze glued to the ground.

Courage places his gentle fingers beneath my chin and lifts my face. He's too piercing, too right, and it hurts. "We want you to be happy. You are Life. If you're not content, we're not either."

My lower lip trembles, and I bite it. I despise weakness; why, then, do I seem to have so much of it? "Nothing happened the way it was supposed to," I whisper, closing my eyes. I remember the desire burning in Fear's eyes, Joshua's kiss in the warmth of his barn, Maggie's bittersweet smile, Landon's blood on my hands. "I just wanted to go to...some quiet place. To forget. To be someone else. Nothing happened the way it was supposed to," I repeat. "And the truth is...I'm scared." Finally, I admit it. My voice shakes, and I utter a cry of annoyance.

Courage smiles. Pinches my chin playfully before releasing me. "My brother will never be far from you," he says. "Best get used to the feeling."

I step away, rolling my eyes, but Courage isn't done yet. "What exactly are you afraid of?" he urges.

A bird passes overhead. Its shadow moves quickly over the trees. I watch it soar. "I'm afraid that if I go on and live as Rebecca James, Landon will think I'm forgetting him."

"If he's watching, he knows that's not possible. After all, even when you were under one of the strongest illusions I've ever encountered, you didn't forget. Did you?" Courage steps away. He's leaving soon. I can feel him gathering power around him.

"Their world is frightening," I whisper. "I don't know if I can go back into it."

His words are so soft a mouse wouldn't be able to hear them, but they waft over to me on the air. "As a wise human girl once told me, you fear what you don't understand."

"Not human," I correct.

"Humanity is a choice, power or no power."

Opening my mouth, I spin to meet him, but Courage is somewhere else in the world, his business with me apparently finished.

He always did have to have the last word.

Life. It's a funny thing. Some want it, some throw it away. Some cling to it, some have it stolen from them. It's terrifying...which is maybe why I was drawn to Fear in the first place. It can't be coincidence that we met and loved in both lifetimes. Rebecca James, Elizabeth Caldwell. He's my match, my equal. And now, finally, I'm willing to admit what I want. Life. With him.

The choice has been waiting ever since the illusion broke. When I was Elizabeth, Fear sought me out time and time again. We both know that it's my turn. I can feel Landon in the back of my head, a kind presence in my shadow, urging me on. And the effects of Courage's touch linger, strengthen, urge me to face my uncertainties. I can't live in the past for the rest of my existence. Denial was right; my time to mourn is done. I'll never forget my twin or what happened to him— that day will always be a dark shroud on my soul—but I can't run from myself anymore.

I do everything I can to bring Fear to me. First I sit in a chair, close my eyes, and remember the entire experience with Nightmare. His teeth, that shack, his knives, my blood spilling to the ground. And my mouth goes dry, my pulse quickens, but still nothing. Next, I go to town and rent some horror movies. Spend two hours watching bloodshed and teenage parties turn into carnage on the ancient television. It works; my palms sweat and it's difficult to keep my eyes open. But he doesn't come.

I'm done with this.

The door slams against the wall when I storm outside. My skirt flaps around my knees as I march toward the ocean, toward the perilous cliff edge. I hold out my arms on either side of me like I'm about to take flight, like I'm one of Sarah's birds. I position my feet so that only my heels are touching solid ground. The rest of me feels the open air. Taking a breath, I look down. The ocean, sensing me so close, pounds against the rocks with renewed vigor. I am Life. I am the ocean.

It doesn't take him long.

"What the hell are you doing?" Fear hisses, wrapping his hand around my arm. I've never heard him so livid.

Terror explodes in my chest. I don't turn, but I wrench myself free of his grip, ignoring how much I want it. "Are you going to let me talk this time?"

Out of the corner of my eye, I see Fear's black coat whipping against his boot. He moves close again, and I know he's thinking about yanking me back. "Why are you doing this, Rebecca?" he asks, his voice low, so serious. *Rebecca*. Not

Elizabeth. For a second I'm tempted to lose my nerve, I'm convinced that he doesn't really love me anymore, I ruined everything.

No. I steel myself. Even though I thought I was immune, I've been letting Fear's essence control my every move. And it stops now.

"I'm in love with you," I blurt, glaring at the sun. "I'm in love with you, not Joshua, and it's you I want to be with. I mean, I want to try. Again." I clear my throat, blushing. I can't bring myself to look at him. The words pound around us, carried in swirls by the wind. *In love with you... not Joshua... try again...*

There's a three-second silence as he processes this. Then he says, "Why don't you step back from the ledge, and I'll let you know what I think about that."

What if you're too late? What if you've lost him? a niggling voice in the back of my head worries. The ocean calls to me: *Life. Life. Yes,* I think. *I am.* And I need to live. So I shuffle back.

I raise my eyes to Fear's, prepared for rejection, for phrases like *too late* and *can't work.* He stares down at me for what feels like forever, those lovely blue eyes so piercing that they poke through my very soul like it's nothing but paper. I swallow. "I—"

He hauls me against him and crushes my lips with his.

I respond instantly, even as his touch invokes goose bumps, raising the hair on my arms. His fingers travel down my spine as I tilt my head. A delicious shiver erupts from the touch. Not close enough, not close enough... I stand on my tiptoes, every part of me fusing to his hard body, and wrap my arms around his neck. A muted feeling of terror edges in, but nothing that would tear me away from him. Thirteen years. After an illusion that changed my face, changed my being, he found me. Thirteen years he's loved me and waited for me.

Distantly, I sense Joy standing behind us, watching. Her hand rests on my shoulder. But she's not alone. There are more, touching me or just watching.

"Take a picture, it lasts longer," Fear growls. His lips move against mine as he speaks. Smiling, I open my mouth, deepening the kiss. We both forget our audience. The rest of the world fades away into beautiful hues of peach and black and white. It's so hard to breathe; no, I can't breathe at all when his tongue does that...but who needs air?

"I never did say it before, did I?" I whisper. He presses his forehead to mine, breathing in the smell of me. I smile faintly. "I love you."

"You can say that as many times as you want," he murmurs. Somehow his embrace tightens, and he doesn't need words to express how much he missed me. We hold each other for so long that the other Emotions get bored and leave. Once we're completely alone, Fear presses his lips to my ear. As he speaks, I can't repress another delicious shiver. "You asked me once if I ever get tired of being who I am," he reminds me. "And the answer is this: only when I have to leave you."

I smile, clutching his coat. My mouth is tucked in the curve between his neck and his shoulder. I could stay like this forever. I imagine us here decades from now, a stone statue entwined in each other. This brings thoughts of the future, and I finally break the blissful peace by asking softly, "How is this going to work?" Things are so different now.

Fear pulls back a little, smoothing damp strands of hair away from my face. His thumbs brush the edges of my jaw. "Easy," he answers. "I show up when you need me, and I show up especially when you don't need me." He grins, an impish light in his eyes. I kiss him again, loving the feel of his skin against mine. So we won't be a normal couple. Since when have I ever been normal, anyway?

Purpose is building up inside of me again, and suddenly I'm filled with the urge to tie up all the loose ends I left behind. To return Life to where it was lacking. "There's something I have to do," I say, pulling myself out of the circle of Fear's arms. "Back in Edson. I'll let you know when I'm done. Okay?"

He kisses my nose. "Just don't go looking for cliffs. I'll know when you want me."

I can't help smiling some more. My face almost hurts. "I'll always want you."

With a tender light in his eyes, Fear vanishes.

I pack the bare essentials, get in Elizabeth's truck, and go.

The hours fly by unnoticed. Late the next day, that sign I've been looking for comes into view: *Welcome to Edson*. The words are chipping, fading. Somehow, I'd expected it to be different, changed in the time I've been gone. But everything in this small town is comfortable, mindless of the rest of the world sprinting by. I pass Hal's Hardware, the clinic, Fowler's Grocery, and the school.

There's a face uppermost in my mind, the person I know I need to see the most. But there's someone else I have to visit before I seek Joshua out. Within minutes, I pull into Morgan Richardson's driveway.

The front door is unlocked. I enter without hesitation, and pause a moment to study my surroundings. The place looks different in the daytime. I remember the ominous air the night of the party, Fear's flight, Morgan's single word: *Run*. Suppressing a shudder, I climb the steps.

The sound of some reality TV show drifts down the hall, and I follow it to Morgan's room. She's sitting there, stuck in front of the television again.

"Excuse me, what are you doing here?"

Morgan's babysitter has noticed me, but she doesn't move from her spot by the window. There's a cell phone pressed to her ear—just like the first time I saw her—and she stares. Still not hanging up, even though there's a complete stranger intruding in the house. There are faint sounds of a male voice on the other end.

I evaluate her quickly. Then, using my full speed, I'm in her face in a split second. She shrieks and drops the phone. She tries to dart to the side in an attempt to run around me, screaming all the while, but I easily corner her. Morgan watches all this silently.

"What are you?" the woman whimpers, holding her hands out in front of her face, like that alone is going to stop me.

My voice is a hiss. "Take your job seriously, or get out so someone more qualified can take your place. If you ever, ever leave Morgan alone again like you did the night of Sophia's birthday party, I'll come back. I don't think I need to elaborate, do I?"

She's already shaking her head vehemently, her blond pony tail swinging from side to side. I smile at her kindly, nodding. "Good."

I turn away, disregarding her completely, and squat down in front of Morgan, blocking her view of the TV. Her watery gaze focuses. I realize how much she looks like Sophia. Two such different girls.

We study each other, and though she can't possibly recognize me with this face, I get the sense that somehow, she does. I sigh. "Morgan, I can't change your parents, and I can't change your sister, but I can help. What you choose to do after this is up to you." I reach up, pressing the heel of my hand against her forehead. I close my eyes, concentrating, using all the power I have to straighten, organize, smooth. Her mind is not completely altered, and it never will be, but with fresh Life flowing through her veins, she'll have more understanding. She won't have to struggle so much, and she'll be able to speak for herself. It's all I can do.

I lean back on my haunches, place my palms flat on my thighs, and jump to my feet.

Morgan sits there, blinking, tasting the new vibrancy of the world around her. She blinks up at me. Her voice, when she speaks to me for the second time ever, is loud and wondering.

"Thank you," she says.

I smile at her, touching her chin. "You're welcome, Morgan. I'll come back to visit you soon, all right?"

She smiles back at me guilelessly, her pasty face glowing. I go to the door, remember the babysitter, and face her again. She's still cowering in the corner.

"Goodbye. I really hope I don't have to see you again."

Eyes wide, she watches me go out the door. I leave it open, just to remind her I was here, lest she forget too soon.

Moments later I'm standing on the driveway, looking up at the big house. It's beautiful in this light, the sun rising behind me. *There*, I think. *That's done.*

Now I have just one more person to see.

———————

I watch him for hours. From behind a tree, I can see the sweat seeping through his jacket as he helps his father harvest the near-worthless crops. They waited too long. When darkness falls I expect Joshua to follow his dad inside, but he still isn't done. He goes into the barn, takes care of the animals. The place where he told me he loved me, the place where we kissed, the place where I was ripped from him.

And as I watch, I'm tormented. Should I go to him? Should I disrupt his existence again in an attempt to give this boy closure? If I leave him alone, will he be able to move on, live his life, be the normal person he needs to be? Or, if I leave now and never touch him again, will he flounder, sink deeper and deeper into dark waters? I think of our kiss, of his gentle hands, of his glowing eyes as he looked at me. He wants Elizabeth back, and she's gone forever. But he doesn't deserve nothing. He deserves a goodbye. I remember Courage's words again. *You will need that boy in the end.*

Now he needs me.

There's no way to deny it. I used him. He was just a key to the door, and even knowing that, I let his feelings for me grow. Now he's suffering for it. There's nothing I can do to bring his joy back, because I can't belong to him. I grip the tree bark, digging my fingers in until it hurts. Dry leaves respond instantly to the touch, becoming more vibrant hues of red and orange. Joshua wheels the barrow around the side of the barn, and at that moment I remember how Susie Yank was looking at him in the hallway. I think of possibilities, maybes, somedays, all the things I am still struggling not to avoid.

As I linger by the tree, Guilt shimmers into view, so close that I can smell her: a combination of sweat and … grease? She claps her hand on my shoulder, grinning, and I give her a baleful look. "Don't be like that," she purrs. "Just doing my job."

"Well, you've done it," I snap quietly, hating the flood of feeling that grips me. "Now go."

With a smirk, she vanishes.

The sounds of the night are all around. Joshua still doesn't go to bed. He tinkers at a workbench, building what looks like a birdhouse. Wind whistles through the tiny cracks in the walls. The gentle light Joshua has on stretches over the hay and out the doorway, toward me.

If we don't take any risks, then we won't find the things worth living for.

The words he once shouted at my back haunt me. It feels so long ago.

It's as I'm watching him work, replaying that sentence over and over in my head, that I make a decision. Joshua is strong. So much stronger than I ever was, and unlike me, he is the kind of person to take risks for happiness. I treated him badly, but he doesn't need my touch to appreciate life. I'm going to leave him with two things. A single memory of me as thanks—words on a page that he can reread as many times he wants—and a way to give him the future he's constantly looking toward.

I run back to the car, hunt down a pen in the glove box. There's no paper but an old receipt to be found, so I write on the back of it. When I'm done, I stick the receipt in the Hayes' mailbox.

Dear Joshua,

~~*I wish this was easier. I wish things were different. You are an incredible person, and you deserve to have everything you want.*~~

~~*I'm sorry for the way things ended. I want you to know that I really did care about you.*~~

~~*There are things I need to do. You don't know everything about my past, and there are still so many unanswered questions.*~~

You're the one that brought me back to life.

Love,
Elizabeth

The second thing is easier. Careful to avoid being seen, I run through the field. The dying land senses me, leans toward me. I can feel it hoping, wondering. Once I reach the very center of the brown crops, I kneel. It's such a simple thing to dig my fingers into the soil. This is what I was born to do. This is what Landon has bequeathed to me to finish on my own.

The power drains from my core, my veins, my very blood. It flows down through my hands into the ground. The surge is a physical sensation, and though I slump in exhaustion, it's still invigorating to watch the change happening all around. The unharvested beans straighten, their stalks reaching toward the sky, becoming triumphant and full. But the crops aren't the end of it. The power seeps deeper, deeper, reaching for the tired earth. *Wake up*, it says. *Here's what you need.* I feel a shift. The moment I know I've accomplished life is when the cracked dirt melts away to mud.

And it's done. My time in Edson, my friendship with Joshua, my ties to the Caldwell family. Gone. It's bittersweet, but for the first time in a long time, I'm looking forward, too. Everyone has a purpose, and these people may not have known it, but they served so many for me. Maggie and her friendship, Sarah and her courage, Joshua and his innocence, Charles and his decision. They'll live in my thoughts until the day the life completely fades from me.

As I'm blearily making my way back to my truck, a scream shatters the air. I pause, smiling.

"What next?" Fear asks from behind, wrapping his arm around my shoulders. Closing my eyes, I lean into him. Visions of horror and panting sweat erupt on the insides of my eyelids.

"I want to find my mom," I tell him.

He doesn't hesitate. "I'll drive."

I raise my brows at him. "Don't you have summons to take care of?"

Fear tries to snatch the keys, but I manage to jerk them away just in time. He scowls down at me. "The world can spin without me for a few minutes, woman. Come on, I've never driven before."

I laugh, a sound that he cuts short with a kiss that tastes like strawberries and terror.

2009 Olivia Wagner Photography

About the Author

Kelsey Sutton has explored a variety of career paths, from fast food to dog training to housekeeping to advertising. Now she divides her time between her college classes and her writing. She lives in northern Minnesota with her pets, Lewis and Clark. Visit her online at kelseysutton.blogspot.com. *Some Quiet Place* is her debut YA novel with Flux.